THE HEIRESS

CYNTHIA KEYES

The Heiress

By Cynthia Keyes

Printed in North America
First edition, 2022

The Heiress

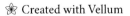

Created with Vellum

PROLOGUE

It was late. The office staff had long since retired for the night. Jem ran a hand over his ancient, scarred face and examined the figures again. He straightened his once massive frame, now shrunken with age, and laid a palsied hand over the evidence of embezzlement before him. *I have failed you Arabella, but perhaps there is still time to right this wrong.*

A long jarring creak broke the silence, interrupting his thoughts. Jem looked up from his work in alarm. Someone was prowling around the office. He glanced at the wall safe across the room, his pistol inside. Not the handiest place to keep it, he acknowledged with a grimace.

Taking a calming breath to settle his beating heart, he lifted his nib pen from its holder and scrawled a quick note into the account book before closing it and sliding it toward the heap of files on his desk. Placing the stopper onto his inkwell with exaggerated care, he rose and silently moved toward the safe. His fingers trembled as he tried to complete the combination. The door burst open, and he froze.

"I knew I would find you here, old man," a rasping voice sounded from the doorway.

With his back to the intruder, Jem tried unsuccessfully to keep the fear from his voice. "What is it you want?" He straightened to his still intimidating height and turned to face him, keeping one hand resting on the dial of the safe. The intruder took a step into the room. Though the man had cloaked his face in the black hood of his domino, Jem knew who he was.

"I want it all. But you know that, don't you?" He laughed, a loud grating sound that echoed in the silent office, as he reached into the folds of his cape and pulled out a pistol, levelling it at Jem's chest. The clicking of the hammer being pulled back on the pistol had Jem gritting his teeth to keep from flinching.

"You had to snoop, then you could not leave it be. And now you'll pay the price. But first let's finish what you started. Open the safe."

Jem tried once more to calm his fumbling fingers while he negotiated the combination. He visualized the gun lying atop his papers. If he could reach inside there was a chance he could get his hands on the revolver.

But it was not to be. The second the safe door swung open; the roar of a pistol reverberated in the room. An icy cold shiver pulsed through his chest as he slumped to the floor.

CHAPTER 1

"Today is the day, Claudia. I admit I am a little nervous about the reading of the will this morning. Are you sure you won't change your mind and come with me?" Eleanora asked.

"No. This one is all yours I am afraid. Besides there is still plenty of unpacking to keep me occupied." Eleanora made a face, and Claudia chuckled. "I am sure it won't be as bad as that."

It had been a week since Eleanora and Claudia arrived in London. Eleanora had been pleased when Claudia agreed to accept the job as her assistant and join her on the journey to London. The first week had been a busy one—hiring staff and settling into the townhouse. The house had once belonged to her grandmother Arabella, and though it was a modest home when compared to its neighbors, its address in the prestigious Mayfair district made it accessible to both the parks and the offices of Pembroke Industries. Facing a small inner-city park with established trees, it gave one the impression of a country home. It was the perfect location and size for two ladies of business such as themselves. Eleanora smiled to herself at the apt description. The friends were indeed beginning what she hoped would be rewarding careers in London.

The breakfast room was her favorite. This morning the sun shone through the windows overlooking the garden, promising an end to the dreary fog and drizzle of the last few days. But despite the promise of a sunny day, Eleanora sighed. The business of reading the will played heavily on her mind. "It is just that I get the impression from my correspondence with Jem's sister, Amelia, that the family is unaware of my business arrangement with Jem. I don't think I could stomach a scene." How wonderful it would have been to spend this sunny day exploring London.

"I wouldn't worry. Mr. Jem Brigg was a power in the shipping industry for a generation. I am sure there will be enough money to satisfy the family…more than enough from my point of view. And it's not like the heirs are his children. He had a sister-in-law and a niece. They should be quite satisfied."

Eleanora smiled at Claudia's no-nonsense attitude. She had been friends with Claudia since her arrival in America more than a decade ago. Eleanora had come to live with her grandmother, Arabella, devastated by the death of her parents. Arabella had immediately found her a companion, Claudia, the daughter of a widowed captain in her employ. After accepting Claudia as her ward, Arabella immediately set about educating the girls, both in the traditional studies of the school room and in the shipping industry. "You need a passion Eleanora, something to keep your mind from your troubles," her grandmother had declared. Ships were Arabella's passion; thus the girls received the unorthodox addition of an internship in her shipping firm as part of their education. Of the two young women, Claudia had shown an aptitude for the financial side of the business. Had she not decided to join Eleanora in England, she would have certainly been offered a position in Arabella's firm in America.

Jem Brigg was given a twenty-five percent share of Pembroke Shipping in London. The same branch of the industry previously owned by Eleanora's mother, and he was assigned the task of managing the business. Jem had been a big man, both in stature and as the dominant force in an industry which had shaped the world. He was a legend on the docks. That he had kept the actual ownership of the company to himself would only have added to the power he exuded in the London markets.

Though she and her grandmother, Arabella Pembroke, were aware of Jem's declining health over the past year, the latest word from him had been that he was recuperating and had even returned to work. The news of his violent death during a robbery had been a shock. Jem had been Arabella's lifelong friend and protector. Her grandmother was heartbroken when word reached them in Boston. Though Arabella declined to make the taxing journey to London, she determined it was long since time her granddaughter returned to England and took up a role in her business.

Eleanora set her teacup down. "I suppose you are right, Claudia. Jem would certainly have provided for his niece, Crystabel. She was his only family after all." It was time to face the day.

~

ELEANORA GLANCED around the small parlor of Jem's London home, where the family had gathered to wait before joining the other minor beneficiaries in the library for the reading of the will. Above the fireplace was a portrait of the man she had always lovingly referred to as Uncle Jem. She smiled at the imposing figure that glared down at them from above, his scarred face so forbidding and unlike the gentle man she had known as a child.

Jem had never married, but after his brother Marion's death, he had taken Marion's widow, Amelia, and her daughter, Crystabel, to reside with him in his home. Crystabel had been Jem's pride and joy. When Eleanora left London, Crystabel had been a debutant, just emerging on the social scene, and now she was married, with a daughter of her own. Today, Crystabel, along with her mother Amelia, and her husband Lord Hargrove, had gathered to hear Jem's will.

"Eleanora, do come sit with me." Amelia bustled over to her and led her to the small settee, where she settled her bulky frame, arranging her skirts. She was a rotund woman, appearing even larger in a day dress covered with bows and flounces. Eleanora was forced to perch on the sliver of seat Amelia had left for her.

"We waited so long for your arrival, and you are home at last. You must tell me all about America."

"We have waited." Stephen Hargrove, Crystabel's husband interjected. Slender and elegant in an impeccably tailored suit, he was the model of the aristocratic gentleman about town. His pale face, too long to be considered handsome, reflected the bored countenance of so many of his set. "Hughes and Barnum refused to read the will until you appeared, though it has been over two months. Apparently, our Uncle Jem has left you a little stipend, and the lawyers insisted we wait for your arrival."

"Yes. I apologize for the delay." Eleanora shifted uncomfortably on the settee. Hargrove's comment added to her growing suspicion that Jem had kept the business of Pembroke and the details of its ownership, to himself. This morning's revelations were sure to be an unpleasant surprise to the family. She contemplated confiding the business arrangement she shared with Uncle Jem, but decided against it. Perhaps the other reveals in the will would soften the blow. "As I intend to make my permanent home here in London, there were my affairs to attend to. Then I was unable to book a steamship passage, thus the journey took longer than I anticipated. I hope you were not too inconvenienced."

"Not at all my dear." Amelia replied, "We are only pleased to have you back once more, is that not so Crystabel?"

"Quite right mother." Crystabel smoothed the folds of her navy silk dress. Dressed in the latest style, with her blond hair pulled back into an elegant chiffon,

Eleanora could not help but admire the picture of perfection Crystabel had become. She was a beauty.

Amelia continued; her round face animated, "It will be so exciting to have a single girl to take under my wing. The season is just beginning, and I have made plans for us my dear. I must say I was dismayed to hear that you had not yet found a husband."

"Amelia, I am not interested in—"

Amelia raised her hand to block her objections and quickly carried on. "I can only imagine that finding a suitable man in Boston was impossible. But not to worry. Twenty-five is a difficult age to be sure, but Crystabel and I will be here to assist, and all will be well." She reached over and patted her hand, while Crystabel nodded her agreement. "You are not on the shelf yet, my dear Eleanora, and you are not to give up hope. I vow before the season is out, we will have you nicely settled. Now, there is the minor matter of the period of mourning, but as Jem was only an uncle, we can correctly re-enter society. And as we have almost reached the required three-month period, all will be well..." She took a breath. "Look at Crystabel, with a fine husband."

Amelia paused and looked up at Lord Hargrove appreciably. Eleanora smiled at the pleased expression on the woman's face. That Crystabel had married into the aristocracy would have been a great boon to the family. After all Crystabel, though an heiress, was the daughter and niece of a merchant. The subject of her admiration ignored the conversation. He rested his arm against the mantle of the fireplace, impatiently waiting for the summons to the library and the reading of the will.

Eleanora took the opportunity to interject. "Thank you, Amelia, but I rather thought I would concentrate on Pembroke Industries for the—"

"Pembroke?" Her statement roused Lord Hargrove from his ennui. "Why would you be interested in Pembroke? The business is hardly your concern Eleanora," he scoffed. "Pembroke is in good hands. Though as a gentleman I could hardly be expected to submerge myself in trade, my man Matheson and I have had the place running smoothly for the past year, while Jem Brigg was so indisposed. It was a burden to be sure, but I take my responsibilities seriously." He smiled down at her. "No, my dear. You should concentrate on more feminine matters. Though it is a trial for me, I will continue to serve the family."

Crystabel nodded. "Stephen has indeed dedicated himself to the business. Why hardly a week went by without him going into the office. Uncle was so thankful, and I could not be more proud. He has been such a treasure."

"He certainly has. A treasure indeed." Amelia smiled at Stephen once more, who acknowledged her praise with a cool nod. "And a wonderful father I might add. Stephen dotes on the child. My little granddaughter Anna has been spoiled rotten," Amelia said proudly. "Is that not so Crystabel?"

"Quite right mother."

Amelia turned back to Eleanora and frowned. "That grandmother of yours has done you no service at all,

Eleanora. Why, you could have children of your own by now. All this nonsense of putting you through training in her operation over there. Look where it has gotten you…twenty-five and no prospects. And you, a relative of the Earl of Pembroke, and a lady in your own right. And why she thought an education in shipping would benefit you in any way is a mystery to me." She shook her head rolling her eyes before continuing. "I would have thought it would have been a simple task to arrange a decent marriage for you. Why, I would have had this taken care of years ago." She shook her head again, this time with a tut-tutting sound. "It is beyond understanding. Arabella was not much for society, but I never thought her so capable of neglecting her duty to you, my dear. Concentrate on business? Huh," she snorted, her double chins trembling with indignation. "I never heard of such a thing. But you mustn't fret my dear, all will be well. Crystabel and I will take you in hand, won't we Crystabel?"

"We certainly will mother." Crystabel answered as though by rote. Eleanora got the impression that Crystabel did not pay much mind to Amelia's constant chatter. She, however, was relieved to have Amelia fill the room with her talk, even if she was not thrilled with the topic.

Amelia cleared her throat, prepared to continue. But before she could, Speers, the butler, announced from the doorway, "The beneficiaries are to assemble in the library. The lawyer is prepared to begin." The family followed Speers into the library, where two rows of chairs were set out, the back one filled with

Jem's friends and employees. The family took their seats in the front row.

Eleanora sat quietly in her chair, twisting the strings of her black reticule. She had a fair idea of what would be contained in the will. She could only hope the disclosure would not be too unsettling for the small gathering in the library.

Crystabel slid her chair next to hers and leaning in close, whispered, "I have never been to a will reading. It all seems too serious. Uncle Jem is sure to have left some of his fortune to Stephen and me. Stephen is so very nervous about it, and I have to say I am—"

The solicitor cleared his throat, interrupting her. He sat behind a huge mahogany desk, surveying the double line of chairs symmetrically laid out before him. "I see I have all the beneficiaries assembled here. I am Mr. Hughes of Hughes and Barnum, the solicitor of the late Jem Brigg. Without further ado we shall begin the proceedings. The will is a recent document, and I personally can attest to Mr. Brigg's sound mind at the time of its creation."

After the initial legal formalities, he started with the minor stipends and pensions for Mr. Brigg's staff, both those from his home and office. After each pronouncement, a ripple of appreciation was murmured from the back row.

"And to my dear friend John Noyes, I leave my four matching grays. He has coveted them long enough." John gave an appreciative chuckle, before the solicitor continued. "To Samuel Marsh I leave my stallion Hercules, a sturdy sire he will prize for his herd."

"Quite right. And I will at that, Jem. May you rest in peace." Samuel nudged his friend John beside him and the two of them shared a grin.

"And now for the bulk of my estate," The solicitor paused.

Eleanora glanced around the room. In the front row Crystabel sat beside her, adjusting the elaborate lace on her cuffs. Next to Crystabel was her husband Stephen, Lord Hargrove, who reclined nonchalantly in his chair, his legs extended and crossed at the ankles. And finally, Amelia, silent at last, sat shifting her heavy form uncomfortably in a narrow, straight-backed chair.

"I leave my home and its contents to my sister-in-law Amelia, together with a pension of 1000 pounds per year for her lifetime, to ensure her continued comfort." The solicitor looked up and nodded at Amelia, who smiled in return, before continuing.

"To my great niece, Anna, I leave the sum of 5000 pounds to be used as her future dowry. The money will not be accessible and held by my barristers until the day following her wedding, or the date of her thirtieth birthday.

To my niece Crystabel I leave the remainder of my liquid assets, a sum of 50,000 pounds, to be administrated as an annuity, with interest paid annually to a maximum of 2000 pounds. The principle is protected and locked to ensure her future security. The details of the arrangement can be explained more thoroughly through the offices of Hughes and Barnum."

"Ah," Crystabel smiled and nudged her husband,

who slowly straightened in his chair, the frown lines between his eyes deepening.

"And finally, unbeknownst to all of you, I have never owned Pembroke Industries, though I have had the privilege of managing it since the death of my dear Arabella Pembroke's daughter, Faith Pembroke-Nyles. Seventy-five percent of the business has always been under the control of Faith's daughter, Eleanora, who graciously granted me my shares when I took over management more than a decade ago. Thus, to her, I return my twenty-five percent share. It is my hope she will be pleased with the assets I have incurred during my guardianship."

An awkward silence filled the room. Beside her, Crystabel could not contain her gasp. Stephen sat up straight in his chair, his shock clearly evident on his paled face. Only Aunt Amelia seemed unaffected, still smiling, and pleased with her inheritance.

Crystabel grasped her arm. "But I had no idea, Eleanora. Did you know about this? Why you are an heiress, you have always been an heiress!"

"I...ah—"

Stephen sprang to his feet. "But this is outrageous! It cannot be! Why was I not informed?" He looked from Eleanora to the solicitor. "Something must be done. I was led to believe Crystabel was the heiress."

The solicitor looked up from his papers, his professional countenance unaffected by the outburst. "Calm yourself Lord Hargrove. Your wife has, after all, just inherited a tidy sum."

"2000 pounds a year! 2000 pounds is a pittance

compared to the value of Pembroke!" He turned his mottled face to Eleanora. "I had never heard of this Eleanora until two months ago, and now to learn she owns the entire shipping firm! It is outrageous!"

Aunt Amelia turned a bright crimson and quickly intervened. "Now that is simply not true." She turned to Eleanora. "We spoke of you often, dearest Eleanora. Why, there was not a day that went by without a mention of your name. Or at the very least, our dear friends in America were always in our thoughts. Is that not so Crystabel?"

"Quite true mother." Crystabel answered, without turning her pale face from her husband's, her voice a quiet monotone. "You were certainly in our thoughts, Eleanora."

"Yes, our thoughts," Aunt Amelia nodded, her double chins echoing their agreement.

"Thank you I—"

"Have you gone mad?" Lord Hargrove glared at his mother-in-law. "You speak of niceties when this woman," he spat the words and flung his arm out in Eleanora's direction, "has stolen what is rightfully ours!" He strode to the desk and placed both hands upon it, leaning into the solicitor's face. "We will contest it. I am entitled to at least the twenty-five percent share owned by Brigg. Furthermore, to have the 50,000 pounds locked into an annuity is unacceptable. The courts will agree with me."

The solicitor was not intimidated. "Sit down Lord Hargrove. There is more." He remained stoic until Stephen swung around and sat rigidly in his chair.

"Now then, it seems Mr. Brigg had prepared for that eventuality." He paused and returned Lord Hargrove's sullen look with a glare. "If an heir should contest any segment of this will and testament, they shall immediately forfeit their inheritance."

Lord Hargrove sprang up, his chair clattering to the floor behind him. Without a further word, he stomped to the library doors, and slammed them hard behind him.

Eleanora broke the awful silence. "Oh dear, that did not go well."

CHAPTER 2

The offices at Pembroke industries had seen several changes over the last week. During her first morning at work, Mr. Matheson, Uncle Jem's manager, had left in a huff when he discovered the company would no longer be overseen by Hargrove, but the new owner—a woman and a young one at that. It was a blow. Eleanora's hopes for a smooth transition had been dashed.

Her grandmother Lady Arabella Pembroke, who owned and operated the American sister company had warned her on this point. "England is not America my dear. You may find some difficulty in establishing yourself in the company. In England, you will be required to manage only from behind the scenes, especially at first."

"But it is 1845 grandmother, the modern age. Why even England's monarch is a woman!"

But her aged grandmother had insisted the transition would not be an easy one and she had been right.

Although it was Arabella who had originally begun the company so many years ago, and it was her grandmother who had turned the company into the success it was, it had not been accomplished without a great deal of difficulty. "Get a good manager, Eleanora," her grandmother had insisted, "someone who will be the public head of the business, but will work with you behind the scenes."

Eleanora had been appalled to see that Jem's office had been left untouched since the dreadful break-in. A dark stain still marred the carpet in front of the wall safe, and the desk was littered with dusty files. She decided the first order of business would be to redo Jem's office, then to reorganize the reception room where the head clerk, Mr. Wicket, kept his desk and files, where she added a workspace for Claudia. With that accomplished, she was left with the task of finding a manager.

Eleanora rapped her pencil on the huge mahogany desk before her as she pondered the problem. Over the last two days, she had interviewed a panoply of applicants for the position. No one had suited her needs.

"Who do we have for our next interview?" Eleanora pushed her glasses up the bridge of her nose and sighed. Choosing the perfect candidate was harder than she expected. What she needed was someone qualified and willing to work in partnership with her. She was more than willing to act behind the scenes. Unlike Claudia, who wanted a career in the day-to-day activities of the firm, she was prepared to leave those decisions to a manager. Yet Eleanora was not interested in leaving the company entirely in their hands. It sounded easy enough, but even in these modern times her candidates had assumed they would be solely in charge of operations, as well as the direction the company would take. They addressed her with a frustrating combination of condescending tones and assurance. It was not what she wanted at all.

Claudia handed her a file. "Your next interview recently returned from India where he served with the British forces for the past six years as a manager for the Governor General. His name is Elliot Sparks. He is thirty-two, qualified...perhaps too qualified for our purposes. I like this one, Eleanora. He would be my pick for the job. You have a few minutes before he arrives."

Eleanora raised her brows. This was the first candidate Claudia had endorsed. She trusted Claudia's judgement above all others.

"Good. I need a little time. When he arrives show him into my office. He can cool his heels while I take a little break." Eleanora laid out his application on the desk and glanced around the room to be sure everything was in order. The massive desk dominated the room with two chairs placed conveniently in front of it. It faced the door, with an elaborate cloak stand parked next to it. To the right an expanse of carpeted floor separated her desk and personal files from a small settee and two straight-backed chairs circled around a low serving table for less formal discussions. A floor to ceiling bookshelf that had been a challenge to fill, covered the far wall. A window behind the clustered furniture overlooked the busy street below. Satisfied that everything was in order, she left for her break.

Eleanora looked at herself in the mirror, pleased with the image of the businesswoman reflected there. Her heavy black hair was pulled back from her face in a bun. By everyone's account she resembled her grandmother Arabella, who had been a beauty in her youth, and but for her green eyes, her grandmother's were almost black, and her height, it was true. She stood on her tip toes for a moment wishing she had a few more inches. An intimidating stance would surely be an asset to her in this situation.

Sinking back onto her heels, she cleaned her spectacles and placed them on the bridge of her nose with a sigh. The glasses were a ruse. Although at twenty-five years of age she was considered on the shelf and well past her prime for marriage, in the world of business she was considered too young to be taken seriously. Thus, the glasses, the conservative bombazine jacket, and the skirt of a working woman. She had also dropped the hyphened Nyles from her name, thinking the surname Pembroke might help the transition.

It was time for her next interview. Hopefully, this candidate would be the combination she needed. As she left the retiring room, she was surprised by the sound of raised voices in the usually subdued office area. She paused.

Claudia sounded annoyed. "Lord Hargrove, I am afraid you will not be able to see Miss Pembroke today."

"Simply tell her Lord Hargrove wishes to be received."

Eleanora closed her eyes and took a breath. Stephen Hargrove had been a thorn in her side since the advertisement for a managerial position had appeared. First, he had demanded the position for himself, though why he thought he was best suited for the role was beyond her. Then he demanded Matheson be reinstated in the position. When Eleanora would not comply, he sent a list of candidates to her office, which she had promptly tossed in the trash. He was simply unable to accept that the company was none of his affair, or that she was capable of taking the helm.

"I am afraid she is interviewing candidates today; she'll not be available—"

"Exactly. And I have the perfect candidate. Whitrow here, is the man for the job." He indicated the robust man at his side.

Eleanora took a breath and strode into the room. "Lord Hargrove, what a surprise." Stephen Hargrove stood in the outer office, flanked by the other man. The two of them faced poor Claudia, who had edged closer to Eleanora's office door in an attempt to bar their way. Mr. Wicket was of little help to her, sitting wide-eyed at his desk across the room.

"Eleanora," he said as he turned to her with an ingratiating smile, "I am so pleased to have caught you. I have brought you the new manager you require. I am sure you will be much relieved. Mr. Whitrow is familiar with the business. He is prepared to take up the task immediately." He again gestured toward the burly bewhiskered gentleman beside him. "The perfect man for the job." Hargrove leaned back on his heels and smiled. "I know it has all been a trial for you, my dear, but rest assured, Whitrow will be able to relieve you of all the pesky little issues with Pembroke."

"Thank you, my Lord. How thoughtful of you." She nodded to Mr. Whitrow. "Pleased to meet you Mr. Ah..."

"Whitrow ma'am. And I am at your service. Prepared to begin today, I am." He reached out his hand and she took it. "You'll not have to concern yourself with this operation for a moment longer."

"Pleased to meet you sir." She said with a stiff smile. "I must apologize for the inconvenience, Mr. Whitrow. Unfortunately, the position has been filled."

"Filled?" Lord Hargrove gasped.

Eleanora took advantage of their momentary shock to hurry to her door. Opening it she turned back to add. "And now if you will excuse me, I really must meet with my new manager."

She stepped into her office hoping to be able to close the door without further ado. But it was not to be. Despite Claudia's quick shift to block his way, Lord Hargrove pushed past her into the office with his man on his heels.

A gentleman stood looking out her window at the far side of the room. He turned and approached her desk as she entered. For a moment she was disconcerted with his presence, before remembering he was her next interview. She purposely stepped behind her desk and glanced down at the name on his resume, Mr. Elliot Sparks.

"Eleanora, this is too important a decision to make lightly. As head of the family, I am obliged to assist you in this trying time. I simply cannot allow—"

She gestured to the imposing man who had just approached her desk. "Lord Hargrove, may I introduce you to my new manager, Mr. Elliot Sparks."

Mr. Sparks looked at her and raised his eyebrows. For the first time Eleanora took in his appearance. He was a tall man, well over six feet, with broad shoulders fitted snugly into an elegantly tailored suit. His brown hair was pulled back into a queue tied at the nape of his neck. Blue eyes looked at her now with just the slightest tinge of amusement glittering in their depths. Despite the formal attire he had the look of an adventurer. She could well believe he had just returned from a sojourn in India. He looked too handsome to be a man of business.

But he handled the current situation with ease. Without hesitation he extended his hand. "Pleased to meet you, Lord Hargrove."

Hargrove automatically took Elliot's hand, then quickly dropped it, and turned to Eleanora. This time he kept his voice soft. "Eleanora, I cannot allow you to make so momentous a decision without consulting me." He gave a condescending laugh. "One cannot simply hire a manager for a business the size Pembroke willy-nilly. I am afraid you are quite out of your league my dear. But not to worry. There is nothing here that cannot be undone. Fortunately, Whitrow here," he gestured to the burly man at his side, "can escort the man out of the building, and all will be well."

"T'would be my pleasure sir." Whitrow stepped forward, eyeing Elliot with an oily grin.

Eleanora's eyes widened in surprise. Clearly Hargrove thought to bully her out of her rightful position at Pembroke. The audacity of the man brought two bright spots of color to her cheeks. She had not anticipated this mode of attack. Placing both hands upon her desk and leaning forward, she used her most professional tone to reply, "The decision has been made and will stand. Mr. Sparks is the manager of Pembroke."

Lord Hargrove was unphased. "I think not my dear. As head of the family, I cannot allow this gross mismanagement. Whitrow will run Pembroke, with my assistance and that is my final word on the matter," he said firmly, then added in a softer voice and a smile, "thankfully my dear Eleanora, you are not without family to help you in these trying times." Whitrow stepped forward to stand ominously at his side. The two of them faced Eleanora.

"My dear Stephen," she said, purposely using his first name, as he had used hers, "while it is thoughtful of you to bother yourself with Pembroke when you have no financial interest in the matter, it is entirely unnecessary. As I said, the decision has been made." It was not without satisfaction that she saw Lord Hargrove's smile falter as he shifted uncomfortably.

Whitrow was clearly not prepared to accept defeat and took another step forward, puffing out his chest and flexing his beefy arms. His stance threatened physical intervention.

Mr. Sparks took this as his cue. Stepping deftly between Whitrow and Eleanora's desk, he said in a dangerously calm voice, "Now then, gentlemen. The owner," he emphasized the word, "has made her position clear. It is time you took your leave."

Whitrow set his jaw bullishly and Elliot Sparks took a step towards him. Eleanora noticed he towered over the other men. His height, with his broad shoulders, rigid countenance, and rugged sun-worn face made for an intimidating figure. His voice was dangerously quiet. "As pleasant as this conversation is, I am afraid Miss Pembroke has much to see to this morning."

There was silence while the three men glared at each other. Mr. Sparks' lips curled into a thin smile when Whitrow took a quick step back. "As I said, Miss Pembroke is much too busy to be receiving today. Perhaps if you made an appointment."

Lord Hargrove flushed a deep red. "Eleanora, you are making a grave mistake. You have not heard the last of this."

"Oh, but I am certain I have Stephen," she said, again purposely using his first name. "And as to our familial connection, let me relieve you of that responsibility. Our relationship is distant at best; my actions are not your concern. The subject is closed."

Mr. Sparks gestured to the office door. "Good day gentlemen."

Hargrove scowled, his eyes darting between Eleanora and Mr. Sparks as though debating further action. Raising his chin imperiously he said, "It cannot be said I have not done all I could to divert this travesty." Finally, he whirled around and strode out the door. Whitrow shot them a glare before following in his wake.

Eleanora sank slowly into her chair and ran a hand across her forehead, smoothing back her hair with fingers that trembled slightly. "Thank you for your assistance, sir." Regaining her composure, she smiled at him. "It was well done, I must say. Please sit down. I do apologize for that dreadful scene."

"It was my pleasure." He took a chair and pulled it to her desk. "But should you decide to hire me, my first order of business will be to bring in some much-needed security here. You are far too vulnerable for my tastes."

Eleanora could not contain her short bark of laughter. It was a release of tension after the nasty confrontation with Hargrove. She was still feeling shaky from the realization she had so underestimated the lengths to which Hargrove would go to take over Pembroke Industries.

She assessed the man across from her. With his tanned face and muscular frame, he looked like a renegade, not a man of business. Perhaps she should have added experience as a bodyguard to her list of requirements in a manager, she thought wryly. Elliot Sparks' other credentials were equally exemplary. As Claudia had pointed out, he might even be too qualified for the role she had in mind.

"I agree. It is not a scene I care to repeat." She

looked at the man across from her with appreciation. "And I will be offering you the position Mr. Sparks."

For better or worse, I have my manager.

She hoped she had not been hasty in her decision. This man was the first to give her the respect she wanted as a businessperson in the industry. Her interviews thus far had shown her how rare that was. There would still be time to change her mind if they could not come to an agreement on the future direction of the company.

CHAPTER 3

When Elliot read the advertisement for a managerial position at Pembroke, his curiosity was immediately sparked. The advertisement had been sent to him in a letter with no return address, and no postmark. It must have been hand delivered. With no note attached, he assumed someone from Pembroke was encouraging him to apply. He immediately cross-checked the item with the Business Chronicle. The advertisement was legitimate.

Pembroke was a leader in the shipping industry and the company owned a fleet of ships. While working in India, Elliot had been interested in the new steamships, with their innovative screw propulsion. He had been able to experience them firsthand when he accompanied the governor on a trip to America, making the journey in record time. While there, he had toured Pembroke's sister company, and even met their matriarch, Lady Arabella Pembroke.

Furthermore, the time and money saved by the British forces in the last few years, especially from their furthest colonies, like India, had been tremendous. Steamships were the wave of the future. He was curious as to whether Pembroke had begun to modernize their fleet.

The advertisement said the selected candidate would be offered a share option as part of their contract, and that was what he most wanted. His goal was to have a share in what he considered the premier industry of the century; to invest in the company and truly be a part of the movement.

Now he examined his new employer with interest. He had never conceived of a woman overseeing so large a company as Pembroke. It remained to be seen how well she could manage, or how active a role she wished to play. He admired her determination to stand up to Lord Hargrove. It had taken no small amount of courage to withstand the man, yet she had not wavered. She appeared determined to take a leading role in the company's operation.

Miss Pembroke looked at him from behind her oversized glasses. She was absurdly young to be an owner of a shipping firm and her short stature did not help the impression of immaturity. "Now then, shall we begin our negotiations, Mr. Sparks. I have read your credentials, and of course a reference from the governor of India is an asset. You are certainly qualified. Pembroke Industries is a good fit for your skills. We have a strong fleet of ships, fourteen of which are currently actively engaged, with six docked here in London." She looked down at an open file and rested her finger on an entry. "But of the fleet, only four have been outfitted with the new steam engines and screw propulsion. What do you think of steam powered vessels?"

He was surprised that her first words so exactly suited his ambitions. "They are the future. In a decade, the galleys will be obsolete. The new steam-powered ships will soon cut travel time to a tenth of what it was." Elliot was finding it difficult to control his enthusiasm. Leaning forward, he added, "Furthermore, the cost and space taken up by the rowers needed in a galley will be eliminated. A company that wishes to survive the next decade will need to adapt now."

Eleanora gave him a wide smile. Her eyes shone with appreciation. For the first time he noticed that beneath her tightly drawn bun, and ridiculously large spectacles, she was a beautiful woman. His stomach tightened and he quickly banished the thought.

"It seems we are like-minded. I could not be more pleased." She flashed him another dazzling smile. "I have concluded that our first order of business will be to continue refurbishing the fleet. Those that cannot be fitted with the equipment will be scrapped and salvaged. It is a task which has already begun here at Pembroke, where we already have several steamships. But there is no time to waste converting the rest of the fleet. Each ship completed will give us a leg up on our competition." A small frown dampened her enthusiasm. "And it will be expensive. It will take everything the company has and more to get the job done. I am afraid we will have some trying times in the next few years, but like you, I believe without this change we are doomed."

Miss Pembroke opened the top drawer of her desk and pulled out a sheaf of papers. "Now then, Pembroke offers a contract with a competitive wage and the option to invest in five percent of shares."

"Five percent? I admit I am most interested in the investment. If I dedicate my skills to this enterprise, I want a stake in the outcome. And you must agree that a manager committed to the success of Pembroke could only be of benefit to you. The standard offer is ten percent, purchased at an assessed price of course. But I was hoping for an opportunity to invest at a higher rate, fifteen or twenty percent."

He watched the frown lines deepen between her eyes as she considered his demands. He added, "Completing the transition to steam engines, as you said, will be costly. Considering the costs of refitting the fleet, an investment at this time can only be a boon to the company. Indeed, I dare say the funds will be needed."

"I will offer you the option to purchase twelve, at assessed value. You are aware sir that an investment of this size will be substantial?" She looked at him quizzically. Clearly, she suspected the price to be beyond his reach.

"Twelve I will accept. But only if any shares put on the market in the future are first offered to me."

Her eyes twinkled as she replied, "You drive a hard bargain Mr. Sparks. You will get the first opportunity to purchase for a five-year period."

"As do you Miss Pembroke. I accept." He stood and offered her his hand. She seemed pleased with the gesture, shaking it firmly.

For better or worse I have tied my future to Pembroke and the new steam propulsion. He looked across at Eleanora and wondered fleetingly if choosing Pembroke, with a female at the head was a mistake. But he was confident the risk would be worth the reward. He was convinced that the next decade would see the dominance of ships powered by engines. And he would be a part of it—and more than that, the investment would provide ample financial rewards.

She closed the file in front of her and rested her hands on it. "I thought today we could take a tour of the warehouse at the docks. A ship is currently being outfitted. Since we share the goal of refitting the fleet, I thought we might see the process."

"Excellent idea. Shall I order a coach brought around?"

To his surprise she laughed. It was a pleasant sound, in sharp contrast to the authoritative voice she had been using. "Oh heavens no. I am not as grand as that. A hackney will do."

He ordered the company coach. If Miss Pembroke wanted to balance her life as a lady with the world of business, then discretion was her best course.

She only raised her eyebrows as he assisted her into

the coach, then hopped in behind her pulling the door closed. The coach lurched forward, with Eleanora Pembroke sitting primly across from him, her bright eyes shining in anticipation. He had the unsettling feeling he was embarking on a journey, one that might be more than he had bargained for.

CHAPTER 4

Elliot nodded to the new security man at the doors of Pembroke Shipping. There would be another in the foyer just outside of Eleanora's office. Furthermore, his office door was just to the left of Miss Pembroke's, and he consistently left it open. If Hargrove attempted another coup, he would not accomplish it easily.

The trip to the docks had been informative, in many ways, not the least of which the role he would be required to play in the company.

Two of their ships were docked next to their warehouse where they were being loaded for transport. In each case they introduced themselves to the captain and toured the ship. After the initial introductions, all comments and questions were directed at him. For the most part, his employer remained quiet, listening carefully to the conversations. On one occasion, when she had asked a direct question, the captain had smiled at her but directed his answer to him.

He glanced uneasily at Miss Pembroke, taking her arm as they walked down the gangplank. "I must apologize for dominating the interviews. I hope you are not offended."

She laughed; her laughter was a heartfelt pleasant sound, and he found he could not resist smiling in return. "Mr. Sparks, I more than anyone, am aware of the discomfort my role in the firm is for the employees. One of my objectives in hiring a manager was to provide a male face for the company."

He nodded at her, relieved. "Very wise. Once the novelty of a young female owner wears off, they will come around."

"I am sure you are right. I can be patient. Employees have a way of determining how best to be heard." She waved her arm as though dismissing the topic. "Now then, we have one ship being outfitted in the slips, and an open berth. With three ships docked, shall we see if it is feasible to immediately begin on a second ship?"

Elliot smiled again. "On to the warehouse then." He took her arm. It was a short walk down the wharf to Pembroke's slips and the warehouse. The sun was warm on his back, and with her arm tucked into his he felt as though they were on a promenade in the park. Somehow, Eleanora Pembroke on his arm felt right. He got the strange sense that they belonged together—a sensation he had not experienced ever before. He tried to shake off the feeling.

The docks were a hub of activity. Despite the noise and bustle around them, he found himself solely concentrating on the feel of her arm in his. He glanced at her. Eleanora seemed lost in thought, no doubt preparing herself for the business ahead. He again forced himself to return to the subject at hand, and once in the warehouse that was not difficult to do. His enthusiasm for the modernization of the fleet preoccupied his thoughts.

Of the three docked ships only one was available to be worked on. One was booked for transport, and the other was too old and small to accommodate the new engines. The latter would be scrapped as planned. Elliot immediately began to mentally arrange the engineers and workmen required for the projects.

It had been a long afternoon, with a blur of captains, foremen, and engineers. It was a relief to be back in the coach at last. However, Miss Pembroke seemed unaffected and even now spoke with zeal. In her enthusiasm she reached forward and rested her hand on his thigh. "I am pleased with the operation at the docks. Our foreman, Mr. Redding, seems to have all in order. I must say I am more than satisfied with the man's capabilities." She unconsciously patted his leg. "The new steamship will be prepared in weeks, and he was quite eager to begin a second and a third. What was your impression?"

Elliot could feel the heat of her hand resting just above his knee. He could concentrate on nothing else while it burned into his thigh. He looked down at her small delicate fingers resting so intimately against him. For an awkward moment they both paused; the world spinning to a halt as he raised his head and met Eleanora's eyes. They both looked down once more at where her hand lay upon him. Her face flushed and she quickly withdrew it.

"Miss Pembroke, I—"

"Please call me Eleanora. The formality of Miss Pembroke grates on my nerves."

"Eleanora..." He paused. Though the name sounded familiar on his tongue, he would have much preferred the more formal address, especially now, with his leg still burning from her touch. Looking at her with her cheeks aglow with excitement, and her eyes sparkling, he felt his stomach lurch. After an afternoon in her presence, he was appalled to discover he had a strong attraction to his business partner. It was disconcerting.

"Eleanora," he began again, "I too was satisfied with the work at the docks and the warehouse. I must say I am pleased with the notion of moving forward with our plans to modernize the fleet. But there will be much work to do. There will be engineers and workers to hire. And before progressing further there will be budgeting of course. Have you had the opportunity to analyze the financials?"

"Claudia and Mr. Wicket have begun the process. We can expect reports later this week. But I think I shall make it my next order of business to assist with the process. There was no year-end report. Poor Uncle Jem appeared to have been in the midst of it at the time of his death, judging by the files I found on his desk."

The coach came to a halt in front of the offices. Elliot opened the door and hopped down, reaching back to assist her. "Good. If you are focused on budgeting, then I shall have our second ship pulled into the slips for refurbishing."

She gave him another dazzling smile. "We make an excellent team Mr. Sparks."

He grinned, unable to resist retorting, "Call me Elliot. I find the formality of Mr. Sparks grates on my nerves."

They entered the building to the delightful sound of her laughter.

~

HE HAD ONLY BEGUN to work the next morning when Mr. Wicket appeared at his door. "A message for you sir. The boy says it is urgent and will wait for your reply."

Elliot took the letter and immediately opened it. He grimaced when he saw the familiar writing of his aunt, Lady Mansfield.

ELLIOT,

I have a matter of importance to discuss. Please present yourself at my home at your earliest convenience. I will be prepared to receive you this morning.

Lady Madelyn Mansfield

ELLIOT SIGHED. Though it was unlikely Eleanora's emergency was anything of importance, he knew it was in his best interest to respond to his aunt's request.

"Tell the boy to inform Lady Mansfield I will visit her this morning."

Elliot decided to finish his paperwork before departing. His aunt could be a little too demanding. Responding too promptly would only encourage her to take further liberties.

It was over an hour before he arrived at her door. The butler took Elliot's coat. "Good day, sir. Lady Mansfield is awaiting you in the parlor."

"Thank you, Grimes. I will show myself in."

Lady Mansfield rose as he entered, offering him her hand. He took it and raised it to his lips. "You look lovely as always Aunt Madelyn. "

"Sit down Elliot. I am sure you are wondering why I summoned you here this morning." She gestured to her maid to pour tea, her fingers glittering with jeweled rings. She settled herself on the settee, adjusting her skirts carefully. She was a woman of a certain age who had always been meticulously fashionable. Even at home she was gowned in the latest style for day wear with her hair done up elaborately.

"Yes, I did wonder. It is not like you to send a message around to my place of work."

"Yes, your work. It is precisely what I wish to speak to you about. Now as you know it is my habit to never interfere in your affairs…" she paused as her maid offered her a dainty, surveying the tray thoroughly before selecting one. "Thank you, Colette, you can leave the tray. That will be all."

Elliot smiled at his aunt's words. The opposite was the case. Since the death of his mother seven years ago, his aunt had done her best to meddle in his life at every opportunity. She had objected strongly when he had chosen to go to India, and still struggled to forgive what she called his descent into trade.

"Now then, where was I? Oh yes, your occupation. It still puzzles me that you decided to take up a trade. I know for a fact you have more than enough money to live as a gentleman. And from what I understand, you have at least tripled your investments. You are a wealthy young man. There really is no excuse for it."

"Surely you have not asked me here to rehash that old topic. I believe there is little more to be said on the issue."

"No, no. I have quite given up that battle. No, it is Charles I am concerned about. My son, unlike you, has little in the way of business sense. It seems he has made some rather poor investments lately. He is so easily taken in, as you know." She sighed and sipped her tea, setting it carefully on its saucer before continuing. "He has asked to have control of his inheritance, and given his recent disasters in the world of finance, it is a request I do not want to grant."

Elliot was relieved. In matters of money, he was more than capable of lending a hand. "What is it you would like me to do Aunt Madelyn? If it is to help Charles arrange his portfolio, I certainly can assist him."

"Yes, yes. That is precisely what I want. But there is another more trivial matter you could assist with." She reached for the tea and poured herself another cup. "Would you care for more tea?"

"No, thank you." Elliot shifted uncomfortably in his chair while he waited for Madelyn to continue. She set down the pot and examined the tray of dainties once again. Her delay tactics could only mean the conversation was about to get awkward. He had the distinct impression he was not going to like her, 'trivial matter.'

"You will of course be attending the ball I am hosting for my daughter Melissa. And Charles will most certainly be there." She took another sip of tea.

He narrowed his eyes, wondering again what scheme she could be enacting, and answered her slowly, "I had planned to, yes."

"Very good. Now then, I received word today that Lord Hargrove will attend, with his lovely wife, Crystabel, and her mother, and we also sent an invitation to Eleanora Pembroke."

Elliot looked at his aunt's determined face with a growing sense of unease. It was clear his aunt was concocting one of her famous plans, of which he wanted no part.

"Do not look so serious Elliot. It is a small matter. Since you are acquainted with Eleanora Pembroke, I simply wanted a proper introduction."

"You wish to be introduced to Eleanora Pembroke?"

Lady Mansfield plucked the little fan from her lap, snapped it shut, and rapped it lightly against his knee. "No, not me, silly. Though I am sure I would be more than pleased to have her in my circle. She is a relative of the current Earl of Pembroke as you know. No. I want you to introduce her to Charles."

"No."

"But Elliot, what harm can it do? It would be a simple introduction, which is all I ask."

"You cannot expect me to play matchmaker. I—"

"I have not asked anything of the sort. I only want the introduction. Really Elliot," she said, giving him an exasperated look, "it is little enough to ask of you. You cannot possibly object to such a small favor."

Elliot sighed. "All right, an introduction if I have the opportunity, but that is all."

"Wonderful!" His aunt clapped her hands together and smiled. "Only think how perfect such a match would be for Charles. An heiress, and one with impeccable bloodlines. And I cannot help but think a more mature woman is exactly what he needs—someone to settle him. It might just be the thing to shake him from this ghastly obsession with poetry."

She smiled with satisfaction, as she raised her cup for a sip of tea. "And as she is new to town, Charles will be the first of her suitors. Surely that can only be an advantage."

Elliot did not share his aunt's enthusiasm. Though he was fond of Charles, he could think of no one less able to cope with day-to-day life. Charles fancied himself a poet and was determined to follow in the footsteps of his hero, Byron. Somehow the image of his beautiful Eleanora with his hapless cousin left a sour taste in his mouth. Even the thought of his Eleanora on someone else's arm made his stomach twist.

It was shocking to realize the depth of his feelings for Eleanora, given the brief time he had known her. Eliot was a man who spent little time analyzing his feelings. He only knew she was meant to be his. The whole experience was unfamiliar to him. As he walked down the steps of Lady Mansfield's townhouse, the image of Eleanora came to mind. He liked everything about her, from her firm resolve in dealing with Hargrove to her shining eyes beneath those ridiculous glasses, and her bursts of easy laughter. *She won't be taken by anyone, Charles included, because one way or another, I am going to make her mine.*

CHAPTER 5

Having accepted an invitation to tea with Amelia, Eleanora was to leave Claudia with the task of interviewing housekeepers. "You are sure you won't need me, Claudia?" she asked as she tied her bonnet and reached for her cloak.

Claudia waved her hand as though brushing Eleanora's concern aside and responded in her usual brusque manner. "I am quite capable of managing. Besides, I found the invitation a trifle half-hearted especially as it pertained to me. I got the distinct impression they hoped only you would attend."

"I am sure that is not the case Claudia."

Claudia smiled. "I am sure it is. And no, I am not offended. But I suspect that family has something in mind for you—heaven knows what it could be. After the incident with Hargrove at the office, I would certainly keep my guard up if I were you."

Eleanora knitted her brow as she considered the

possibility. "I cannot imagine Amelia being in any way confrontational."

"Still, take care. Now you had best be off. The hansom has been waiting at the gate for a while."

As Jem Brigg's townhouse was only a few blocks away, Eleanora was still contemplating Claudia's warning when she walked into the family's large salon. She could not shake the uncomfortable suspicion that Claudia was right, and Amelia had a scheme in mind. She was not to be disappointed.

"My dear Eleanora," Amelia crooned and bustled over to her as she entered the room, her face flushed with excitement, "I have such a pleasant surprise for you." Eleanora shot her a look which she ignored. She led her into the parlor where Crystabel sat entertaining a heavyset young man who awkwardly levered himself to his feet as they entered.

"Lord Manford, may I present my niece, Lady Eleanora Pembroke," she said, and turned to Eleanora to explain, "You have always been like family to me my dear, a true niece of my heart." Taking Eleanora firmly by the arm, she pulled her to the settee where Lord Manford stood. His short coat was pulled taut against a massive belly. "As you know, Eleanora has just returned from America. A trial, I am sure. But she is here with us now and we could not be more delighted." Amelia's eyes twinkled as she gave Eleanora a wide smile, pulling her close to add quietly, "Lord Manford is a widower, and long past his mourning stage. Is that not so Lord Manford?"

"Quite true. It is time I found a worthy countess.

Perhaps my search is over?" He chuckled as he reached for Eleanora.

Eleanora offered her hand politely. He raised it to his lips, then continued to hold it in a firm grip while he took his seat, forcing her to sit beside him on the settee. Aunt Amelia settled herself into the couch across from them with a satisfied smile.

Lord Manford had a round face, with eyes clouded by thick spectacles. His upper lip was hidden beneath a heavy mustache. He smiled. "I have heard so much about you Miss Pembroke. I must say I am pleased to meet you at last. You know, I am a particularly good friend of your manager Mr. Matheson. Thick as thieves we are."

"Oh, you are a friend of Mr. Matheson?" she asked, thinking he could not have been too good a friend, as he appeared to not know of him leaving the company. Or perhaps he had?

"As I said, thick as thieves. We have had many long talks about the future in shipping. With me in commodities and he in shipping there was a handy profit to be made there to be sure." He nodded and lowered his voice as though to share a secret. "Yes, I must say I was interested to hear about your inheritance." He chuckled before continuing, "You represent a sizable market share, and would be a fine investment as a countess, a splendid partnership! Commodities and shipping, Pembroke and Manford." He giggled at what he assumed to be a quaint financial joke. His voice was high pitched for a man his size, and Eleanora found herself repulsed by his reference to her as an heiress. Her shoulders stiffened as she forced a smile.

Crystabel joined her mother on the opposing couch. She chimed in, as she poured Eleanora a cup of tea, "I have been telling Lord Manford of your interest in business."

Lord Manford's eyes lit up. "Yes, and I am quite intrigued. As I said, Mr. Matheson and I held many a conversation on this topic. Though I am sure as a lady, you can hardly be interested in the mundane operations of a firm, let me assure you it is an occupation at which I am most adept. I have been managing my family's finances for years. Then of course, my late wife left me a sizable sum. I have done rather well." He leaned back and puffed out his chest. "I am more than capable of managing a large firm like Pembroke. I've made quite a name for myself at Capel Court. The word maverick has even been tossed about." He winked at her.

Eleanora forced herself to smile politely and said, "How nice for you." She looked towards Amelia and narrowed her eyes. Amelia gave her a winning grin in return.

Eleanora sighed and resigned herself to the inevitable. She would remain polite and force her way through this afternoon's tea. Reaching for the platter of pastries, she said, "Can I offer you a dainty Lord Manford?"

"Why thank you." Lord Manford selected a biscuit. "Now then, as I was saying, if you are looking for financial advice I can—"

Mr. Speers, the butler, interrupted from the open doors of the salon. "A Mr. Arthur Weins for you Madam," he said, stepping aside to present a tall character dressed in the latest fashions. His dark suit and trousers were highlighted with a red velvet waist coat, topped with a neckcloth in an elaborate flourish and held by a diamond pin. His dark hair had been liberally smoothed back with pomade. He sported a narrow mustache, also dark, and waxed into the perfect line. He was the epitome of all that was fashionable.

The party rose in greeting. Lord Manford eyed the new guest with a frown.

Crystabel immediately stepped forward to take his arm. "Ah, Arthur. How kind of you to accept our invitation. I am sure you have met Lord Manford, and of course you know my mother. But I must introduce you to my esteemed friend." She led him to Eleanora. "Eleanora, may I present Arthur Weins. Arthur is a dear friend of Stephen's."

Mr. Weins took her hand and raised it to his lips with a flourish. "I am honored to meet you, Miss Pembroke. I admit I had heard you were a lovely young woman, but you have far surpassed my expectations." He kept her hand at his lips as he graced her with a smile.

She tugged her hand from his grasp. "Thank you, Mr. Weins."

"But I insist you call me Arthur. All my friends do, and I am sure we shall be great friends." He had brown eyes, so dark they looked black, and a perfect smile.

Crystabel took Mr. Wein's arm. "Do sit down

Arthur. Let me serve you a cup of tea." She offered him a cup and saucer and settled him in a chair next to the opposing sofas. Eleanora could not help but admire Crystabel's easy graciousness. She was the portrait of the gentile young lady in a soft violet day dress of the latest style, with her blond hair coiled atop her head, and wide blue eyes welcoming.

Lord Manford cleared his throat and said, "Now then, as I was saying Miss Pembroke, the word at Capel Court is that no one is more qualified than I—"

"Oh, surely not, my Lord," Mr. Weins interrupted, "we cannot plague Miss Pembroke with talk of finance. No, no. There are more pleasant topics. The Mansfield soiree will take place next week. You will be attending Miss Pembroke? It promises to be the event of the season. Everyone in society will be there."

Her aunt quickly responded, "Of course she will be attending." She shot Eleanora a warning look, as though afraid she would deny it. "I sent our replies just this morning. Eleanora, I am sure, will do the same. She is thrilled to be active in society once more after such a long while in America. Are you not my dear?"

"I had not given it much thought." She caught Amelia's glare and quickly continued, "Perhaps I will attend."

"Perfect. Then you must reserve a dance for me, Miss Pembroke." Mr. Weins gave her a practiced smile, his head held stiffly erect as though his neckcloth were too crisply starched. He was a man who played the role of gentleman a little too well. Slender, with his dark hair and eyes, he personified the current trend of handsome.

Before she could reply, Mr. Speers cleared his throat from the doorway and announced, "A Lord Douglas Farrow for you Madam."

"Wonderful." Aunt Amelia smiled broadly as she heaved her heavy frame from the couch to greet her new guest. "Come in, come in. I am so pleased you accepted our invitation to tea."

Lord Farrow was a small man. He appeared a trifle awkward standing at the doors to the salon, surveying the room as though reluctant to enter. Aunt Amelia grasped him firmly by the arm and pulled him toward her assembled guests for introductions.

"P-pleased to meet you all," Lord Farrow stammered, his face flushing a deep red. Eleanora sympathized with him.

The room had become a little crowded, the couches were taken up by Crystabel and her mother on one side, her and Lord Manford on the other, with Mr. Weins on a chair between her and Crystabel. Speers pulled another chair up next to Lord Manford for Lord Farrow, who seemed pleased to have a gentleman to share the tales of his investments with.

"Have you invested in coal, Lord Farrow? One hears of fortunes to be made..." Eleanora let the conversation fade from her consciousness. Crystabel continued to play the role of hostess perfectly, filling teacups and offering treats from various platters, as she engaged their guests. Perhaps she could sit quietly and get through the afternoon without too much difficulty.

But it was not to be. After a discreet nudge from Aunt Amelia, Crystabel turned to her. "I have heard so much about knickerbocker society in America. You simply must tell us about it Eleanora."

"Yes, do tell. Miss Pembroke." Mr. Weins interjected, adjusting his laced cuffs until they fell perfectly over his slender fingers, "I too have been curious, though I cannot imagine the entertainments compare to those here in London."

"Actually, I resided in Boston, where the elite social circle is given the rather sarcastic title of Brahmin caste."

Mr. Weins gave her an oily smile. "How quaint."

A movement caught her attention from the doorway. Surely not, Eleanora thought with a growing sense of horror, not another single man.

Speers cleared his throat once more. "A Lord Brambury ma'am," he announced in his deep baritone. Eleanora found herself suppressing an urge to giggle. The afternoon had gone from annoying to ridiculous.

An older heavy-set man pushed past Speers into the room. "No, don't get up Amelia," he said as the party rose to greet him. "I came at once to meet your little filly." He ploughed into the room, nudging poor Lord Farrow aside to take Eleanora's hand. "And you must be Eleanora Pembroke. Can't say I am disappointed. Heard you had the look of your grandmother about you and so you do." He grasped her hand. For a moment Eleanora thought he would give it a hearty shake. But he brought it to his lips before extending her arm to examine her person, concentrating on the corseted vee of her gown where it hooped into its belled skirt. "A healthy young woman to be sure. And good, fine hips."

Eleanora had no idea what to say in response and could only mutter the usual niceties. She was thankful when Crystabel skillfully intervened to settle Lord Brambury into the company. Her head began to pound. Dealing with social situations had never been her forte. It was particularly uncomfortable when she was the object of attention as she was today.

The next hour passed in a blur of conversation. Try as she might it was impossible to withdraw into her usual quiet repose. Arthur Weins fawned over her the entire time, but he was not alone in his pursuit. Even the shy Lord Farrow managed to edge a few words in her direction. She felt like a commodity, newly launched on the market.

When the last of the gentlemen finally took their leave, Amelia stood at her side and patted her shoulder, her face flushed with pleased satisfaction. She had been uncharacteristically quiet during afternoon tea and broke her strained silence now with a rush of conversation, "There, my dear. As you can see there will be no shortage of suitors for you. No need to despair. By the end of the season, we will have you nicely settled." She clapped her hands together. "So many men for you my dear. I must say we had a wonderful turnout this afternoon. And we have just begun. Once you have been introduced at the ball there will be more. Oh, it's so very exciting!"

Before she could reply Crystabel took her arm and

said, "Mother, do not rush her. Although I do think out of the gentlemen today, Mr. Weins is by far your best prospect. Stephen suggested him and I quite agree. A true gentleman, and handsome. Don't you think?"

"Crystabel, I truly am not searching for a husband. I have—"

"No need to rush as I said. But do keep him in mind Eleanora. He will be at Mansfield ball. You simply must grant him a dance, my dear. Oh, but put him on your dance card early as he is much sought after, a popular gentleman of the ton, Eleanora. Perfect for you!" She smiled and squeezed her arm. "It will be something to look forward to."

A little girl peeked into the room, then ran to Amelia and plopped down beside her, momentarily distracting Crystabel. The child could not have been more than five years old, and unlike her mother was dark-haired with huge brown eyes. "Anna! What are you doing here? I specifically told the nurse to keep you upstairs. Off with you."

"Can she not stay and have a dainty?" Amelia pleaded. "The guests are gone and there is no harm in it." She reached forward to hand the child a square.

Crystabel stepped forward and snatched the dainty from the child's hand. "She must do as she is told," she said firmly.

Crystabel waited until the little girl had stomped indignantly from the room, then grasped her arm once more. "My apologies Eleanora. Stephen and mother have indulged the child. She has become quite the little tyrant."

She pulled Eleanora in close, returning to the subject of marriage. "As an heiress and a lady in your own right, you need not be concerned with financial prospects, or even a title for that matter. You will be able to pick and choose as your heart directs. So many young women would envy you, my dear." Eleanora wondered fleetingly if Crystabel had been forced to choose a husband for his prospects or title. Based on her interactions with Lord Hargrove it could not have been his charm that sealed the match.

"I cannot wait until the ball. One dance with Mr. Weins and you will be swept off your feet." Crystabel giggled girlishly.

Eleanora was not looking forward to the ball at all. Amelia and Crystabel had certainly announced her status as an heiress to society. The very last thing she needed was a host of fortune hunters plaguing her all evening.

She wondered if Elliot Sparks would be present at the event. If so, the evening would not be a total waste of time. An image of his handsome rugged face flitted across her mind, and she smiled to herself. She quickly squashed the thought. If she had learned anything from her experience working for the firm in America, it was that work and romance were not compatible.

CHAPTER 6

Eleanora frowned over the maze of bank statements in front of her. The accounts contained far less money than she had anticipated. She reached again for the file of expenditures, going over the lists of costs carefully. Somewhere there had to be a substantial investment to account for the missing revenue, but she could not find it. The huge amounts missing were large enough to be an investment in a ship—an 11,000-ton steam ship costs about 22,000 pounds.

Costs for each ship were precisely recorded, the amounts matching the final ledger summarizing each shipment's costs and total expenditures for Pembroke. Nowhere was there an entry of a new build or any other investment. According to the reports a sum of over 10,000 pounds was unaccounted for. It was a disaster.

She flipped open the files for revenues once again, carefully examining each line. About four pages into the documents her heart stopped. Scrawled into the margin in shaky handwriting was a note. It overlapped the entries. ***The Guardian and the Elizabeth have listed no income for the past year, despite numerous runs.***

The Guardian and the Elizabeth were two of the company's ships which had been converted to steam by Jem. Leaving the file open, she quickly checked the expenses for the ships. They had indeed gone on numerous runs, with the associated expenses and wages listed. Flipping back to the income file she let her finger run down each page as she searched for an entry from either of the two ships. There was none. Not a single entry.

She pulled the revenue file in front of her and stared again at the message written there. It looked to be in Uncle Jem's hand. She slowly closed the file and laid her hand upon it as though securing its contents. Her company had been the victim of theft—an embezzlement had taken place. So massive in fact that Uncle Jem had recognized it almost immediately upon his return to work. There had been little attempt to disguise the activity. They must have assumed Uncle Jem would not be returning to the office.

She closed her eyes for a moment trying to digest the information. When she opened them again the file lay on the desk before her. For the first time she noticed a small dark stain on its far-right corner. She tossed her fake glasses off her face and held up the file. It looked like a blood smear. Was it possible the file was on the desk at the time of the murder? Jem's death took on an entirely different aspect. The handwritten note could well have been his last words. It was no coincidence Jem had been killed so conveniently during his first few days back at the office.

Her stomach churned. She reached for the little bell she used to summon her assistant. Claudia appeared in her doorway. "Claudia, ask Mr. Sparks to come to my office please."

Elliot settled himself across from Eleanora, looking at her curiously.

"We have a problem." For a moment she was unsure of how to break the news. Taking a deep breath, she decided to get directly to the point. "At least 10,000 pounds has been embezzled from the company in the past year." Opening the revenue file to the page with Jem's scrawled note, she indicated the line with her finger, and then set the banking and expenditure files next to it. She could not seem to find the words to explain it all. "You can confirm for yourself. I find I am quite nauseous. While you do so, I believe I will see to tea. I am in need of...something to settle my stomach."

Eleanora gave Elliot a full half hour before returning to the office with a tea tray. She set it carefully on the desk and poured for the two of them, handing Elliot his cup, before settling into her chair. "I find that a bracing cup of tea can settle the nerves."

"I think a brandy might be more in order," Elliot answered. His face was grim. "We have a serious problem. There is no doubt the money has been taken. The question is, how will we deal with it?"

"I thought we might call in the constables immediately."

Elliot took a sip of his tea, then set the cup down carefully. "I wonder if that is our best route. This theft had to be done by Matheson or at the very least, with his cooperation. If we call in the constables, they might be able to arrest him, if they can find him. You may or may not get your money back and the company will be the center of a public scandal."

He leaned back and rubbed a hand over his eyes. "I am not sure now is the time for Pembroke to be in such a position. Your customers want to hear that the company has smoothly transitioned to new management. We are already a novelty, with a young female as owner. Hiring me, the face of the business as you put it, was an important move, but make no mistake, the business community will be watching with interest. A disclosure of this nature will make your customers doubly nervous."

"So, what do you suggest?"

"We need to find Matheson. With luck the man will not have gone to ground just yet. If we can locate the scoundrel, we may be able to recoup our losses."

Eleanora pressed her lips together stubbornly. "The man is more than an embezzler. I believe he is also a murderer." She flipped the file closed and indicated the blood smear on its corner. "That Uncle Jem was shot just days after returning to work is no coincidence. And it appears he was killed with this particular file on his desk. I want the culprit prosecuted."

"Eleanora, we can still have Matheson prosecuted. But first let's see if we can track down the man. I have a friend, a former runner, who operates a detective agency, I will put him on the task. But first, there is one man who may know where to find him."

"And who would that be?"

"Our Mr. Wickett. In my experience no one is more informed than a secretary. Shall we summon him?"

Eleanora gave the little bell on her desk a shake. Claudia appeared in the doorway. "Claudia, would you ask Mr. Wickett to join us?"

Elliot added, "And could you write a note for me, to Mr. Peter's detective firm? He is at 224 Fleet Street. Ask him to meet me here this afternoon."

"Certainly, sir."

Mr. Wickett hovered in the doorway, shifting his feet nervously. He was a small man in a short suit jacket, one size too small. With his round spectacles, on a face that was marred with dots, he gave the impression of a lad just out of short pants. When first meeting him last week, she had wondered how the shy young fellow had achieved the position of head clerk. She concluded the man must have hidden talents, which would hopefully become apparent over time.

"You wanted to see me sir?" He flushed and quickly added, "Ma'am."

"Yes." Elliot rose and pulled a chair from the settee to the desk. "Come in, sit down. We have a few questions to ask you."

Mr. Wickett gingerly settled in the chair. His cheeks flamed.

Elliot began abruptly. "When you worked for Mr. Matheson, who handled the accounts?"

"I...I wasn't allowed the a-ac-accounts." His face was

turning a ghastly shade of pink. "Mr. Matheson insisted on handling th-those himself."

"Never? Are you saying you never saw the accounts? How is that possible?" Mr. Wicket winced as Elliot's voice rose in disbelief.

Eleanora shot Elliot a warning look, which he ignored. "Mr. Wicket," she said, purposely keeping her voice soft and low. "Explain how the accounts were handled."

Mr. Wicket turned to her with some relief. "I compiled the expenses, did payroll, and made up deposits, but all the files were kept with Mr. Matheson." His eyes darted back and forth between Eleanora and Mr. Sparks. "I... I was not p-privy to the whole picture sir. Mr. Matheson always insisted on handling the accounts himself." The poor clerk's face reddened even further as he sat twisting his hands nervously in his lap. Eleanora was beginning to understand Matheson's purpose in having this man as head accountant. He was certainly not a person who would question an employer, or heaven forbid, alert Jem to any discrepancies or concerns at Pembroke.

Eliot glared at the man; his brows lowered in a menacing scowl. Mr. Wicket seemed to shrink under his scrutiny.

Eleanora intervened once more, attempting to reassure the clerk with a smile. "I understand Mr. Wickett. No one is accusing you sir. Now then, what we need is the address of Mr. Matheson, and any ideas of where the man could be found."

He shifted his body in her direction, seeming to

prefer her approach to Mr. Sparks', who continued to glower at the man. "He has a residence here in town, number 105 Bassett Street. But if we needed to message Mr. Matheson, we first tried his club. The Businessman's Haven, just off St. James."

Mr. Sparks grimaced. "Ah. Well, it is a place to start. That will be all for now Mr. Wickett." Mr. Wickett rose from his chair and hurried from the room.

Elliot stood and strode to the window to gaze out at the street in contemplation. He rested his hands on the windowsill, his suit jacket pulled taut against his broad back. "I think I will pay a visit to Bassett Street, and then perhaps to Mr. Matheson's club."

"Why not wait for the runner you wish to hire? Surely given the circumstances it would be best to have someone with you?"

He turned to face her. "It is unlikely Mr. Matheson will have remained at home, waiting for us to discover him. My guess is he is long gone. Still, I may be able to get some idea of where he went before meeting Mr. Peters, my detective friend, later in the day."

"Alright, if that is the plan, then we best be off." Eleanora stood and walked to the door, grabbing her cloak and bonnet from the stand.

"Where do you think you're going?"

"I am going with you of course." She draped her cloak about her and began fastening her hat.

"Oh no, you are not." Mr. Sparks walked briskly across the room and took an intimidating stance between her and the door.

Eleanora resisted the urge to take a quick step back.

Mr. Sparks loomed over her; his sharp features set in firm lines. Everything about his stance was intimidating. Eleanora refused to be cowed by his bluster. "You are not going alone. If you will not wait for Mr. Peters, then I will accompany you," she said as she tied her bonnet ribbons into a brisk bow.

"No."

She raised her eyebrows and shot him a glare. "No? I would remind you, Mr. Sparks, that as owner of this company I am affectively your employer."

Mr. Sparks was unmoved. "Part owner. You are forgetting my twelve percent shares."

"Majority shareholder," she retorted, raising her chin a notch and placing her hands on her hips. "And as such I have final say in all decisions."

"Not in this decision you don't. Mr. Matheson has proven to be an embezzler and could be a murderer. It is too dangerous. I will not have you in harm's way."

"I fail to see the danger. You said yourself he is unlikely to be there waiting for us." Having draped her cloak about her, she walked back to her desk, and pulled her reticule from the top drawer, snapping it open to ensure she still had several pound notes inside, before tucking it under her arm. "Shall we?"

He scowled down at her. "If you come, you will not leave the coach. I will simply see if the man is at home, then return here to meet the detective, Mr. Peters."

Ignoring both his disgruntled face and high-handed tone, she gave him a gracious smile. "I am sure you are right, and there will be nothing to discover. We will be there and back in no time."

The ride across town was a quiet one. Eleanora glanced at Mr. Sparks. He had spent the entire journey looking out the coach window with a stoic expression on his face. She could not resist breaking the awkward silence. "Do you intend to ignore me for the entire ride?"

He turned towards her at last, a hint of amusement in his eyes. "As we are almost at our destination, the answer to that would be yes."

"Hmm," Eleanora responded, scowling at the smug expression on his face.

Before she could reply the coach slowed to a stop in front of a prestigious, white-bricked townhouse. It had three columns at its entry and rose two stories. Next to it, a stable, echoing its neoclassical design was tucked back from the street, its double doors currently open. A stable hand could be seen moving amongst the stalls.

"Quite elaborate for a man of business. And not abandoned by the look of things. I thought Matheson would have closed the place and left town. Interesting." Mr. Sparks opened the latch and swung gracefully into the street without waiting for the coachman. He narrowed his eyes at her. "I would remind you of your promise to remain in the coach," he said before abruptly closing the door.

The nerve of the man. Eleanora slid across the seat to watch from the window. Mr. Sparks approached the house and to her surprise the door was opened for him. The home was indeed occupied. After a short conversation with a man, who she assumed was a butler or servant of some sort, Elliot stood for a moment on the step, then walked over to the stables and disappeared into its open gates.

As she peered through the window, a robust woman carrying a basket made her way from the rear of the house toward the street. Eleanora quickly opened the coach door and hopped down.

"Good morning, ma'am," she said, giving the woman her best smile, "I'm looking for Mr. Matheson. I wonder if you could help me."

The woman looked her up and down, unimpressed with her workday clothing and practical cloak. "Are you now?" she responded before turning away and heading down the street, dismissing her.

Eleanora hurried to her side. "I am here from Pembroke, where Mr. Matheson worked. I must speak with him." Her words had no effect on the woman, who held her face steadfastly averted and hurried on her way.

While scrambling to keep pace with her, Eleanora reached into her reticule and pulled out several pound notes. "I can make it worth your while."

That slowed her down. She paused and looked at the money Eleanora offered. "Well now," she glanced again at the money in Eleanora's hand before she asked, "what is it you want to know?"

Eleanora laid a pound note in the woman's basket. "We are looking for Mr. Matheson. Any information about his whereabouts would help."

"You won't find him here. Haven't seen the man for days. Not a moment's notice either. Left the house one evening after supper and hasn't returned."

"Do you have any idea of where he might be? Did he pack a case?"

The woman snatched up the bill from her basket and slipped it into her apron pocket. "Packed nothing. We all thought he was spending a night or two with his light skirt, as he sometimes does. But this time he hasn't come back. The staff are all getting nervous here at the house—quarterly wages were due two days ago and not a word from the man. Just like the nobs to think nothing of the help, I say."

"One more thing ma'am. Is Mr. Matheson a social man? Did he have any guests the week before he left?"

"Well now, not that I know. He kept to himself, he did. And it was a good thing. I wasn't cooking for all and sundry, just a few bits for the master and a' course the staff. Made for a good shift most days."

"He did not entertain then, no guests. No one came by last week?"

"Not for meals, thank the Lord." She looked at Eleanora with a sly smile and then looked meaningfully down at her basket.

Only when Eleanora had dropped a second note into the basket, which was quickly whisked away, did the woman continue. "He had a lady come by last week. She's been here before. Wears a veil so there is not much I can tell you about her, except she looked right fancy. Never stayed for a meal though, not even tea. Just in and out. We figured she was his lady friend."

"Oh! Do you happen to know her address—the address of the lady friend?" she asked, unable to contain the excitement in her voice.

The cook smiled. "I do. I sent a cake to the house just recent-like, a birthday cake. But my memory gets a bit foggy if you know what I mean."

Eleanora was quick to drop another note into the basket.

The cook grinned as she tucked it into her apron. "Number twelve, Brightline Street. I remember it, because an old friend lives right next door. And that is all I can tell you."

"Thank you, Mrs.—"

"Bixby, ma'am."

"Thank you, Mrs. Bixby. If you hear any word from the man, if he returns or if you can think of where he might be, send word to Miss Pembroke at the offices and there will be a reward in it for you."

Mrs. Bixby rubbed her apron pocket and flashed her a toothy smile. "I will at that," she said and hurried on her way.

Turning toward the coach, Eleanora found herself facing an aggrieved Mr. Sparks. His arms were crossed, and he glowered at her forbiddingly. She flashed him a wide smile which did not soften his disgruntled expression. Flinging the door to the coach open, he wordlessly offered his arm.

He waited until she had settled before he spoke. "I thought I told you to stay in the coach."

"I don't recall agreeing to that particular instruction. Now then, what did you learn?" She decided to let him share his information before she gave the news about Mr. Matheson's mistress, but it was hard to hold back her excitement.

"I learned you do not take orders well. You promised to remain in the coach."

Eleanora was not about to let him dampen her enthusiasm. "I made no such promise, Mr. Sparks. Has anyone ever mentioned you have a nasty habit of issuing orders a little too liberally?"

He raised a single eyebrow and looked at her with an amused expression. "So, it is back to Mr. Sparks, is it? I thought we agreed on first names?"

"It is. Let's drop this argument for now. I am interested to learn what you found out." She leaned forward expectantly.

"Wherever he went last week, he took a hackney and no luggage. He apparently was in a hurry and did not wait for his carriage to be brought around. Odd that. But it does mean that wherever Mr. Matheson is, he is likely to be in town. A hackney would only take him to a city address."

She frowned. "That is odd. And it is stranger still that he has been gone for days, but packed nothing. What puzzles me is the man must have known it would only be a matter of time before his embezzlement was discovered. I would have thought he would have packed his prize possessions and been on a ship to the Americas by now." She grimaced and added, "With our money in his pockets. Is that all you were able to learn?"

"It is not much to go on I am afraid. We will have to begin our search for the man with next to no leads."

She could not resist a grin. "Not quite. While you

gained little information there, I, on the other hand, learned a good deal more from his cook."

His eyebrows furrowed into a frown, which she ignored. "It is true Mr. Matheson left without notice last week and hasn't been seen since. He must have gone out directly after he quit Pembroke. As you said, he took nothing with him." She paused for effect, waiting until he raised his eyebrows expectantly before continuing. "But I also learned he kept to himself. He had no visitors before he left, except for a veiled woman the servants thought might be his mistress. And..." she paused for effect, "I have her address."

"You have her address!"

"I do." Eleanora could not contain a smug smile.

"It will be an excellent place to start. If nothing else, she may be able to give us an idea as to Mr. Matheson's whereabouts." He paused and leaned forward awaiting her response. "Well? Where is it?"

"You will get it only if you agree that we question the woman together. I have no intention of giving you the address if you intend to go without me."

Eleanora watched as his lips tightened into a frown, and she quickly added. "I might be helpful. Think of it, Mr. Sparks. She will be much more inclined to speak to a woman."

Elliot groaned. "Fine. You may come. But only if you remain in the coach."

"But that is ridiculous. How can I question her if I remain in the coach?"

Mr. Sparks glowered at her from beneath furrowed

brows. "Has anyone ever mentioned that you are a willful young woman?"

She gave him her best smile. "Never. I have always been described in the most flattering of terms."

"Hmm. That I doubt. All right, we shall compromise. I will go to the door. If only the mistress is home, I will signal for you to join me. I do not want you there if we are to confront Matheson. Now the address if you please?"

Eleanora could not resist a triumphant smile as she recited the location.

In only a few moments they arrived at a small home, tucked behind a tangle of shrubbery, and set back discreetly from the street. Unlike Matheson's residence this house had an air of desolation about it. Even the windows placed symmetrically on each side of the door were completely shuttered. Eleanora felt the skin on the back of her neck prickle in warning as the coach slowed to a stop at the gates. She could not shake the feeling that there was something ominous hidden in its depths.

CHAPTER 7

Sliding the coach window back to get a better view, Eleanora watched as Elliot approached the front door and rang the bell. She was not surprised when he received no response. Another shudder of dread rippled through her stomach when he walked around the corner to the back of the house. Something was not right. Opening the coach door, she hopped deftly to the street, and followed him to the back of the house.

Elliot stood on the back stoop. In front of him the door to the kitchen hung slightly ajar. Coming up silently behind him, she watched as he used his foot to nudge the heavy wooden door. She took a silent step forward and peered around him as the door swung open to reveal an abandoned kitchen, with an empty hearth to the left and a spotless worktable parallel to barren sinks. Across the room a swinging door was propped wide to reveal an empty dining area.

At this time of day, the area should have been busy

with preparations for luncheon. "How odd," she whispered at his back.

He straightened abruptly, bumping her back a pace, then spun around to glare at her. "Bloody hell Eleanora!"

She ignored his exasperated look, pushing past him into the room to touch the charred walls of the hearth. "It is cold. No one has lit this fire in a while."

Elliot leaned against the door frame. "You realize you have just committed a break and entry?"

She rolled her eyes at him. "I did no such thing. The door was open." She walked to the swinging doors and peered inside. "Hello. Is anyone about?" she hollered, her voice echoing in the still house. After a pause to listen for a response, she tried again, this time drawing out the word, "Helllllloooo!" Nothing.

She looked at Elliot and raised her brows, surely he was thinking the same as her. A peek around the home could do no harm and might give them information on the whereabouts of Matheson.

Elliot pulled the kitchen door closed behind him. "We will take a quick look. But you my dear will stay behind me." He stepped past her into the dining room. Eleanora followed, scanning the room for anything untoward. Everything appeared in order.

They made their way to a small salon. With its windows shuttered, the room was a gloomy cavern. At one end it opened to the front entry and stairs leading to the upper floor, at the other a desk sat in front of heavily curtained windows. Between the two, was an arrangement of furniture next to the fireplace for entertaining. In a small house, the room would have served several purposes. It too was chilly, with a cold hearth; its fire long since burned out. Eleanora could not suppress a shiver. By the settee, two glasses sat on the coffee table, one still partially full. Elliot picked up the glass and sniffed its contents. "Brandy," he said and set it down.

A shawl was draped across the couch, but otherwise nothing was out of order.

Eleanora made her way to the desk. "Perhaps we'll find something here." Its top was bare, with only an ink jar and quill at its furthest corner. Elliot joined her and together they began going through the drawers.

"What are we looking for exactly?" Eleanora asked, as she tried to sort through the top drawer. It was filled with odds and ends—bits of broken porcelain, parts of quills, old nib pens, broken, and even an assortment of used paint brushes.

"I am not sure. Anything that might tell us who this woman is and where we might find her," he said as he sorted through a stack of bills. "Work quickly. I do not relish the idea of explaining our presence here," he added as he flipped through the papers. "Ah. An invoice addressed to Madam Rose Ingram. We have a name. It is not much, but it's something." He tucked the letter into his inside pocket and continued sorting through the pile of paperwork. "She was not much for organizing her accounts. And not a single personal letter."

"I don't know that a woman in her occupation would have many social connections. Still, you would think that there might at least be a note from family," she said as she pulled open the second drawer. A stack of paper, a few crumpled envelopes, and nothing else. The bottom drawer held more miscellaneous pieces of junk. There were several broken picture frames, with a shard of glass lying at the top. But tucked sideways beside the frames was a little black book.

She snatched it up and immediately opened it. "An address book!" The book was tattered and old. When she flipped through it there appeared to be only a few entries. Its yellowed pages were interspersed with adolescent drawings and what looked like bits of poetry. "It might be of some help." She handed it to Elliot who scanned it before slipping it into his inside pocket.

Elliot walked to the foot of the stairs, and Eleanora quickly followed. He turned to glower at her before ascending. "Stay behind me," he ordered.

Eleanora only rolled her eyes at him once more. But as they stepped up onto the upstairs landing Eleanora lost her bravado. A shadowed hallway loomed before them, the doors to rooms on the left and right closed, and a bathing room at the end of the hall open and dark. An unwholesome odor assaulted them; it was the unmistakable smell of death. Eliot too must have smelled it, because he paused briefly. This time she had no intention of pushing past him. Instead, she found herself hesitating, her heart pounding, and her fingers curled into sweaty palms.

She remained at the top of the stairs, gripping the handrail as Elliot stepped to the first door and after glancing in her direction to ensure she stood safely back, turned the knob.

She closed her eyes briefly as the door creaked open wide. Light from the room's window poured out, illuminating the hall. Eliot stood for a long second, surveying the scene before entering. Eleanora too, waited a moment before tentatively approaching. Releasing her breath, she scanned what appeared to be a spare bedroom which did double duty as a dressing room.

On the far wall of the room a daybed sat undisturbed, but for a carpet bag left open on its covers. On the opposite wall the closet door hung open with its contents spilling into the room. The chest of drawers too was in disarray, with clothes spewing from open drawers. On the floor what looked like a sheer nightgown and silken robe lay in a heap near the closet.

Eleanora peered into the closet. A few dresses were still there, but there were many empty hangers. "It looks as though someone packed in a hurry."

"I agree." Elliot picked up a lantern left on the bedside table. "And in the evening. This lamp was left here to burn out on its own."

Eleanora plucked the silken robe from the floor. A brown stain marred its front. "Elliot, I think it's blood," she said, holding out the dressing gown, her eyes wide.

Elliot took the offending garment and examined it carefully. "It appears to be. But it is a smear. Whoever wore this wasn't injured, rather they brushed against something," he grimaced before adding, "or someone, who was saturated in it." He dropped the robe. Both looked at the closed door across the hall with similar expressions of dread.

Eleanora's stomach turned. "This doesn't look good. I'll stay here while you check the other room."

"An excellent idea." Elliot strode across the hall and, hesitating only briefly, pushed open the last door. Immediately a rank smell overwhelmed them. Eleanora began to gag, quickly pulling her handkerchief from her pocket to cover her face. She watched Eliot pause and do the same before entering the room.

Her curiosity overwhelmed her. With her handkerchief securely over her mouth and nose, she took a few steps forward to stand at the open door. Elliot stood over a rumpled bed. Its white sheets stained a grotesque deep brown over a misshapen mound. She watched wide-eyed as he pulled back the sheet and stared at the mass beneath it.

Her stomach lurched, and she could not hold back a groan. Elliot looked at her, dropped the sheet and hurried to her side. "Come on, we have to get out of here," he said, taking her arm. Eleanora tried to hold her breath as they negotiated the stairs and scrambled through the kitchen to the back door.

On the back step they stopped at last. She bent over, coughing, and gagging to still her churning stomach. Eliot's arms slid around her waist, holding her from behind. His firm embrace helped her regain her equilibrium. She held tight to the strong hands at her waist while she gulped the fresh air. Only when she was sure she would not vomit did she turn to look up at Elliot, who kept his arms firmly about her waist.

"Are you all right?"

She nodded. His blue eyes examined her face carefully before releasing her. "It seems we have found our Mr. Matheson. Apparently, he has not left town as we suspected."

"No," she replied weakly, still recovering.

Taking her arm, he led her back to the waiting cab. "I must get you out of here Eleanora. You cannot be associated with this murder," he said as he helped her into the coach, giving quick instructions to the driver before climbing in behind her.

He settled her in the seat and slid open the window, before sitting across from her. "A little fresh air will help put some color back into your face," he said, scanning her as though looking for other issues with her person. "I told you to stay in the coach Eleanora. You have a great deal of difficulty taking instructions, even when it is for your own good. That was a scene you should not have been subject to."

Eleanora ignored his lecture. "He was murdered then?"

"That appears to be the case. He had a bullet wound to the chest." He grimaced. "And I think we can safely assume the event happened several days ago."

"Yes," she answered, thinking of the horrendous stench, and swallowing her horror. She leaned a little closer to the window, enjoying the cool wind on her face. "Do you think it was his lover then, Rose Ingram?"

"She was either present at the shooting or arrived shortly after, judging from the blood smears on the night gown." He frowned. "But it is too handy by half that the man was killed by his lover just as we discovered his role in the embezzlement."

"I agree. There must be some connection between this murder and the stolen money at Pembroke. It is simply too coincidental." She shuddered once more at the memory of the little house on Brightline Street.

Eliot looked grim. "We must find this woman. If we are right and she is not the killer, she may know who is, or at least have some idea who is responsible."

"If someone else killed Matheson, why would they leave her alive to tell the tale?"

"I can think of two possible reasons," Eliot answered. "The first is that she was not in the room. Matheson was killed in her bed. Yet there was no blood spatter on her robe, only a smear as if she later leaned over the body. If she were out of the room, she could then have hidden from the killer. And my second idea is that the killer left the woman alive knowing she would be blamed—which I am sure she will be."

Eleanora considered the possibilities. "It could be both."

The coach came to a stop in front of Pembroke. Again, Elliot did not wait for the coachman, opening the door and assisting her to the street. With her arm firmly in his, he silently escorted her into the building. It was as though he was determined to see her back to safe ground. There was something comforting in his grip, as though his calm strength was seeping through her arm as he held her tight against him. She stole a glance at his face; he wore a stoic expression which gave no hints as to his thoughts. Only when they entered the outer office did he relax his hold.

A man in a dark suit coat and bowler hat rested nonchalantly against Claudia's desk. Whatever he had been saying to her assistant had her smiling. Her face glowed with a soft pink blush.

The man slowly straightened as they entered. Claudia quickly rose to her feet. "Mr. Peters is here to see you Mr. Sparks." Eleanora looked at her curiously. If anything, Claudia's face had become even more flushed. Interesting, she thought to herself.

Elliot held out his hand to the man. "Sorry to keep you waiting Will. Thank you for coming down so promptly." He turned to Eleanora. "This is Miss Eleanora Pembroke. Eleanora, I would like you to meet an old friend of mine, Mr. Will Peters."

"Pleased to make your acquaintance sir." She held out her hand to shake his and was surprised when he lifted it to his lips.

"Honored Ms. Pembroke," he said with a wide smile. The man did not fit her idea of a detective. There was a charm about him, opposite to her expectations of the dour investigator.

Elliot addressed him, "I have a job for you if you are willing to take it on. And then I think a visit to the constables will be in order. It has been an interesting day." Mr. Peters only raised his eyebrows in response. Elliot turned to her. "Would you care to join us?"

"No. I will leave you to it. Claudia and I have appointments this afternoon." Eleanora answered remembering their fittings for the ball tomorrow night. "But I wonder if you could stop by the house later today to apprise me of the events."

Eliot took her hand, giving it a gentle squeeze while searching her face. Whatever he saw there seemed to satisfy him and he nodded. "Later then."

Eleanora was surprised to see Mr. Peters turn in Claudia's direction and wink before following Elliot into his office.

Once in the coach, she told Claudia of the startling discovery on Brightline Street.

"They must be connected. It is too much to assume the murder a bizarre coincidence."

Eleanora nodded. "Exactly what we deduced. Matheson had to have a partner. And I cannot help but make the obvious connection to the arrogant Lord Hargrove."

"I agree. And I am confident your Mr. Peters will be able to catch the culprit. He gave me the impression he was quite astute in these matters," Claudia said.

Eleanora looked at her with interest. Before she could comment the coach rolled to a stop.

An afternoon at the dressmaker was the perfect distraction. Eleanora and Claudia were to try on the final product and determine if any last-minute changes could be made before the dresses were delivered.

They were welcomed into the shop and outfitted in the new gowns. The dressmaker, Madame Bovine circled the women, testing the snugness here and there while nodding with satisfaction.

"You will be the finest young ladies at the ball. Perfection!" she said, in a French accent that was a trifle overdone. "Excellent, n'est ce pas?" Madame waved a white cloaked arm extravagantly. She was in a black dress, with white sleeves and collar, topped with a pristine white apron, pulled tight across a massive bosom, and tied on her heavily corseted waist. The unfortunate effect reflected her namesake of the Holstein variety.

"They are lovely." Eleanora smiled at Claudia's grand appearance in a soft emerald gown. Its hooped skirt was embroidered in bright green and the flowers of spring. The same pattern appeared in a stream across the bodice. The dress was cut in the latest fashion with a wide neckline and tightly corseted waist.

Eleanora ran her hand down the silken fabric across her waist and turned to the full-length mirror to examine her own gown. The apricot tones suited her dark hair and complexion. Her dress too was the latest in London fashion, sporting an off-the-shoulder neckline, softened with silken folds of a sheer, darker shade of apricot silk. The cinched waistline fell to the hips in a vee, where her skirts flared into a bell. The skirts themselves had alternating vertical panels of the light soft material of the gown's bodice and the sheer darker silk, heavily layered into the panels, and gathered periodically into sculpted silk flowers of the same material.

"I wonder if it is too much?" Claudia asked with a frown. "We are a veritable garden of blooms."

Eleanora laughed at her disgruntled expression. "It is time we had a little fun Claudia. We cannot be wearing our work suits to a ball."

"No, no." Madame Bovine insisted, taking offense with Claudia's comment, "Not overdone at all. You are conservative—the trend is for wild colors with bouquets of blooms. Be assured you are the very height of fashion. I would even suggest a few flowers in the hair, yes?"

Claudia widened her eyes in an exaggerated expression of horror, causing another burst of laughter from Eleanora.

"I thought I heard you in here. What lovely gowns." Crystabel poked her head into the dressing room, then stepped into the room in a swirling flurry of blue frills to give Eleanora a hug in greeting. "I hope this means you will be attending the ball tomorrow night."

"We are indeed."

"Wonderful." Crystabel stepped back to grace the women with a wide smile. Eleanora could not help but admire the perfect picture she made. Her blond curls peeked out of a stylish little hat perched at a saucy angle. Her azure day dress, with its ruffled skirts, suited her pale complexion and gave her an air of feminine delicacy.

"You must remember to seek out our Mr. Weins. I saw Arthur today. He was raving with praise for you my dear. You have made quite an impression!"

"Yes." Eleanora quickly changed the subject. "May I

introduce you to my friend Claudia? Claudia, this is Lady Crystabel Hargrove."

"Pleased to meet you, Lady Hargrove."

Crystabel acknowledged Claudia with a nod before returning her attention back to Eleanora. "As I said Mr. Weins was quite taken with you. And his dancing is divine. There is no one, my dear, more sought after in a ball."

"I will keep that in mind."

Madame Bovine greeted Crystabel with a bobbed curtsy, "Lady Hargrove, so glad you are here. I have finished your gown! It is marvelous, perfection! Just as you ordered. Come, come, we will do a final fitting." Madame leaned into the hall. "Adele, come at once!" She gestured to Lady Hargrove to follow her. A harried Adele bustled into the room. "Assist these ladies, and box the gowns for delivery."

"As you can see, I must be off. Until tomorrow my dears." Crystabel followed the modiste in a whirlwind of azure.

"Who is this Mr. Weins?" Claudia looked at her curiously, as she stepped carefully out of her gown, allowing Adele to whisk it away onto the waiting hanger.

"One of the many suitors Amelia and Crystabel have arranged. And all of them eager to wed an heiress. Amelia and Crystabel seem to think I should be focused solely on finding a husband." Eleanora sighed. "I am not sure I can stomach another round of fortune hunters." She turned her back to allow Adele to manipulate the myriad of tiny buttons on the ballgown.

"Not every man is a fortune hunter Eleanora. It is time you let go of that whole unfortunate experience with Sir Robert. It was three years ago, after all. I hope you are not still carrying a torch for the man."

"Oh, heavens no. It is not Robert that plagues me. It is that I was unable to see his true nature despite numerous warnings from both you and grandmother. I stubbornly insisted he genuinely loved me, until I heard the words from his own mouth. I am sad to admit I was flattered by his relentless charm. I think I must have enjoyed the constant praise. It has quite soured me on the whole suitor business."

Eleanora shuddered as she replayed that terrible scene in her mind. Her grandmother had maneuvered her onto the balcony, and there the two of them had stood cloaked in shadows, listening to her fiancée below declaring his love for another. And worse, the man was reassuring his woman that she, Eleanora, once married, could be whisked away to an asylum, or meet with a fatal accident. It was a night she could hardly forget. It had been enough for her to abandon the notion of love forever. All the pretty words Robert had bestowed upon her were lies, lies she had been too eager to believe.

"Phew!" Claudia snorted. "The man was a villain. And you, my love, were too innocent by half. Besides, I think part of your attraction to the beast was to flaunt your independence. Arabella, who as you know I love dearly, was nothing if not controlling. Your grandmother disapproved of him from the start, which I am sure, made him more delicious in your eyes." She paused as Adele assisted her into her day dress and began cinching up the ties at the back. "In my opinion, it is time you looked again."

"Not you too, Claudia." Eleanora gave a little laugh. "In the words of the bard, 'I'll look to like, if looking liking move.' Maybe I will find someone of interest this season."

Eleanora smiled as the image of Elliot flashed across her mind. "Perhaps this time I will look to marry as a business arrangement." She allowed Adele to make the final adjustments to her dress. "Thank you, Adele. We love the new gowns. The Madame has our address for delivery, but please be sure they are sent today. The ball is tomorrow night."

"Yes, my Lady."

As the ladies left the shop, and were assisted into their waiting carriage, Eleanora contemplated her statement about marriage as a business deal. The more she thought about it, the more she liked it. Most marriages among the elite were exactly that, arranged by families to ensure the benefit of both parties.

"Only think of it, Claudia, I could arrange a partnership. Someone who could contribute to Pembroke. We would have a relationship based on mutual respect, rather than this sordid business of love and trust. Then I could forego all the insincere prattle of a superficial courtship." And I could keep my heart safe, she added silently.

"You are not serious?"

"Why not? It is done all the time. The only difference is I would get to do the interviewing as opposed to a guardian handling the affair."

Claudia laughed. "Rather like interviewing for a manager you mean?"

"Exactly."

Claudia rolled her eyes. "I suppose we could advertise," she said and laughed again, "Unless you have someone in mind?"

Eleanora looked out the coach window at the busy streets. Here and there pedestrians picked their way between the many coaches passing this way and that. "No. But I do want to marry at some point. Amelia is unfortunately correct when she suggests time is against me. I just wish I could do it without all the shallow niceties of the courtship," she said, still focusing on the lively streets. Men in bowler hats and topcoats were in abundance. Surely there would be someone out there perfectly suited to the position of husband.

Mr. Elliot Sparks came to mind once more, and she smiled to herself as she imagined his chagrin if she approached him with such a proposal. She touched her waist, remembering the feel of his arms around her.

The thought of a romantic liaison with the man brought with it a delicious shiver of excitement. She pictured his broad back and strong capable hands. His rugged handsome face, with its chiseled features was one she found particularly attractive.

"What do you think of Mr. Elliot Sparks as a candidate?"

"Mr. Sparks?" Claudia laughed. "You cannot be serious! Elliot Sparks has all the charm of a distempered dragon. I hate to admit it, but the man intimidates me." Claudia shook her head in disbelief. She raised her handkerchief to her mouth and muttered to herself. It sounded like, "I have no idea what Arabella was thinking."

"What was that?"

"I said, I have no idea what concoction you're drinking." She colored slightly and explained, "I mean, to find Elliot Sparks as a candidate for marriage. The man is blunt, with no regard for the more delicate sensibilities, and that may be suitable for a manager of Pembroke, but it is not the best criteria for a husband."

"Nonsense Claudia. Elliot is a kind man, courteous in every way. It is just that he looks like a renegade, what with his height and his rough features." When Claudia rolled her eyes in response she added defensively, "And his talk is just bluster."

"If you say so my dear."

"I do. And I am sure that once you have gotten to know him better, you shall see for yourself."

The ball would be the perfect venue for her to charm Mr. Sparks. She wondered if Elliot would be attending. If so, surely there would be ample opportunity to make her interest known. She smiled to herself, at the idea of an evening spent in his company. Who knows what the future might bring?

CHAPTER 8

Elliot stood back from the little house on Brightline Street, watching Will as he attempted to glean more information from two constables assembled in the front yard. Although they were keeping the curious passersby and the press from the scene, a small crowd had gathered. Several of the onlookers scribbled into notebooks. Elliot would not be surprised to see lurid headlines tomorrow. He was sure that within a week the penny dreadfuls would be awash with the gruesome murder of a prominent businessman by his illicit lover. The story was too titillating to resist.

Even if poor Rose Ingram were innocent, she would be tried and convicted by the London mobs. The search for Miss Ingram would be on. Though it was imperative they find the woman, he almost hoped for her sake she was long gone.

He had given his statement, careful to leave out any mention of Eleanora's name in the process. He simply said he had arrived to seek out Mr. Matheson. Finding the door suspiciously ajar, with no one responding to his calls, he searched the place. When the constable asked him his reason for searching out Matheson, he considered hiding his true motives, but decided against it. The truth was certain to surface eventually and given this was the second murder, the constables would need to be informed. The constable had simply nodded and scribbled the information into his notebook.

Will Peters approached him. "We are done here. I have gotten what I could from my friends on the force."

"Would you care to share a hansom cab? I can drop you at your place, if you don't mind a quick stop at Miss Pembroke's place along the way."

"Perfect."

The events of the evening made for a somber ride with both men lost in thought, processing the day's revelations. When the coach slowed to a stop in front of Eleanora's small townhouse, Elliot was surprised when Will jumped down from the cab to join him.

When he rang the knocker, he was taken aback when Eleanora herself answered the door. He could not help but admire her in a light-yellow day dress with her hair pulled back in a casual braid. This relaxed persona was much different than the woman who worked at the office in a dark jacket and skirts with oversized glasses. For a moment he was dumb-founded and could only stand awkwardly by the door.

"Do come in gentlemen. Let me take your cloaks." He had planned to simply inform Eleanora of the latest developments and leave without interrupting their evening. But before he could get out the words, Will handed her his coat and Eleanora was arranging the items on the rack in the entry. "I am afraid we are still interviewing staff and are at odds and ends here." She gave them a wide smile. "But we do have a little brandy and a warm fire."

"I certainly could do with a brandy. It has been a long day," Will said.

She led them to a small parlor, just off the entry, where Claudia rose in greeting. "Do sit down gentlemen," Eleanora suggested and motioned to the arrangement of chairs and a settee before the fire, "Claudia and I were just now having a glass of wine. But as I said, I have a good French brandy." After pouring a glass of brandy for the men, she joined them in front of the fire, sitting beside Elliot on the sofa, with Claudia and Will taking the chairs.

"Now then, how did you manage with the constables?"

Elliot cleared his throat, still a little unsettled with her feminine appearance. "I informed them of our discovery of the body, leaving out only your role in the matter. I even told them about the embezzlement. Yet I got the distinct impression the authorities see this as a cut and dry case, with Rose Ingram as the culprit."

"I wouldn't be sure of that. Mcgowan is on the case. He was an excellent bow street runner in his day and has made a cunning investigator in the new police force." Will sipped his brandy before continuing. "It will be difficult finding Rose Ingram now. She has either left London or disappeared into the stews."

Eleanora added, "And I wish her all the luck. I am convinced she is only a witness in this affair. We do have the book. It is likely outdated, but it is a place to start."

Elliot reached into his inside pocket and pulled out the tattered black book, handing it to Will. "We found this in her desk. It appears to have been unused for a while, but it might be a place to start."

Will lay the book on the coffee table. Claudia shifted her chair forward to get a closer look. As Will slowly turned the pages the four of them studied what was written. There were many blank pages, each page headed with an elaborate letter of the alphabet as though the book had been intended as an address book. But though they had reached J, there were no addresses. Instead, there were bits of poetry and drawings, brightly colored and all done in a rounded adolescent hand. The images were of rainbows, butterflies, and the like. Occasionally the name of a girl appeared. Emma Fairbanks under F, and Elizabeth Kipple under K, but no addresses.

Will closed the book with a disappointed sigh. "I suspect this is not going to be of much help."

Eleanora agreed. "It does appear to be a memento, something Rose kept from her youth. Leave it with me. I will take a closer look at it when I get a chance." She set the book to the side and addressed Will. "I assume Mr. Sparks informed you about the embezzlement, and our assumption that the murder of Matheson must in some way be connected. What do you think, Mr. Peters? Do you too believe it likely?"

Will leaned back and took a sip of his brandy. "Oh, I agree. It is altogether too much of a coincidence. But if we are correct, and Matheson was an embezzler and a murderer, who himself was killed for his efforts, then we must look for a partner. Someone who needed to remove Matheson before he could give up his associate."

Claudia interjected, "I agree. And I believe it is Hargrove. The man is an absolute bully. Last week he attempted to muscle his way into the firm. He was determined to take control. Had he succeeded, it is likely the embezzlement could have remained hidden."

"And one must not forget Hargrove believed Crystabel to be the inheritor of Pembroke. Jem's death would have been a windfall for the man if that had been the case," Eleanora added.

Will nodded. "Lord Hargrove is an excellent place to start. I will be looking into his lifestyle and finances. But for now, I think it best to keep the missing money and any suspicions concerning Mr. Brigg to ourselves. I cannot see inspector Mcgowan announcing the information. He likes to keep his theories to himself and is known for sharing little with the press. We will let the conspirator, if there is one, think himself safe. With luck, the press will focus on the lover in Matheson's murder."

Elliot grimaced. "I don't think that will be a problem. The reporters at the scene were eager to scoop up the lurid details of an illicit affair gone wrong—makes for exciting reading."

"We might want to keep an eye on Hargrove, keep

him close. He is the one with the motive..." Will paused to take a sip of brandy while he contemplated. "Watch who he interacts with, and where he goes. In my experience a lord always has someone else do his dirty work. Maybe the fellow will slip up and we can get him." Will set down his empty glass. "For now, finding Rose Ingram, and taking a close look at Lord Hargrove will be our starting point."

"He will be at the Mansfield ball tomorrow night. Claudia and I will be attending. I can try to monitor him," said Eleanora.

Elliot was quick to respond. "No Eleanora. I would prefer you to stay out of this. I will be attending and can manage that task."

"Really Elliot, must you argue with me at every turn. I am quite capable of watching Hargrove. I would remind you it is my company we are investigating."

"Our company. You keep forgetting my twelve percent shares."

"I am the majority shareholder and as such I believe it is both my responsibility and duty to take an active role in all this." Eleanora crossed her arms and set her chin at a determined angle. Elliot wondered for a moment how so much stubbornness could be held in such a small frame. He glowered at her, achieving only a scowl in response.

From the corner of his eye, he caught Will and Claudia exchanging a look.

Claudia interceded, "It seems to me, Eleanora, that you have a solid connection with Crystabel. Why not try to gather information from her. There may be more opportunities to learn about Hargrove through his wife. After all, if Hargrove is our villain, he is bound to be more careful in his actions at this time."

Will smiled at Claudia. "Excellent idea, Miss Claudia. You have the makings of a true detective."

Eleanora sighed. "Fine. What sort of information should I look for?"

"I am not sure. At this point we know almost nothing about the man. Finding out about his relationship to Matheson, or his previous role in the company, may help. I will have some of my men investigate his financials and after I leave here tonight, I will put a tail on him. With any luck he will meet with his conspirators to discuss the discovery of the body." He shrugged. "I am hoping Elliot can check out his club." He looked at Elliot who nodded. "I doubt there will be much to learn at the ball, but we can keep an eye on him."

Will set his empty glass on the end table. "And now I best be going. I have a few things to tie up tonight. Thank you, ladies, for the brandy."

Eleanora and Claudia walked them to the door. As Elliot pulled his cloak over his shoulders he turned to Eleanora. "Since I too will be attending the ball, I would be honored to escort you ladies, if that is your pleasure."

"Thank you. That would be lovely." she replied, giving him a wide smile. He was relieved to note that the disgruntled Eleanora of the last few minutes seemed to have disappeared.

Once in the carriage, Will turned to him. "I must say she is a fine figure of a woman."

Elliot looked at him warily. "Yes, she is."

"She has a sound mind. Rather surprising to find such intelligence in so fine a form. Can't say I am not impressed."

"She is intelligent." Elliot answered slowly, eyeing Will suspiciously.

"I would love to take her for a turn around the dance floor. Sadly, I did not receive an invitation to the Mansfield ball. Apparently, detectives were not high on the guest list." He grinned, then looked at him hopefully. "Lady Mansfield is your aunt is she not?"

"She is." Elliot did not like where this conversation was going. He turned to stare out the coach window, refusing to acknowledge Will's less than subtle hint.

Will persisted, "I wonder if you could snag me an invitation. I plan to impress the woman with my charm and agility." Will chuckled to himself, unaware of Elliot's growing annoyance.

Elliot scowled at him. "I doubt you will get the chance for a dance. Miss Pembroke will likely be swarmed with admirers."

"Miss Pembroke? Who said anything about Miss Pembroke? It is Miss Claudia I mean to court."

Elliot laughed. "In that case my friend, I will be happy to get you an invitation."

"Excellent." Will grinned, before looking at Elliot speculatively. "I take it you have an interest in Miss Pembroke?"

"I do, though I am not sure why. She is the most irritating woman I have had the honor to meet."

Will laughed. "This is so unlike you; I must say I am

intrigued. Picturing you as the charming suitor is a bit difficult to be sure. One gets the impression you would have done better a few thousand years ago when you could just hoist the woman over your shoulder and carry her off." Will laughed again, considerably pleased with the image.

"I am glad you find this so amusing."

Even in the dim coach light Will's eyes twinkled with amusement. "My apologies old friend. Feel free to ask for my assistance at any time. I can put in a good word for you. I would even be more than happy to scrawl a sweet poem for you, should you need it."

"Drop the topic Will."

"Fine. But I do suggest you use the opportunity of tomorrow's ball to relate to her on a social level, away from the office routine. And for God's sake, be sure to dance with her," he said in more serious tones.

Elliot remained stoic, refusing to discuss his personal issues, even with Will. "Sound advice, I am sure," he said. Thankfully, the coach was pulling to a halt outside Will's apartment. "I will send the invitation over as soon as I get it tomorrow."

Will let himself out onto the street, with a smile and the tip of his hat before closing the coach door.

Elliot leaned back in his seat as the carriage swung around to head back the way he had come. His apartment was only a few short blocks from Eleanora's townhouse. A shorter distance if one cut across the park in front of her home.

He thought about Will's advice. Yes, he wanted to dance with Eleanora. And though aware he was not the most charming man in the vicinity—fine words and flirtations were a skill he had found impossible to attempt, let alone master, nevertheless, he hoped to make a positive impression on the woman.

He scowled when he remembered his promise to his aunt to introduce his cousin Charles to Eleanora. Perfect. Now he would be competing with a poet to charm his Eleanora.

CHAPTER 9

Breakfast was a slow affair the next morning. It was usually a pleasant chance to linger over tea and discuss their day. Despite her initial lack of enthusiasm for the ball, Eleanora now found herself in a tangle of anticipation. Having Elliot escort them made all the difference.

Claudia, however, was her usual practical self. "We have one more interview for housekeeper this morning, before we can think of preparations for tonight. I am hoping this will be the one. So far, we have had a former butler in his seventies, a young man still wet behind the ears and a woman of questionable integrity." Claudia reached for the teapot and refilled her cup. "This was a last-minute resume. It was delivered just this morning, and not by the agency, which leaves me hopeful. I replied that if she could present herself here today before noon, we would interview her."

Eleanora sipped her coffee, then set it down and

responded, "After this I should think we shall have ample staff. We have a cook and scullery maid, and our Anna as a lady's maid—I am still thankful she agreed to come with us from America. We even have a gardener."

"Yes. The British are over-staffed in my mind." Claudia gave a heartfelt sigh. "It seems ridiculous for a house this size. But we do need a housekeeper or butler, one who is willing to do double duty helping where needed and to oversee the lot. If we are frequently at Pembroke, someone will have to be in charge here. This Mrs. Bixby sounds promising. She has worked as a housekeeper and more recently as a cook. I am hopeful."

Eleanora gasped. "Mrs. Bixby! Matheson's cook was Mrs. Bixby. I wonder if it is the same woman. She seemed a bit rough around the edges, but perhaps she would do."

Claudia smiled. "I would remind you, that having just arrived from the Americas, I am sure the two of us are considered 'rough around the edges' as well."

Eleanora laughed. "Quite true."

The sound of the knocker at the front door interrupted their thoughts and Anna entered. "A Mrs. Bixby to see you, Miss Claudia."

"Thank you, Anna. Send her to the library. I will be right there."

"I will leave you to the interview, but I do think I will take a quick peek to see if it is the same woman," Eleanora said as the ladies both rose from their breakfast. "If nothing else the woman is punctual. You could not have sent your note more than an hour ago."

"As I said, we can be hopeful. It seems the old adage, 'good staff is hard to find,' certainly applies in London."

When they entered the library, a buxom woman wearing the short jacket and skirt of a working woman with its dark toned shades, rose to meet them. It was indeed the same Mrs. Bixby of Matheson's household. She had certainly lost no time before searching for another position. Matheson's death would only have been announced yesterday afternoon.

Eleanora shook her hand. "Why Mrs. Bixby, I wondered if it might be you."

Mrs. Bixby colored slightly. "Yes. I saw no reason to delay looking for employment, what with the dreadful news and all. A woman's got to look after herself these days."

"I am sure it was a shock to all the staff."

"Oh aye, it was. Terrible situation that. And what's more it left us all at loose ends in the house. As I said, there was no point in delaying. I decided right then and there to move on and be done with it."

Claudia took up a position behind the desk. "I agree Mrs. Bixby. The practical route is always the best one."

"I will leave you to it Claudia." She turned to Mrs. Bixby and smiled. "Good luck."

ELEANORA WAS NOT SURPRISED to learn Mrs. Bixby had been hired as their new housekeeper. She would begin immediately.

The ladies spent the rest of the day preparing for

the ball. A last-minute shopping trip to pick up some needed accessories: gloves, fans and even a tiny clutch purse for Claudia, had been accomplished.

Anna was just finishing the last touches on their hair when Mrs. Bixby entered the dressing room to announce, "Mr. Sparks has arrived with your carriage. He is waiting at the entry."

"Thank you, Mrs. Bixby. You can tell him we will be right down." Eleanora turned and smiled at Anna. "We look lovely. You have outdone yourself Anna." Both women wore their hair up. Anna had added sprigs of flowers to Eleanora's, and she turned her head to admire the coronet of tiny colorful blooms. Claudia had refused to go with the fashionable choice of flowers. Instead, her hair was arranged with delicate pearl beads woven into her chestnut braids then coiled into a lace chiffon.

All that was left was to drape their shawls about them.

Claudia positioned herself for a last moment before the full-length mirror as she pulled on a long silken glove. For once she appeared nervous. Eleanora stood beside her and gave her a hug. "You look beautiful Claudia."

Together they glided down the stairs. Below Elliot was framed at the threshold. He was all that was proper, in a formal long coat over glossy vest and trousers all in black, his white cravat and gloves standing out sharply against the elegance of his perfectly tailored suit.

He made a short bow when they reached him and

held out his arms. "I am honored to have two lovely ladies to escort."

Eleanora smiled. "Thank you, Elliot." The evening was beginning as she had imagined. This was to be her first London ball. In Boston, the young women who had spent a season in London, raved about the pomp and circumstance of a London affair. In her mind she had romanticized the ball into a glamorous event, and tonight she would be part of it. She hoped reality would live up to her fantasies. Her one concern was that having been in America for over a decade, she would be frowned upon for what might be considered her provincial ways.

Her concerns evaporated when they entered the ball. She was surprised by the gracious welcome she received at the door. Lady Mansfield took her hand and smiled warmly. "How lovely you are my dear. I am so pleased you decided to attend our little soirée." She waved a bejeweled hand at her son who stood slightly back from the entry and away from the queue at the door. "Charles, you must escort Miss Pembroke and her party to the very best seats." She turned to Eleanora and added, "I do hope you enjoy your evening," before she was obliged to return to the ever-growing crowd of guests arriving.

Elliot led them away from the entrance to the ladies' receiving room where they left their cloaks and checked their appearance in the full-length mirrors. When they returned to the ballroom he stood with the young Charles at his side.

"Your dance cards ladies." Elliot's face was grim, and

she wondered what could have irritated him so. "Miss Eleanora Pembroke, Miss Claudia Whitfell, may I introduce to you my esteemed cousin, Charles, Lord Mansfield."

Charles did a formal bow, before raising each of their hands to his lips. He was a young man, very debonair in a perfectly tailored suit. His blond hair was fashioned into the curls so popular among the young aristocrats of the ton. "Honored to meet you. Two such lovely flowers, shining in a veritable garden of blooms." Eleanora could not resist a quick glance at Claudia, and the two of them shared a smile. "You must allow me to be the first to write on your dance cards. I am sure we can add Elliot as a fourth for the first quadrille."

Before they were settled the master of ceremonies announced the quadrille. The four of them took their positions and the orchestra began to play. The ballroom became a sea of vibrant color as the ladies twirled their elaborate gowns in unison.

The next two hours passed in a blur of dancing. She was seldom able to return to her seat, before being whisked away for the next set. Since her arrival she had seen little of Elliot. Indeed, had it not been for Elliot's height she would not have caught a glimpse of him at all. She knew she should be pleased with her social success, but the constant crowd around her was beginning to wear.

Her most persistent admirers were Charles and Mr. Weins. So far Mr. Weins had twice insisted on a dance. It seemed she could not move without finding him at her elbow. Though it was considered rude to refuse a dance, Eleanora decided to sit the next one out. She looked around the room for Claudia and smiled when she saw her on the arm of Mr. Peters. Spotting Elliot near the open patio doors by their seats, she made her way toward him with some relief.

As she approached him, Charles stepped deftly into her path with a bow and a glass of punch. "A glass to cool my lady's fair throat, though nothing here can chill the ardor, or demote, the emotions now ignited in our hearts."

"Ah...yes...thank you, Charles," she said, taking the glass and leaning around him to give Elliot a tentative smile.

She was about to speak to him when someone grasped her arm. She turned to see an elegant Crystabel with Mr. Weins. "I have found a moment with you at last. You look lovely as usual Eleanora."

Mr. Weins graced her with a bow. "I agree. The perfect picture my dear. You are a jewel in this gilded setting. You have made the evening a memorable one—truly the bell of the ball."

Eleanora flushed slightly and turned to Crystabel. "As do you Crystabel." Tonight, Crystabel wore a dark red gown, with her hair in a fabulous array of curls, adorned with a red and black ostrich feather. She could only be described as stunning.

"Arthur and I were just discussing a walk in the park tomorrow afternoon and hoped you and your friend Claudia might join us."

To her surprise Elliot stepped forward and announced, "I am afraid Miss Pembroke and Miss

Whitfell have accepted a stroll through Hyde Park with me tomorrow afternoon."

Crystabel was not deterred. "How wonderful. We will make a full party. I shall even convince my husband Steven to join us." She turned to Eleanora. "Shall we meet at the south gate? I think two o'clock would be a fine time."

"Hyde Park? I would be delighted." Charles interjected. "I can think of nothing more delightful than a stroll with such lovely ladies—the very blooms of spring, so suited to those green environs."

"Well then," Elliot said with a sardonic smile, "it seems we will indeed be a full party." The orchestra began a waltz. "And I believe this is my dance, Eleanora." Before she could reply he took her hand and pulled her towards the dance floor, giving the company a nod before swinging her into his arms.

Eleanora had time for only a quick glance at the little gathering before she was whisked away. For the briefest moment, she saw a flash of anger marring Crystabel's normally charmed expression. But there was no time to contemplate it as Elliot's arm circled her waist and they began to move to the music.

She allowed herself to enjoy the feel of Elliot's warm hand on her back as he glided them across the floor, masterfully maneuvering through the dancers before she addressed the issue of the walk in the park. She stole a look at his face. His expression was stoic as usual.

"You certainly managed to plan my day. Has it

occurred to you that I may have made my own arrangements for tomorrow afternoon."

"Did you?"

"No. Fortunately I have not. But that is not the point." She paused for a moment while they executed an elaborate turn. "I can think of any number of activities I would prefer to an afternoon stroll with the Hargroves and Arthur Weins."

"Let's not forget Charles." Elliot broke into a grin, then continued on a more serious note. "I apologize Eleanora. I genuinely thought I was saving you from an unwanted engagement."

"Be that as it may, I am still obliged to spend an afternoon in their company. I am not sure I can take the attentions of two so persistent suitors for an entire afternoon." Eleanora grimaced at the thought.

"If it is any consolation, I shall be there as well. As will Claudia."

"If I can convince Claudia to attend, which is unlikely." She furrowed her brow at the thought. "And you had better be there. In fact, I will expect you at my home with your carriage in ample time to take us to the park."

Elliot laughed. "I shall arrive in my very best walking boots." He concentrated for a moment on negotiating them around a slow waltzing couple. "Think of it as an opportunity to learn more about Hargrove."

"There is that."

The music wound slowly to a halt. Elliot walked her around the edge of the dancers as a second waltz began. Two waltzes danced consecutively with the same partner was a major breach in etiquette, thus Elliot was compelled to return her to her seat. Eleanora scowled as she realized she had blown her opportunity to charm him. The evening was certainly not going as planned.

Being encircled by his arms was where she wanted to be. She decided to assign the laws of etiquette to perdition. It was time to take the matter into her own hands. Let the gossips talk—she could blame her lack of manners on her decade in the Americas. "I do love the waltz. Shall we have another dance?" Eleanora realized with dismay that she had breached a second rule of etiquette—a lady did not ask a man to dance.

Elliot raised his eyebrows and with only a sardonic half smile in response, swung her around, as the music began to play.

This time she tilted back her head to avoid getting dizzy and gazing at the glittering chandeliers above her, concentrated only on the feel of Elliot's arms about her and his body close to hers. Elliot held her scandalously close as they twirled expertly around the room. Her world narrowed until she was only aware of his delicious scent and the strength of his arms around her. The lights began to blur as they moved together in a perfect rhythm. When the music slowly came to a stop, Elliot held her still against him and looked down into her eyes.

It felt as though they were frozen in time. She was transfixed by the clear blue depth of his gaze. Her heart was pounding in her chest, and her cheeks burned. She wanted this man—this was the man of her dreams.

Elliot broke the spell with a quick nod, silently taking her arm to walk back to her seat. She was thankful to be well across the room from her party, hoping to use a few moments to try to regain her composure.

As they approached the patio doors, Elliot looked down at her. "Shall we get a little fresh air?"

"Thank you, yes." The words were barely out of her mouth when Elliot pulled her through the open doors and into the cool night air.

The patio was lit with colored lanterns, illuminating several groups of people who had taken a moment to escape the stifling heat of the ballroom. In the distance a fountain was glowing with a soft blue light, giving the yard a magical quality. But they did not pause to enjoy the scene. Instead, Elliot led her briskly away from the doors and into the shadows beneath a potted palm.

Without a word, he rested his arms on her shoulders, turned her body into his and kissed her. At first his lips were gentle, raining soft tentative kisses along her lips, seeming to ask a desperate question. When she responded by putting her arms around him and pressing her body into his, it was as though the flood gates opened.

Her world shattered as her senses exploded. The feel of his hard back beneath her hands, and his unique manly scent overwhelmed her. She gasped and Elliot used the opportunity to plunge his tongue into her mouth. She groaned and tightened her arms around his body, relishing the taste of him. He pressed his body against her, holding her tightly against him as he assaulted her mouth. She felt him lift her off her feet. Never in her life had she been so thoroughly kissed.

And then very slowly he gentled, brushing his mouth against hers with the softest of caresses. He let her slide seductively down his body until her toes once again touched the floor. He ended the kiss as he began, showering her with soft kisses as he withdrew. For a moment he rested his forehead against hers before his arms found hers as he stepped back from her, letting his fingers trail down over the satiny smoothness of her gloves, until he held her hands in his. Never once did his eyes leave hers.

Neither spoke. Eleanora could only look helplessly into the dark pools of his eyes, wondering at the passion that held her so enthralled.

"There you are." Charles' voice interrupted from across the patio. Elliot took a quick step back, releasing her hands, and turned to face Charles as he hurried towards them. "I saw you step onto the patio looking a trifle flushed. It is frightfully warm in there, thus I thought to bring you a glass of iced punch."

He executed a perfect bow and handed her the glass with a flourish. "For my lady."

Eleanora reached out for the glass, thankful for the shadows which hid her burning cheeks. "How thoughtful of you." She took a drink to calm her shattered nerves, enjoying its cool sweetness.

"Yes, thoughtful indeed." Elliot said dryly.

"I could not let my esteemed cousin take sole credit for rescuing a damsel in distress." He did a second bow. "I braved the crowds, completing the arduous task of tracking down a footman to bring my fair princess an ice in her time of need."

"You sound as though you climbed a mountain to its snowy peaks," Elliot said, failing to hide his sarcasm.

"Rest assured I would not hesitate to do exactly that, my fair Eleanora. And seeing your eyes outshine even the brightest star in this dark night is reward enough." He took her hand and raised it to his lips. "With eyes aglow and ebony hair, was ever a lady quite as fair, as the beauteous Eleanora."

Eleanora laughed, in part as a response to Elliot's disgruntled expression. "Shall we return to the ball? I am feeling quite revived with all this attention."

Charles was quick to take her arm, and with Elliot trailing behind them, they returned to the hall.

A small group had gathered around her chairs, with Amelia beaming at its core. She wore a mauve gown, its excessive flounces, and ruffled layers cascading over her wide girth. "There you are my dear. My, but it has been hard to find you in this crush." She leaned in close and whispered, "I have let it be known that my wealthy niece will select a husband this season. Not to worry love, plenty of suitors now." Amelia giggled and whispered for her ears only, "A little pressure does a world of good." Then she stepped back, and in a grand gesture indicated Lords Manford, Farrow, and Brambury. "Look who I have found for you, my dear." All three gentlemen did the required short bow.

Eleanora saw Crystabel on the edge of the crowd. When she caught her glance, Crystabel rolled her eyes with irritation. At least she had an ally there.

Lord Farrow stepped forward. "My Lady Pembroke, I w-w- wonder if—"

Lord Brambury plunged forward and grasped her arm, shoving poor Lord Farrow to the side. "There you are my little filly. It is time I took you for a turn around the dance floor." Before she had a chance to answer, she was being pulled along.

She could only glance back at Elliot helplessly before Lord Brambury plowed forward into the dancers.

After Lord Brambury it was Lord Manford. Unfortunately, it was a waltz. She had spent the entire dance attempting to lean back to create space between them, while he was intent on the opposite.

After the dance, it was a relief to find Crystabel waiting for her at the edge of the dance floor. Before Lord Farrow could stutter out his request, Crystabel grabbed her arm. "Miss Pembroke and I need to visit the retiring room," she announced. Eleanora happily took her arm and let her lead her away.

Once in the ladies' room, Eleanora basked for a moment in the cool quietness. A cabinet of sorts had been set against the wall with several basins filled with cool water, in front of a large mirror. A young maid worked as an attendant and was busy at the moment stitching the hem of a lady's dress on the far side of the room.

Crystabel took a clean white cloth and after wetting

it, dabbed it gently on her face. "It is far too hot in there. I hope you do not mind me stealing you away for a few minutes of peace."

"It was a perfect idea," she said following Crystabel's lead and cooling her cheeks with a cloth.

"I thought you would welcome a break." Crystabel set the cloth aside and turned away from the mirror to look at her. "I fear I must apologize for my mother's zeal in finding you a husband. Is it a little too much?"

"It is. But I do understand that she means well. It is the suitors themselves. They are relentlessly persistent. I have always been an heiress, but Amelia's announcement that I will be choosing a husband this season appears to have added a competitive fervor which is entirely too much."

"Oh dear," Crystabel lamented and laid a hand on her arm in sympathy. "You mustn't rush Eleanora. I admit I was a tad jealous. You have what I never had—the option of choosing a man for his charm alone. It is a great boon my dear. So few women have the privilege of owning both wealth and status. I would encourage you to do what I could not. If you want a husband, choose one who is charming and elegant—a man like Mr. Weins who can be admired." She squeezed her arm and smiled. "And then I can live vicariously through you."

Eleanora realized Crystabel had just shared her past challenge in choosing a mate. Lord Hargrove was certainly not a man of charm. His face and demeanor were arrogant. And though he seemed fit enough, his long face and thin features could not be described as handsome. Crystabel had obviously made an arrangement where she received a title, and he the money he needed to save his estate. Such a bargain was a common one in the ton.

Crystabel reached into her reticule and took out a small pot of rouge. Eleanora watched as she put a small amount on her cheeks and blended it in. Rouge was a secret amongst the women of the ton. Though no one admitted to using it, almost everyone did. She offered the pot to Eleanora with a mischievous smile.

"Oh no," Eleanora laughed, "the last thing I need is to have rosy cheeks. Young Charles would be sure to produce some poem to hail them."

Crystabel laughed too. She looked at her through the looking glass. "I can help you sort through some of the suitors. For instance, my advice is to stay away from Lord Manford. His first wife had a great deal of money. Her early death was suspicious."

"Suspicious?"

Crystabel grimaced. "It was said to be an arranged marriage, her money for his title. Both families were pleased, and the gossip was they forced the match. There were rumors the two of them did not get on. She fell down the stairs shortly after the marriage leaving him her fortune. There were no witnesses. Very convenient." Crystabel told the tale as though the whole thing were commonplace.

Eleanora could not help but feel a pang of sympathy for the unfortunate Lady Manford.

Crystabel returned the rouge to her reticule and snapped it shut. Taking Eleanora's arm once more to return to the ball she said, "I do not need to warn you off Farrow, he is far too shy for someone as outgoing as you. But what do you think of Charles?"

"He is too charming. I would be forever swimming in poetic verse," she answered and the two of them laughed as they reentered the ballroom. The music was too loud for further conversation.

The rest of the ball passed in a blur of gentlemen eager to have a chance at the latest prize. By the end of the evening, her toes were blistered, and her lips ached from the permanent smile plastered on her face. If she could have strangled Amelia, she would have. The very last thing she wanted was a trail of fortune hunters tormenting her. She had learned her lesson well enough through her former fiancée Robert. The fawning and flattery had no effect on her this time, other than irritation.

The ride home began in silence. Claudia appeared lost in thought, gazing out the window at the passing gas lights. Elliot sat stone-faced across from her, his arms crossed on his chest, and his legs stretched out before him. She wondered if he was regretting their kiss on the patio.

Eleanora broke the silence. "For all that I wanted to monitor Lord Hargrove tonight, I don't believe I even saw him this evening. Was he in attendance?"

"He was," Elliot responded.

"He could not have been dancing. I would have noticed if he had taken to the floor," Eleanora said.

"Yes. You certainly would have. It was where you spent the entire evening."

Eleanora ignored Elliot's surly attitude. "He spent no time with Crystabel. Each time I looked at her it was Mr. Weins beside her, not Hargrove. Where was the man?"

"Lady Mansfield supplied a games room. Whisk has become quite popular in the ton. Fortunes can be won and lost at those tables. Our Lord Hargrove spent the night in deep play. When I last looked in on him, he was down on his luck."

The comment caught Claudia's attention. She turned from the window to join the conversation. "Now that is interesting. If Hargrove has a gambling problem, it will certainly provide a further motive for the crimes."

"It would indeed," Eleanora mused. "I wonder what Hargrove's financial status was before he married Crystabel. After all, Crystabel is the daughter of a merchant, and Hargrove is an aristocrat. From Hargrove's point of view, it would have been a considerable step down."

"Quite true," Elliot agreed. "I would guess the marriage settlement was a substantial one. And if you are correct, and Hargrove expected to inherit Pembroke, then he would have seen it as marrying into a fortune." Elliot shrugged and said, "But we should not jump to conclusions. It could have been a love match. Crystabel is a beauty."

Unable to keep the bitterness from her voice, Eleanora replied, "He would not be the first man to propose with the sole purpose of gaining a fortune."

Elliot raised his eyebrows inquiring, "You sound as though you have experience in the matter."

"I do. But that is neither here nor there." She waved her hand as though dismissing the topic. "Tonight, Crystabel told me a piece of gossip about Lord Manford. His first wife fell down a set of stairs to her death in a suspicious set of circumstances." Eleanora frowned. "I cannot help but remember he told me that he and Matheson were, in his words, 'as thick as thieves.'"

Her comment roused Claudia from her thoughts. "Now that is interesting. Though I cannot imagine anyone using that particular expression if he were involved in the embezzlement." She considered it for a moment. "And it is difficult indeed to conceive of the fellow involved in anything outside the stock exchange."

"Quite true." Eleanora was still set on Lord Hargrove as the prime suspect. "It will be interesting to see what Mr. Peters discovers about Lord Hargrove's finances. He did say he would be checking into that aspect."

"Yes," Claudia added with some enthusiasm, "We must invite him to the house to share his discoveries."

"We can do that. But it certainly would be ideal if we had some information to share with him. Unfortunately, we learned little at the ball. Mr. Peters will be quite disappointed in our progress…" She paused and looked at Claudia with a speculative expression. "Luckily, we have accepted an invitation to do a walk about with Crystabel tomorrow afternoon in Hyde Park. I had hoped you would join us, perhaps take Hargrove's arm, and learn what you can."

Elliot chuckled. Eleanora flashed a scowl at him before turning back to Claudia. "It would be a boon to at least have something to share with Mr. Peters," she repeated.

Claudia sighed. "I suppose I could."

"Wonderful!"

Eleanora sat back against the seat, satisfied with her success at getting Claudia to join them tomorrow.

She stole a glance at Elliot, who leaned back in the shadows, with only the sharp features of his face illuminated by the weak coach lamp. With his black domino open over his black suit and matching top hat he looked like the villain in a penny dreadful novel.

She smiled at the memory of the kisses they had shared on the Mansfield patio. He had been both fiercely passionate and agonizingly gentle. Looking at him now, she could understand why Claudia called him a distempered dragon. It seemed impossible that this large, hard figure of a man could have such a soft touch.

She unconsciously lifted her fingers to her lips and traced the path of Elliot's sweet kisses. She was determined to taste those kisses again, perhaps tomorrow. Looking up, she met Elliot's eyes and quickly withdrew her hand, feeling her face burn. Thankfully, the coach lurched to a halt outside their townhouse, and she was able to busy herself preparing to exit. Tomorrow could not come soon enough.

CHAPTER 10

The parlor was full of flowers. To Mrs. Bixby's horror the doorbell had been ringing all morning with deliveries of bouquets. To add to her strife, since luncheon a panoply of male guests had arrived, each determined to enjoy a short tete-à-tetes with the ladies. It was proper to visit a young lady after a ball, especially one you wished to court. However, those visits were strictly confined to fifteen-minute intervals.

They had just said their goodbyes to Lord Farrow when the doorbell rang again.

Mrs. Bixby bustled through the sitting room to the foyer muttering as she went. "Land sakes! Had I known I would be run off my feet, I would never have taken this position. It's a regular Pall Mall in this house. What with the constant goings on."

She stepped back into the parlor moments later. "A Mr. Sparks and a Lord Mansfield to see you."

"Send them in, Mrs. Bixby. And we will be going

out. If there are further guests, have them leave their card," said Claudia.

"Well thank the Lord," their housekeeper muttered.

Elliot and Charles stood under the arched entry to the parlor, each with a bouquet of flowers in their hand. Elliot looked at the masses of flowers covering every available surface with a grimace.

Charles, however, was undaunted. He did a short bow, "A posy for two lovely ladies," extending his arm to display a cluster of yellow roses interspersed with white lilies.

"How lovely." Claudia took the flowers from Charles and turned to Elliot who handed over his red roses without a word, his brows furrowed into a deep frown.

Mrs. Bixby scowled at the men, clearly unimpressed with their gifts. She turned to Claudia. "Gimme those. I'll put them in vases for you." She bundled up the flowers in her arms. "If I can find one." she added as she proceeded to the kitchen.

"Mrs. Bixby, please put the red roses in my room," Eleanora added, smiling at Elliot. Mrs. Bixby only grunted in response. "It looks like a lovely day, perfect for a walk about. Shall we proceed to the park?" The ladies had only to grab their parasols at the door. The parasol was the required accessory of every fashionable woman in the park—the more elaborate the better.

Charles immediately took her arm. "Your carriage awaits you, my lady."

Mr. Weins and Crystabel stood near the park gates and approached the coach as it rolled to a stop. Mr.

Weins was quick to assist her from the carriage, firmly holding her arm.

Crystabel greeted her. "I am afraid it will be just Mr. Weins and I this afternoon. My Lord Hargrove was not available today."

Eleanora could not help but sigh in relief. A conversation with Lord Hargrove after their last encounter would only be awkward. Besides, there was their deepening suspicions about the man. How did one chat with a suspected embezzler and murderer?

They soon joined the throngs of people strolling the pathways. The promenade was a ritual for Londoners, particularly the upper class. The object was to see and be seen. Claudia and Charles took the lead, followed by Elliot and Crystabel, and finally Eleanora and Mr. Weins.

They meandered along the walk, nodding at acquaintances as they passed by. It was a lovely day, after weeks of chilly fog, and as a result the park was busy. Ladies in colorful day dresses held frilled parasols as they walked sedately down the pathways, accompanied by men in casual suits with the required top hat and cane. Along the drive that circled the perimeter of the park, visible intermittently through the trees, open carriages displayed a kaleidoscope of gay color as further patrons chose to ride, and sleek horses mounted with gentleman accompanied them. It appeared as though the entire ton was in attendance.

"It is unfortunate that Steven Hargrove was not able to be with us today," Eleanora said, attempting to make casual conversation with her partner.

Mr. Weins gave a sardonic half smile. "Yes. Under the weather, I assume."

"Crystabel tells me the two of you are friends. Have you known each other long?"

"A few years. Crystabel introduced us when I first arrived in London." They paused for a moment allowing a party of strollers to pass by.

"You are not a Londoner then? I would not have known by your accent." Eleanora asked.

Mr. Weins laughed. "Thank you for that. I am a Yorkshire man. My family comes from Scarborough. We have operated a shipping company there for generations. Not the size of Pembroke to be sure, but a viable business." He smiled and looked at her meaningfully. "So, you see my dear, we have more in common than you think. When I heard you were to take an active role in Pembroke, I must say I was intrigued. I support a woman in business. Like you, I am a product of the new age." He leaned in close and added, "If you are looking for a man to support you in all you do, you need look no further than me."

Eleanora noticed Elliot, who held Crystabel's arm just in front of them had slowed. She was sure his shoulders had stiffened with Mr. Weins' words. Choosing to ignore Arthur Weins' comments about what a fine partnership they would make, she said, "How very interesting. You have known Crystabel for a long time then?" She had assumed the friendship with Arthur Weins originated with Lord Hargrove.

"Since we were children. But enough of me. How are you finding London my dear?"

"I am afraid I have not toured about much as of yet. It has been a busy time for us, settling in." The party approached the lake, and Eleanora looked longingly at its crystal waters.

"Then it shall be my duty to take you for an excursion around town." He flashed her a smile.

Eleanora tried to change the topic. The very last thing she wanted was another outing with Mr. Weins. "What a beautiful sight. Why look, there are swans."

"Not as beautiful a sight as you my dear." He tucked her arm in, pulling her closer. Eleanora forced herself not to rudely pull away. There was something unwholesome in his touch, something which had the hair on the back of her neck prickle with warning.

She squashed the feeling, deciding that her impressions of the man were tainted by his resemblance to her former fiancée. A lock of his pomaded black hair had fallen over his eye. He brushed it back nonchalantly, then gave her a wide smile. Perhaps she judged him too harshly. She smiled in return. "Thank you, Mr. Weins for the compliment."

"But you must call me Arthur. As I said, we will be great friends. I look forward to spending a great deal of time with you."

Elliot turned back towards them. "Shall we feed the Queen's swans? There is a boy selling bits of bread."

"What a wonderful idea." Eleanora used the opportunity to break away from Mr. Weins. Except for Charles, the group gathered on the manicured bank to toss bits of bread to the majestic birds. Charles had settled onto a park bench, where he scribbled into a tiny notebook, the view apparently providing inspiration.

Eleanora took the opportunity to stand next to Elliot, who silently handed her bits of bread to toss to the waterfowl. His face masked his emotions as usual, but she got the distinct impression he was not enjoying the outing.

"Are these actually the Queen's swans?" she asked, tossing a bit of bread onto the lake, and watching the elegant birds hurry forward to scoop them up.

"The crown owns all the swans in England by an ancient decree. But her majesty claims only those in the parks of London." Elliot answered, flashing her a smile, and handing her another morsel of bread. He watched while she tossed it to the water, then took her hand. "Have you forgiven me then for forcing this excursion on you?"

"Not yet. You will have to be especially pleasant before you receive complete absolution," she laughed. She glanced at Crystabel and Arthur Weins who stood a little apart from the group, talking quietly to each other, their faces serious. When Crystabel looked up, she caught her gaze and quickly left Arthur's side to stand beside them on the bank. Eleanora could not help but be disappointed that her moment alone with Elliot was interrupted.

"How are you enjoying Hyde Park?" she asked. As always, Crystabel was in the height of fashion. Her parasol was a lacy pale blue, adorned with turquoise bows, which perfectly matched a fully ruffled walking dress. "We have a pleasant day for it, so clear and sunny, and not a hint of the usual fog."

"It is lovely. I had no idea the park was so large." She waved her hand, turning slightly to indicate the expanse. A movement coming down the path caught her eye and she paused, unable to contain her gasp. Lord Manford was jogging awkwardly toward them, his outstretched arm held a bouquet of tattered flowers, which he swung wildly as he lumbered his heavy body toward them.

"Ah, another admirer, how marvelous." Elliot sniped.

"Lady... Lady Eleanora," he called, panting as he approached, "So glad I caught up with you. Quite the trek. Whew!" He tried to catch his breath for a moment. Beads of perspiration had gathered on his brow, and he reached into his pocket to pull out a handkerchief. He began mopping his reddened face with his free hand, while the other held a dangling bunch of what had been violets. "Ms. Amelia told me I would find you here."

For a moment Eleanora could only stare at him open-mouthed. "Lord Manford, what a...a surprise." She glanced at Crystabel, hoping she would contribute something to the conversation, but Crystabel only pressed her lips together and glared at the man.

He mopped his face once more. "Yes. I knew you would be pleased. I brought you some posies." He held out the unfortunate flowers. "For you, my dear."

"Thank you, Lord Manford." She took the bouquet

and made a futile attempt to arrange the drooping blooms. "They are lovely."

Charles chose that moment to burst upon the scene, his notebook open at his latest poem. "Ah, but what finer gift is there than the poem? Only words can capture a fair maid and immortalize her for the eons." He held out his poem, and in a grandiose stance began to recite. "The glorious dawn wept upon the dewy grass, knowing its promise was soon to be shadowed. Branches sway, fanning the empress as she passes, even the elegant swan bows its regal head in honor of her beauty…For nature has achieved its final splendor, in fair Eleanora."

She could only smile at Charles before Mr. Weins interjected, "Such praise for our Eleanora is certainly warranted, but now I think it is time we continued on our way." He took her arm and began to pull her toward the walking path.

Lord Manford quickly stepped up to take her other arm, and ignoring the black look on Mr. Weins face, added, "Yes, I look forward to a stroll with you, my lovely. I have much news to share with you from the exchange. Why just this morning I was praised for my insights in the market. It seems I have impressed..."

Eleanora let his words fade from her consciousness. She looked up helplessly at Elliot as she was being led away. His stern expression had been replaced by an amused half smile. He shrugged and grinned at her before taking Crystabel's arm to follow down the walkway.

Lord Manford continued his tirade, this time

including her in his business plans. "I have been thinking of you a great deal, Miss Pembroke," he leaned in close to her and continued in a quiet voice, "only think, my dear, of what we could accomplish. Pembroke and Manford, commodities and shipping! It is a partnership sure to make us the richest couple in England." He paused for a moment, perhaps aware that his enthusiasm had not moved her.

Mr. Weins intervened at last, clearly annoyed. "Manford, can you not see that you are boring the woman. I demand that you drop this subject." He pulled her close and added, "I can see that my first order of business will be to protect you from such talk."

Her plans to share at least part of the walk with Elliot were dashed. The afternoon only got worse as they progressed. Somehow, they managed to attract two more suitors to their party. Mr. Weins had been nudged aside during the introductions and replaced with a Lord Salsbury, who was eager to impress her with his charms.

Not so Lord Manford, who steadfastly held her arm, still sweating profusely, and regaling her with stories of his prowess in his business dealings. Each time he patted her arm, and he did so frequently, she thought of those same pudgy fingers pushing his first wife down a staircase to her death. It was a disconcerting image. She had even begun to anticipate Charles' interruptions to recite his ghastly poetry celebrating her beauty.

It was a relief to be back in the carriage at last. The four of them were silent. Mercifully, Charles sat quietly scribbling in his notebook as they traversed the distance to the townhouse. The afternoon had left her with a pounding headache. Amelia's announcement that the Pembroke heiress was looking for a mate this season, had certainly inspired a host of gentlemen determined to have a chance at the prize. If she were to survive in London this fiasco could not continue.

Something would have to be done. She determined that the only way to end it all was to take the commodity off the shelf—by announcing she was no longer available. And there was only one way to accomplish it. Her conversation with Claudia about selecting a husband had been in jest. But as the afternoon wore on, she began to see it as a distinct possibility.

It was time to announce an engagement. She stole a glance at Elliot, who sat stone-faced across from her. Arabella had raised her to boldly pursue her dreams and shape her own destiny. Well, she thought wryly, what was more pivotal to her future than acquiring a husband? She had made her choice and was certainly not going to wait around for him to take the first action.

She peeked again at Elliot from beneath her lashes. He looked formidable. Fortunately, she was not one to be intimidated by a challenge.

CHAPTER 11

Another full day of ardent suitors clamoring at their door had Mrs. Bixby in a foul mood. Charles had arrived with his latest poem, and Arthur Weins had insisted on another stroll, this time in the park across the street. He had fawned over her as usual, taking her arm and pulling her too close to him. He spent their time together hinting about how wonderful a match they would make. At one point he had even leaned in as though to kiss her. Eleanor had been quick to take a step back. It was with some relief that she saw the epitaph ahead, signaling that they had completed a circle of the park, and could return to her home. Mrs. Bixby waited at the door, sourly announcing that guests awaited her in the drawing room.

Lord Salsbury, and another gentleman eager to meet her, waited in the drawing room. Eleanora was truly thankful for the laws of etiquette which limited afternoon visits to fifteen minutes. Still the afternoon had dragged on.

The house was crammed with flowers of every sort. The one suitor she had hoped to see, Elliot, was absent. It had been a long and exhausting day, and not one she wished to repeat.

This morning, Mrs. Bixby set the tea service down with a clang. "Can't say I am looking forward to the day. You will have to increase the budget for tea and dainties if this business is to go on much longer. Those men stuff them down faster than the poor cook can get them out of the ovens. The staff will be surly if it is to be another day the likes of yesterday. We have been run off our feet."

"It is a bit much," Claudia agreed.

"It is too much," Eleanora concurred. "We will not be receiving today, Mrs. Bixby. Outside of Mr. Sparks and Mr. Peters, you can have them leave their cards."

"Thank the Lord," Mrs. Bixby muttered as she left the room.

Claudia looked across the breakfast table at Eleanora curiously. "You have been in the oddest mood since the walk about at Hyde Park. It is as though you are not quite with us. Would you care to tell me what is going on?"

"I have made a decision Claudia. I have chosen a husband."

"What? Who? I can't say I noticed anything usual in your interactions yesterday. Has someone proposed? Surely not the too elegant Mr. Weins? He did insist on a walk in the park yesterday afternoon, but I hardly suspected—"

"No. You may rest easy. It is not Mr. Weins."

Eleanora paused while she meticulously buttered her toast. She could feel Claudia's eyes on her, as she waited for a response. She was unsure of what Claudia's reaction to her news might be. Given her opinion of Elliot, Claudia was not likely to support her choice. Claudia had made it clear she did not consider Mr. Sparks husband material.

She reached for the marmalade, and began to meticulously spread it on her toast, ignoring Claudia's curious stare. Claudia finally lost patience. "Tell me who this suitor is."

Eleanora set down her toast. "Mr. Elliot Sparks." Claudia gasped and was about to comment, but Eleanora held up her hand to forestall her and quickly continued. "And no, he has not proposed. I intend to do the proposing. I wanted to send him a message yesterday to come to the house, but I lost my nerve. And then when the house was filled with suitors all afternoon, I was too busy to consider it. But I am determined to do it today."

For once Claudia was speechless. She could only stare at Eleanora open-mouthed.

"I am unsure as to how one does a proposal. I suppose I shall just come out with it." She looked at Claudia. "I was hoping you might help me with this task."

"But Eleanora, Mr. Sparks! Surely you cannot be serious! You must think this through."

Eleanora sighed. "I have thought of nothing else. If we are to exist here in London, and take part in the social scene at all, I must be at least engaged. This business of fighting off a train of fortune hunters is quite beyond me. I cannot bear it."

"But to marry Elliot Sparks is a bit extreme, even for you Eleanora. You cannot possibly marry simply because you are annoyed. Marriage is a lifelong commitment—not to be taken lightly."

"But I don't have to actually marry the man. Think about this as an engagement of convenience. I will be taken off the shelf as it were, and free to go about my business without this constant barrage of fortune hunters plaguing me. And if it does turn out that Elliot and I suit, well, all the better. Amelia is quite right when she says I am nearly on the shelf. I will have chosen a solid match. It will be a relationship built on mutual respect, where both parties can go about their business with the support of the other. More like a partnership."

Claudia was flabbergasted. "Eleanora you are talking about a business associate, not a marriage."

"Exactly right. It is what I want. And I intend to make this arrangement with Elliot Sparks." Eleanora raised her chin and set her lips in a firm line.

Claudia looked at her warily. "I can see that you are determined to do this thing. I have no idea how to stop you." She ran her hand across her forehead and sighed. "For the first time I wish your grandmother Arabella were here with us. Perhaps she could talk some sense into you." She leaned forward and asked, "Can you not at least take a little more time?"

"Time will not change my plans. My mind is quite made up."

Claudia sighed. "Oh Eleanora. I can only hope that Mr. Sparks has enough sense not to agree to this plan."

"Don't try to stop me, Claudia. Instead, I need your help." Reaching across the table and grasping her hand, she said, "It is the right action for me. Mr. Sparks is the perfect man for the role. I want your support, but if I must, I will proceed without it."

Claudia looked down at their joined hands. "I just cannot see the man agreeing to this ruse, Eleanora. But if this is what you genuinely want, then you know I will help you."

She flashed Claudia a wide smile. "Perfect! And now we must plan! I will need to do this right if I am to get the answer I want. The man might be a little finicky about the whole scenario."

It was decided the ladies would invite Elliot to supper that very night. He would have no idea he was to be the only guest. Claudia would then feign a headache, leaving Eleanora and Elliot alone for the evening. The invitation was sent immediately.

To Eleanora's delight, Elliot responded promptly with a positive reply.

"Everything must be perfect, Claudia." She looked around the dining room. They had removed the leaves from the table to create a more intimate setting. The table was set for two. The elaborate candelabra needed only to be lit. More candles filled the sconces on the walls, and a second candelabra was set upon the side-board. Flowers in a low arrangement made the perfect centerpiece and more bouquets graced the hutch, filling the room with the sweet scent of lavender.

Eleanora surveyed the room. "It will do. Now then, we will serve brandy in the parlor, when he arrives. And we will fill his glass at every opportunity. I want him to imbibe as much brandy as we can pour. When we go in for supper, you will complain of a headache."

When Claudia frowned, she was quick to reassure her. "It is all you are required to do. Just the headache, the rest of the evening will be my responsibility. I have asked Anne to serve the table. I thought Mrs. Bixby might be a bit much," she said and chuckled at the thought. "Anne will only bring in the courses, then discreetly withdraw. I will serve plenty of wine. It will hopefully have him a little off balance."

"Eleanora, I am not sure of this plan. Your schemes always seem to go awry. Why not just ask the man, and forego the attempt to get him intoxicated?"

Eleanora sighed. "But plenty of alcohol may just be the thing. I want him to be pliable. I will be sure to keep his glass full." She put her hands on her hips and surveyed the scene. "And the room looks lovely. All that remains is the perfect proposal."

"Eleanora, this is bound to be a disaster."

"Nonsense, my dear, it will work wonderfully. Now I need a gown which will truly entrance him. I must look seductive, but not too seductive. I want to be a fiancée, not a mistress." She laughed and tugged Claudia toward the stairs. "Cheer up, it will proceed perfectly."

Anne did Eleanora's hair up, with a few curls falling seductively onto her shoulders. Eleanora walked to the full-length mirror to examine the results and was satisfied with her appearance. They had chosen a pale emerald gown which fell low across the shoulders, showing an expanse of her neck and chest. Her decolletage was discreetly covered with creamy lace, matching ribbons and bows twined elaborately through alternating panels in the belled skirt. It had all the fripperies of the latest fashions but was considerably subdued when compared to the latest trends.

Eleanora smoothed out its silky folds as she inspected herself in the mirror. She wished she could smooth her frayed nerves in the same way. All day she had been in a state of nervous excitement. If she could get Elliot to agree to her proposal, she would be engaged. She secretly hoped the arrangement would evolve into a permanent one. She would marry a man of her choice. Their union would be one of mutual respect and of course, the ideal business arrangement. The fiasco of suitors would be over, and she would have the perfect partner for Pembroke.

Claudia came up beside her and smiled at her reflection. "You are lovely. He will be enchanted."

Mrs. Bixby announced from the doorway. "Your Mr. Sparks has arrived. I put him in the drawing room with a stout glass of brandy as you asked. Picked the strongest brew we had; I did."

"Thank you, Mrs. Bixby. We shall be right down. Are you ready Claudia?" Eleanora said, and then turned to Miss Anne. "Now remember our plan. You are to ply the man with alcohol. At every opportunity I want his glass refilled."

"I shall do my best ma'am." Anne smiled, pleased with the idea of being a part of the conspiracy.

Eleanora took a deep breath. Though she had told Claudia this would be a business arrangement, and temporary, she had not been entirely truthful. She admitted she had chosen Elliot for more reasons than just his talents with finance. She remembered his kiss, both gentle and passionate, and felt her stomach quiver in anticipation.

Elliot Sparks might even be the man for her. Tonight, she needed only to convince him of the rightness of this arrangement, and then with time, who knew? At the very least the problem of her suitors would be solved. With a little alcohol to help persuade him, she was sure her plan would succeed—how could it not?

CHAPTER 12

The parlor was still cloaked in flowers. The gifts of her many admirers, Elliot thought with a grimace. He wandered over to the fireplace and made himself comfortable, sipping his brandy, while he waited for other guests, or the ladies to come down. Leaning against the mantle, he pulled his pocket watch from his coat. He must be early. He gave his watch a little shake, deciding to have it checked at the jeweler's tomorrow. One must have a reliable time piece—he valued punctuality.

His biggest concern for the evening was that he be a charming guest. Lady Mansfield and Charles were forever admonishing him for his lack of polish socially. He hoped there would be plenty of guests to cloak his inadequacies in that department.

The housekeeper appeared in the arched doorway, her hands on her hips and her expression irritated. "The ladies will be down shortly. I am to ask if you would like another brandy."

"Thank you, no, this will be good," he answered.

"Well, you can help yourself if you change your mind. Brandy's on the side table," she said and bustled from the room. Obviously, he had disrupted the household, irritating the staff by arriving far too early. After several minutes, when no other guests came to the door, and Elliot had checked his watch numerous times, Eleanora and Claudia entered the room.

He was entranced by Eleanora as she glided towards him. Her hair shone in the soft amber light of the lanterns, and everything about her was soft and feminine. He felt his heart pounding in his chest and marveled at the response she could instill in him with her mere presence.

He made his short bow in greeting. "Good evening, ladies."

"Elliot, I am so pleased you could join us tonight," Eleanora said, taking his hand and leading him to the settee by the fire. "Do sit down." She settled in beside him, with Claudia taking the chair opposite. Turning to a young serving girl she said, "Some wine for Claudia and me, Miss Anne. And please freshen Mr. Spark's brandy. Or no," she amended, "make mine a brandy as well."

The servant handed them their drinks. Eleanora reached for hers and to his surprise, immediately took a hearty gulp. Predictably, she reacted by coughing and sputtering.

Reaching over and pounding her back, he instructed, "You are supposed to sip it."

"I know how to drink brandy," she gasped, her face

a rosy color. She raised her glass and purposely took another hefty swallow. He shrugged his shoulders, smiling as her eyes widened with the second swig. It was strong alcohol, and certain to burn.

"Now then," Claudia intervened, deftly changing the subject, "I have always wondered about India. Since I first noticed you had spent several years there in the King's service, I have been curious. Do tell us some tales about the far east."

Determined to be engaging, Elliot took a breath and began, "I am not sure what I can tell you. Society is much the same there as here. Except, of course, that it is ridiculously hot. At this time of year, the season is ending rather than beginning. It is impossible to remain in the city during the spring and summer. Most people, including the governor, thank goodness, retreat to the mountains to escape."

He glanced at Eleanora. She twisted her hands in her lap when she was not nervously sipping her brandy. She seemed agitated.

How odd the other guests had not arrived. Perhaps that is what was bothering Eleanora, he thought. He cleared his throat and continued, "But the food was marvelous. I believe the English will forever love the fabulous curries of India."

"I dare say you are right. Can I get you another brandy?" Eleanora asked. Before he could protest, she motioned to her servant to refill their glasses. The poor woman had no idea how to serve brandy and filled his glass to the brim. He grimaced. When she stood in front of the ladies to refill Eleanora's glass, he took the opportunity to pour a sizable dollop into the massive rose bowl of flowers beside him. Though it was a waste of good brandy, he had no intention of drinking too much in the presence of Eleanora.

For thirty minutes he regaled the ladies with stories of the bright colors, the sounds, and the splendor of India. He described the crowded streets, the elephants with their houdah—canopied seats decorated extravagantly, parading down the boulevards. He attempted to describe the lively marketplaces, filled with the smell of incense and spice, and wares of every variety. For once he was feeling quite pleased with his contributions to the conversation.

Claudia was listening intently, but when he glanced at Eleanora, she was still nervous and distracted, concentrating on drinking her brandy. Something was certainly plaguing her.

The servant, Miss Anne, was forever topping their drinks, several times he had to put his hand over his glass to stop the woman from overfilling it. He even had to make use of the unfortunate rose bowl once more, pouring another full glass into it at the first opportunity. Eleanora seemed to not have an issue with the copious amounts of brandy, holding out her glass for a refill and nodding toward his. Despite the overzealous servant, and Eleanora's preoccupation, he found he was quite satisfied to have the ladies to himself for once. He was working hard to be entertaining and believed he was doing rather well.

The housekeeper interrupted from the archway, "Dinner is ready ma'am."

Claudia put her hand to her forehead and groaned. "It seems I have developed one of my headaches. I hope I do not offend if I retire. It is simply impossible to carry on when I am in its grip."

Eleanora rose and assisted Claudia to her feet. "Oh dear. I am so sorry Claudia. Of course, you could not offend." She turned to Elliot, "When poor Claudia is so afflicted, she simply must rest in a quiet darkened room."

The two ladies swayed for a moment. Elliot was quick to hurry over to take Claudia's arm, thinking she must be dizzy. Eleanora gave a little giggle as he helped hold the two of them upright.

Anne stepped forward. "Allow me to assist Claudia. The two of you can go in to dinner."

"Yes, I will be fine," said Claudia as they made their way to the stairs.

Elliot took Eleanora's arm, "Shall we?"

When Eleanora giggled again in response, he looked at her curiously. She had an impish grin on her face.

"I have a marvelous surprise for you." She stumbled a little, and he tightened his grasp on her arm.

She is tipsy, he thought with shock. If she had finished that second glass of brandy, filled to the brim as his had been, it was not surprising. Obviously, someone had neglected to teach these women the finer points of serving and drinking brandy; it was not to be guzzled by the mug. He had been so busy trying to impress the woman, he had failed to notice the amount of alcohol she was consuming.

He helped her to the dining room, where two place settings were placed intimately at one end. The room was lit with the soft yellow glow of candles. Every surface sported a bouquet, filling the air with the soft scent of lavender.

He graciously pulled back her chair, noting she wobbled slightly as she seated herself.

"Shall we have a glass of wine? I chose a special bottle for this evening." Without waiting for a response, Eleanora filled their glasses with extreme care. Smiling triumphantly when she accomplished the task, she said, "It is a lovely red, from the Burgan...Burgundy region." She laughed again. Her face was flushed, and her eyelids drooped.

The brandy was now having an obvious effect. And indeed, if she had consumed all that was served to him in the parlor, she would certainly be experiencing some difficulty. "Do you think this is the best idea, Eleanora. Perhaps if we had a little something to eat—"

"It's a perfect idea. We must celebrate our, our partnership." She took her glass and held it up in a toast. "To us and to business deals," she said, taking a long drink. She belched. "Oh, excuse me," she said with a wide grin.

"Well, this is certainly going to be an interesting evening."

"Yes, it is. You are so right." She laughed again, "I have a proposal for you. And that is funny. It is a proposal, an actual proposal." She took a drink of wine, then waved her arm extravagantly. The wine slopped from her glass to the linen tablecloth. "Whoopsie daisy," she said, fumbling for her napkin and plopping it down onto the offending stain.

Mrs. Bixby chose that moment to push through the doors with trays of food. "As Anne is not down yet, it is up to me to serve table," she muttered unhappily as she plopped the dishes unceremoniously onto the table. Eleanora indicated the wine with a nod, and the woman snatched up the wine bottle and refilled their glasses, then placed a second open bottle on the table before lumbering back through the swinging doors to the kitchens.

He raised his brows as Eleanora took another swig of wine. "Perhaps we should try some of this delicious food." he suggested again, hoping to avoid the inevitable scene.

He winced as she gulped down more wine, then awkwardly refilled her glass. "Not...not yet. There is something I need to talk to you a...about." She rested her elbows on the table, braced up her chin and looked at him.

"Eleanora, I wonder if we should ask for some assistance." He looked longingly at the swinging doors. "You are not feeling yourself just now—"

"No, no. I've something 'portant to ask. Planned it all day, but I can't seem to remember the words. I need a little drink first." She took a hefty swallow. "Guess I'll jus' out with it."

She pulled herself awkwardly to her feet and stood swaying. "I want you to m...m... marry me. Wha' do ya say?"

His mouth dropped. Before he could answer, her

swaying took a dangerous lurch. She reached for the table to steady herself, grabbed the table linen and took several quick steps in reverse. Both place settings, at least two dishes of food, and a rose bowl center piece clattered and smashed to the floor, splattering the room and her dress. The two bottles of wine tipped over, spewing their contents across the table linens before following in their wake. As a final encore, her wine glass rolled from the table and shattered amongst the carnage.

For a second, Elliot sat frozen in the scene.

"Oh dear," Eleanora said in a child's voice, as she began to sink to the carpet.

He leapt to his feet, oblivious of the chair clattering to the floor behind him and caught her before she fell, swinging her up into his arms.

Mrs. Bixby burst through the swinging doors, standing with her hands on her hips. The parlor maid peered over her shoulder. "What in heaven's name goes on here?"

Elliot ignored the servants as he resituated the drunken Eleanora in his arms. She managed to wrap her arms around him. When he looked down at her she gave him an impish grin. "You're very strong," she said, massaging his back, "Always good in a husband." She rested her head against his shoulder and sighed.

He stood amongst the ruins of supper, holding a grinning Eleanora tight against his chest. "I fear Miss Pembroke has taken ill. I will carry her to her room if one of you leads the way."

Eleanora lifted her head from his shoulder and

looked about as though she would speak to them, then emitted a loud hiccup. “Excuse me,” she giggled.

There was a pause, with each of the servants wearing identical expressions of confused horror before the parlor maid quickly stepped out from behind Mrs. Bixby. “Yes, yes of course.” She carefully picked her way across the room to the archway leading to the foyer. “If you will just follow me.”

As she led him from the room Mrs. Bixby bellowed, "A fine mess this is. And I am expected to clean the lot. The goings on in this house—run off my feet morning to night, and now this. Cook! Send the scullery out! Land sakes. Cook!” her shouts followed them up the stairs.

They were met on the landing by a distressed Claudia, still wearing her finery from early on. “Why all the shouting? What has happened?”

“Miss Pembroke is not feeling herself,” he said, negotiating the doorway into Eleanora’s bedroom. She groaned as he placed her carefully on the bed. She was a fine mess. Her lovely emerald gown was splattered with a tomato sauce of some sort, and dark red wine.

“Goodness, oh my dear Eleanora, what has happened?” Claudia repeated.

“I believe it was the brandy. It might be wise not to serve it for future gatherings, or at the very least, not consume it.” He looked at Eleanora who had turned a ghostly pale. “I suggest a bucket. I have a feeling she will need it.”

The maid nodded and pulled a chamber pot out from under the bed.

He turned to Claudia. "She will be all right, although I am certain she will suffer a headache in the morning. I suggest purging if she does not accomplish it on her own. And now I believe it is time I took my leave."

Eleanora braced herself up onto her elbows, objecting, "But you haven't agreed to my p...p... proposal."

He looked back at her. But before he could answer, she flung herself to the side of the bed. The maid was quick to ready the chamber pot and the retching began.

Claudia grasped his shoulder and turned him away. "Come Mr. Sparks, I will walk you to the door."

They were silent as they proceeded down the stairs to the entry. Miss Claudia handed him his hat and cloak, her face a mask of formal civility. "I must apologize for this unfortunate evening. I can only assure you that Miss Pembroke is not a drinker. She will be quite devastated with this ghastly scene."

"Yes, I gathered she was not an experienced drinker," he said with a wry smile as he pulled his cloak across his broad shoulders and adjusted his hat. "Tell her all is forgotten. I will stop by tomorrow to see how she fares."

He opened the door to leave, adding as an afterthought, "And you might mention to her that I accept her proposal."

CHAPTER 13

Even the muted sun filtered through the breakfast room's windows hurt her eyes. It must be past noon, Eleanora thought as she settled herself into a chair with her back to the offending window.

Mrs. Bixby pushed through the swinging doors with a tray, set it on the sideboard and handed her a glass filled with a reddish substance. "Drink it. You'll feel better. The one thing I learned from my drunken father, was how to fix a body sickened from the drink."

She stood over her until she had consumed every drop of the vile substance. "Now a bit of food, and you will be right as rain." She readied a plate from the sideboard and set it in front of her. "Miss Claudia said to inform you she would pop in this afternoon to see how you are doing. Gone to work she did," she said before retreating to the kitchen.

As though Mrs. Bixby had conjured her up, Claudia stood in the archway. She leaned against the doorway dressed in the jacket and skirt of the working woman with her bonnet in her hand. "I see you have survived." She scanned her appearance. "You are looking fit. How do you fare?"

"I am feeling much better, with just a bit of a headache." While physically she now felt she could survive the day, emotionally it was an entirely different matter. Unfortunately, she could remember most of the evening. It was a disaster. What Elliot could be thinking of her just now, made her squirm. She closed her eyes to banish the thought.

Claudia pulled back a chair and poured herself some tea. "I cannot think there would be much left in your stomach to bother you. Mr. Sparks suggested a purging and you certainly managed that."

Eleanora felt her cheeks burn. "Yes." She hesitated before asking, "Was Mr. Sparks in the office?"

"He was."

She waited for Claudia to expand on her comment, but she sipped her tea, ignoring her. "Claudia, please do not torture me. He must have said something about the incident?"

"Actually, I didn't see much of him. He went down to the docks and spent the morning at the warehouse."

Eleanora groaned, rubbing her hand against her forehead. "I am not sure how I will ever live this down."

Claudia sighed, set her teacup in its saucer, and said, "As much as you deserve to suffer the consequences of this fiasco, I do have some news which may brighten your day. Before Mr. Sparks left last night, he asked me to inform you that he would accept your proposal."

"He did?" Eleanora brightened. "Does this mean I am engaged?"

"It would seem so." Claudia did not seem enthusiastic about the match.

"But this is wonderful! My plan worked!" Claudia rolled her eyes as Eleanora clapped her hands together.

"Did you manage to tell the man the whole thing is a ruse? What if he took you seriously Eleanora?"

"I do not think I did. But it makes no difference. We could just consider the whole thing a trial engagement. It might work out for the best."

Claudia shot her a disapproving look. "Eleanora, I insist you inform the man of your plans. It would be unfair to lead him on so. If you don't tell him, I will."

Eleanora sighed. "I will tell him today."

Mrs. Bixby entered with her distinctive frown firmly in place. "A Mrs. Amelia Brigg and Lord and Lady Hargrove to see you ma'am. They say it is an emergency and won't be turned away."

"Heavens, whatever could they want?" She looked up at Claudia as if she might have the answer. The very last people she wanted to deal with today were the Hargroves and Amelia. That all three of them were at her door was disconcerting indeed. "I best see them. Put them in the drawing room, Mrs. Bixby. We shall have our tea there." She looked up at Claudia. "You will stay, won't you? I have a feeling I will need your support." She rose from the chair and took her arm. "Whatever it is, I am sure it is not going to be pleasant."

Claudia frowned. "I will stay. If nothing else, I am curious as to what those three are up to."

When they walked into the drawing room, Mrs. Bixby had already settled Amelia into the sofa. Amelia was once again decked out in cascading ruffles which enhanced her robust physique. Lord Hargrove and Crystabel stood by the fireplace.

Lord Hargrove did his formal bow. "Ladies," he said in greeting. Eleanora could not help but look at him suspiciously. Her stomach lurched at the thought that she may have a murderer and thief in her drawing room. But his impression was far from the scoundrel she had conjured up in her mind. Instead, he was impeccable in his three-piece charcoal morning suit, every inch the aristocrat, and not at all what she imagined a murderer to be.

"What a pleasant surprise. Do sit down." She said, careful to keep the disdain from her face. If the man was the murderer, she thought him to be, he must not suspect she had any notion of it. She glanced at Claudia while she waited until the company had settled. Claudia too wore the mask of a polite hostess.

Crystabel sat on the settee next to her mother, and Lord Hargrove took a chair. She and Claudia took chairs across from them.

Mrs. Bixby entered with the tea tray and set it firmly on the side table. Eleanora quickly rose to assist, saying, "Thank you, Mrs. Bixby, that will be all. I shall pour," before the housekeeper could mutter a complaint. She turned to her guests. "We were about to have tea. Won't you join us?"

Amelia immediately burst into conversation. "Tea will be just the thing. We have such exciting news for you my dear. I told you we would find you a husband and we have. And a good catch too, I might add. When Crystabel asked me to join them in breaking the news to you, I could not resist. It is all such a thrill. And quickly accomplished! I have no idea how Arabella could have had such difficulty with you, my dear. The season has hardly begun, and we have offers." She paused to accept her tea and take a sip.

Lord Hargrove cleared his throat. "Yes Eleanora, we have indeed had an offer for your hand." When Eleanora opened her mouth to protest, he held up his hand to ward her off and continued. "Now I understand you may consider this a slight against your independent nature," he chuckled and rested his hand against his chest. "And I of all people have surely learned the offense you take at such an intrusion. But in this case the man is certainly correct in doing all that is proper. And since you have no other family here in town, I believe he has approached the whole issue correctly."

"Lord Hargrove, I—"

Crystabel interjected, "Darling, you are so fortunate! I was thrilled to hear such happy news! It is Mr. Weins!"

"Mr. Weins? But—"

"He has made a fine offer, very fine." Lord Hargrove raised his chin and adjusted his tie. "And as I said he has correctly asked permission to approach you. A gentleman to be sure." Lord Hargrove was obviously pleased with his role as guardian in the whole affair. Eleanora bit her lip to hold back an angry retort.

Amelia leaned forward. "And to think you were introduced to him at my home. I am more than pleased to have had a hand in this. I cannot wait to write Arabella and tell her all about our success." Amelia chuckled happily. "I am sure she will be pleased to have you settled at last. Again, I am shocked she had such difficulty. Why I have accomplished it with no trouble at all."

Eleanora looked at Claudia who wore a broad smile. "I think you had better tell them your news Eleanora."

"Yes. I do have some news for all of you." She looked at each of her guests in turn. "Mr. Weins' offer has arrived too late. I became engaged last night."

"You what?" Crystabel gasped.

"Mr. Elliot Sparks and I have agreed to marry."

There was a long pause. Crystabel looked horrified. "This cannot be true. Mr. Elliot Sparks? But Eleanora. There must be a way to undo this ghastly mistake. You have a good offer from Mr. Weins. Had I known you were so eager to wed, I would have had him speak to you sooner. This is a disaster." She rose to her feet and took Eleanora's hand. "Have you announced it in the papers? Perhaps we can salvage this situation."

"Yes," Lord Hargrove also rose to his feet. "It cannot be too late to change your mind. Is it not a lady's prerogative? And if it is not announced, I am certain it can be arranged."

Amelia had recovered from her surprise. "Let's not be too hasty. Mr. Sparks is the nephew of Lady Mansfield. His late mother was her sister, I believe, and a lady in her own right. And better still I have heard the man is as rich as Croesus. It might be a fine match. In fact, I think it a better offer."

"Mother!" Crystabel dropped her hand and turned to Amelia with such a look of outrage and anger, it took Eleanora's breath away. It was only the briefest flash, gone so quickly she assumed she must have imagined it.

"Yes, but the man is in trade, as was his father," said Lord Hargrove. His comment silenced them all.

Amelia's face colored, and even Crystabel had the grace to lower her head. After all, the Brigg family had made its fortune through Jem, who had rose from the ranks of the working man to become a powerful businessman.

"Be that as it may, Mr. Sparks and I have agreed to marry. I am happy with the match. And..." she raised her chin and turned to Crystabel. "If the announcement has not made it to the press in time for this morning's papers, I am sure it will appear tomorrow."

"I don't know what to say. You are apparently set upon this decision. I am at a loss Eleanora." Crystabel had paled. "Is there anything I can say to change your mind? Perhaps now that you know you have another offer you will reconsider?"

"My mind is made up. I am determined to accept Mr. Sparks as my husband."

Crystabel shook her head, as though denying her words. There was a moment's silence before she turned to Lord Hargrove. "We are finished here Steven. I would like to leave." Claudia moved to show them to the door. "Don't bother Miss Claudia, I can show myself out."

"Very well, my dear." Lord Hargrove turned to Eleanora and did his formal bow. He could not hide his chagrin. "I congratulate you on your engagement Miss Pembroke. Once more you are one step ahead of me."

"Thank you, Lord Hargrove." She replied as the couple turned to leave.

Amelia struggled with her bulky frame to rise to her feet, taking Eleanora's hands for assistance. She whispered, "I for one am pleased with the match. Mr. Sparks is a fine choice, wealthy and well connected," and with a wink followed her daughter and Lord Hargrove out.

Mrs. Bixby appeared in the archway. "A Mr. Sparks and Mr. Peters to see you ladies. I suppose you'll be wanting more tea?"

"Yes. I will greet them." Claudia hurried to the door. "And tea would be lovely. With the gooseberry tarts, Mrs. Bixby."

"Gooseberry tarts indeed. Pall Mall on a Saturday in this place," she muttered as she gathered the teacups from the Hargrove party, loading the tray and retreating to the kitchen.

A flushed Claudia returned with the gentlemen.

"We certainly could not have received a frostier greeting from your previous guests. I take it the biscuits were not to their liking," a cheerful Mr. Peters piped from the doorway.

"Meeting Mr. Sparks at the door could not have been a pleasant surprise for them after I shared my news." Eleanora answered as she gestured to the seating, "Please make yourselves comfortable. I promise not to serve the biscuits," Eleanora grinned.

"You shared your news? Our news?" Elliot asked.

At the sound of Elliot's voice, all the memories of last night's debacle came back to haunt her.

"She did." Claudia quipped. "Of the three only Amelia thought you a worthwhile catch."

Mr. Peters laughed. "My felicitations. I for one, think you have made a brilliant catch Miss Pembroke."

It appeared Mr. Sparks had also announced the engagement. The idea pleased Eleanora. "Thank you, Mr. Peters," she answered, as she took a seat next to Elliot on the sofa.

She glanced at Elliot from beneath her lashes. As usual he looked serious. She wondered if he was remembering last night, and felt her cheeks burn. The scene in the dining room flashed across her mind. She had to forcibly prevent herself from covering her face with her hands.

Mrs. Bixby chose that moment to enter with the tea tray. While she served Mr. Peters and Claudia, seated in chairs across from them, Elliot leaned in close and spoke quietly. "It pleases me to hear that you told the Hargroves about our engagement. I wanted to have a chat with you before I sent off the notice to the papers. I thought you may have changed your mind."

"I have not," she answered, finding the courage to

face him at last. She was relieved to see no traces of remonstration or disgust in his expression after last night's humiliating events. The man was behaving like a true fiancée, considerate and appropriately attentive. Eleanora pushed aside her feelings of guilt. She would explain it all soon enough.

He took her hand and gave it a gentle squeeze, before accepting his teacup from Mrs. Bixby. "Now then," he said, raising his voice, "I invited Mr. Peters along to allow him to share his findings with all of us."

Mr. Peters nodded, waiting for Mrs. Bixby to leave the room before saying, "I have done a thorough investigation of our Lord Hargrove. There were no surprises there. In fact, he lives his life as I suspect most of his peers do. He is at his club most days, attends the races at New Market occasionally, and plays whist at parties, but as far as I can tell, is not a compulsive gambler. Still, the cost of his play with the monied crowd would begin to add up. We checked the gambling hells in the city; he is not a frequent customer there."

"I suppose that rules out the simple motive of Hargrove needing funds." Claudia mused.

"Not quite. As I said the cost of play mounts, and sadly Hargrove is not the sharpest at cards. The Hargroves are living beyond their means. One does not need to be a gambler to accomplish that. They attend constant parties. Crystabel has worked hard to make a name for herself in the ton, mixing with a fast crowd, and that costs money. She has hosted a number of lavish balls which swallowed up a sizable chunk of their funds. The bills for those events have been paid—where they got the money is unclear. There is new jewelry, notably a diamond necklace and earbobs purchased at Garrod's, also paid for with cash."

"But what of Hargrove, does he not have income from his estates?" Elliot asked.

"He does, but unfortunately not enough to support the extravagant lifestyle they lead here in town. We were right when we assumed Lord Hargrove had married for money. Jem Brigg settled a huge marriage settlement on the man at the time of the wedding. But that money was taken up to pay the debts of his floundering estate. An estate that is only now beginning to pay for itself. What was left was used to purchase a townhouse in London, one of the best, which costs a fortune to maintain."

"Then money would certainly have been a motive for him," Eliot mused.

"Oh yes. The Hargroves' spending is out of control. Their creditors would have been assured of a huge inheritance to settle the accounts, one which is now not forthcoming. They will be closing in on them. For example, four months ago, Lord Hargrove purchased a new coach and four prized horses. The bill has yet to be paid. The owners of the livery are about to repossess. And Crystabel has had to change modistes after charging up a sizable bill. It will not be long before word leaks out and none of the shops will extend credit to the family." Mr. Peters took a sip of tea, setting his teacup carefully on its saucer before continuing.

"Furthermore, from what I have gathered, Jem Brigg was concerned with all the extravagance. He met with the lawyers just before his death to rearrange his will, adding the restricted trust for Crystabel to protect her inheritance."

"Well, that confirms our suspicions about Hargrove," Eleanora said. "But we still have no proof he committed the embezzlement or that he is a murderer."

Mr. Peters sighed. "No. But we have a motive. And Hargrove does appear to be the likely suspect. If he was the culprit, he had to have accomplices, Matheson for one. But I believe there must be a third conspirator. I cannot shake the idea that Hargrove hired someone to kill Matheson. He does not strike me as the type to do the job himself."

Elliot asked, "Have you had Hargrove tailed? Surely the man would meet with an accomplice, if there was one, after the murder of Matheson was discovered."

"We have kept a close watch on the man. Oddly enough there has been nothing unusual in his movements. No messages sent. From what I can tell he has gone about his days in a normal manner. He spends a great deal of time with his daughter, unusual for a man of his class. There have been no meetings or even conversations with anyone outside of his set of privileged friends. The man has a predictable lifestyle. He spends mornings in his garden with the child and afternoons at his club, when he is not out with his child taking in museums or events in town, then returns to the house in time to dress for an evening out, or a quiet night at home. He attended two events this week. Both times we were able to slip a servant into the home to watch the man. He keeps to his crowd of friends, usually at the card tables. Not once has there been even the suggestion of something suspicious going on."

Claudia offered Mr. Peters a gooseberry tart. "That is disappointing. The man must be particularly good at the business of being a fiend."

"Or he is innocent," Mr. Peters added, helping himself to two tarts. "Nothing in his behavior indicates he is anything other than the titled gentleman he portrays. The jewelry and expensive entertainments could have been paid for by Crystabel's uncle before his death. There is always the possibility Matheson was the sole villain, who was subsequently killed by his lover."

Eleanora snorted. "I am not ready to declare Hargrove innocent. As you said, he has a motive."

"Nor am I," said Elliot. "It looks as though our best chance of discovering the truth is to find the lover, Rose Ingram. Have you made any headway with that?"

Will Peters shook his head. "Everyone is looking for the woman. I talked to Inspector Mcgowan this morning. They cannot find a trace of the woman; she had no connections that they have found. The woman kept to herself. Mcgowan has not even been able to determine her past. It is as though she came to London from nowhere."

Claudia commented, "Surely, they have something to help locate her—a photo, or even a sketch?"

Will Peters sighed. "There is a drawing circulating, but it is vague. It could be any dark-haired woman. The papers have had a heyday reporting the heinous crime, and their drawings are more detailed, and less accurate. Each day Miss Ingram looks more and more like a villain in a fairy tale. There is even a penny dreadful circulating, with Rose as the wronged lover, killing Matheson in a bloody rage. You would think with all of London aware of her crime, it would be an easy find. But she has disappeared." He looked at Eleanora. "Did you glean any information from the little notebook?"

"I admit I haven't had the opportunity to analyze it. It has been a busy time here, I am afraid." She rose and walked to the sideboard, retrieving it from the top drawer. "I can do that today. If there is anything helpful in it, I will let you know."

Eleanora held the little book in her hand, but her thoughts were on her conversation with Crystabel about Lord Manford. "There is one further possibility. Crystabel shared some interesting gossip about Lord Manford." Eleanora told the story she had been told in the ladies retiring room.

"Very interesting indeed. I remember Manford. I was a constable when his wife's death occurred. Very suspicious. We had no proof of foul play. And of course, as always it was near impossible to get information from the parties involved." He grimaced and added, "Nothing protects you more from the law than the title of Lord."

Mr. Peters set his cup down and adjusted his jacket. "I will add Lord Manford to my list of suspects. We will take a closer look at his financials and movements. Perhaps we have been on the wrong track." He stood, preparing to leave. "There is nothing more I can offer you for information. I will continue to monitor Hargrove, and certainly check out Manford. But I think we may have to concentrate our efforts on finding Rose. She cannot have vanished without a trace." He bowed to Miss Claudia. "Thank you for the tea, ma'am, I must be off."

"You are welcome Mr. Peters." Claudia stood. "And I too must return to the office. There is still much to be done with the accounts."

"The fog has begun to descend and threatens to become a regular peasouper. Even hailing a cab will be a problem. Perhaps we could drop Claudia at the office. Elliot, what do you say?" Will Peters asked, not looking at Elliot who remained seated, instead he held Claudia's gaze with a smile. "I believe we are going your way."

"The two of you may take my coach." Elliot turned to Claudia. "And instruct my coachman to return for you after you have finished your day, Claudia. I have no need of it. My place is just a walk across the park." He waved his hand as though indicating the expanse. "There are a few things I would like to discuss with Eleanora."

Eleanora's stomach quivered at his words. She was not sure she wanted to hear what he would say to her. She hoped he would continue to ignore last night's fiasco. And despite her bold statements about determining her own destiny with an arrangement of mutual convenience, she was suddenly feeling shy about the whole enterprise.

Mr. Peters held out his arm. "Shall we then?" Claudia took his arm and the two of them left the room without a backward glance.

There was a moment of awkward silence. Eleanora found she was still standing at the sideboard clutching the notebook. For the life of her she could not think of a word to say.

"Come and sit down, Eleanora." Elliot patted the couch beside him. "We have a few things to sort out."

Eleanora took a bracing breath, crossing the room to settle as far away from him on the couch as possible. It was time to explain her proposition to him. She only hoped she would be able to find the right words.

She cleared her throat. "First let me apologize for my behavior last night. I swear it is not a habit of mine to imbibe."

Elliot was quick to interrupt. "The incident is forgotten. But I assume, from your announcement of our engagement to the Hargroves, the proposal still stands."

"It does." She looked at him from beneath her lashes. He was so serious and thoughtful. "May I ask why you accepted?"

"Only if I can ask what prompted the proposal?"

Eleanora felt her cheeks burn. Elliot remained silent, waiting for her to answer. This was not going to be easy, she decided. If only Elliot was not so straight and stiff beside her. He looked impossibly forbidding.

She sighed. There was nothing for it but to plunge forward.

"I have a host of suitors, as I am sure you noticed. I hate the whole experience of being courted." She paused and chewed on her finger before quickly pulling it from her mouth and grasping her hands together. She was unsure of what to tell him. "I was courted before, you see, and it turned out that all the pretty phrases which turned my head were lies. I am much pursued for my fortune. I cannot bear it."

"So, you asked me to marry you to avoid a courtship? That cannot be all of it." Elliot looked at her and raised an eyebrow, willing her to continue.

"No. Of course there is more. I asked you because..." she paused, debating whether to give him more of her motivation, "because I want to be off the marriage mart. You will not truly have to marry me; an engagement will be enough." Eleanora met his eyes, narrowed now as he considered her statement and quickly added. "We can think about it as a business arrangement, one from which both of us will benefit. An engagement of convenience as it were. You can change your mind, Elliot. It has not been announced."

Elliot furrowed his brows. "And how exactly would I benefit from this arrangement?" He waited for her response, but she had none. Eleanora's face colored. "No," he continued with his face set, "I don't think I will call off the engagement. And furthermore, I am going to accept the proposal as a reality. You are not going to get off the hook so easily Eleanora."

"What?"

"From my perspective we are engaged to be married. If I am to get something from this bargain, then it will be the opportunity to convince you that a marriage to me is indeed the right choice." He rose, walked to the sideboard, and poured himself a brandy from the decanter. He tilted his head and drank it in one gulp, then set the glass down and met her eyes.

"I want a true engagement. And after a decent length of time, say three months, you may call it off if that is your wish. But until that time, you will be my fiancée, and I will treat you as such. You want to avoid suitors and a courtship, and you will, but for one—me."

"This is the bargain you wish to strike?"

"It is."

Eleanora considered the arrangement. It solved her problems, at least for a time. And to have Elliot say he wished a true courtship caused a ripple of excitement in her belly. There was no question she was attracted to the man. She would have to be careful to keep her heart well wrapped while she fulfilled her part of the bargain.

"I accept," she said.

"We have an agreement then." He looked at her with a half-smile. There was a glint in his eyes, and she could not discern thoughts.

"Yes." Eleanora replied, warming to the deal. It was, after all, remarkably close to what she had initially proposed. "We have a partnership. Each of us with roles and responsibilities, rather like our bargain for the management of the firm. I want an engagement in the same sort of pattern. This will work splendidly."

And she added silently, after a few months, she could just negotiate for an extension.

Elliot laughed at her attempt to fit their agreement into a business contract. "And what percentages have you carved out for this engagement? Am I to be relegated to a twelve percent share in this partnership?"

"No, no..." She furrowed her brow. "I had not thought of that. No, I suppose the split would have to be fifty percent."

Elliot smiled at her. "That is reassuring."

"You are laughing at me!" She shoved his shoulder in frustration. "I am serious about this Elliot. I do not intend to lay out our responsibilities, not specifically. But I do think we can have a relationship that is a partnership, based on mutual respect, much like the deal struck between us to operate Pembroke." She glowered at him.

"Hmm. No feminine talk of affection or even attraction in this proposal?" His face was serious once more.

Eleanora felt her face burn as she considered sharing her feelings for him. He watched her carefully and nodded.

Eleanora ignored the question. "You must tell me why you want an engagement."

"I have several reasons. The first is that I want you as my wife and believe I will convince you to make our arrangement permanent. When I returned to England, it was with the objective of settling here and raising a family. I hope to have children one day. And I want a woman of some maturity and intelligence. You meet those requirements."

He paused and smoothed back a lock of long brown hair which had somehow escaped its leather thong. "I could leave out the fact that you have Pembroke, but it would be dishonest of me. Of course, your ownership of a company which aligns with my current passion for shipping is a factor. But I can tell you truthfully that you would still be my choice in a bride without it."

"Are those your only reasons?"

He laughed. "There are others. One I would like to keep to myself for now. And there is this." He reached over and drew her into his arms. His mouth found hers and he rained gentle kisses along her lips until she raised her arms and held his shoulders. Then he deepened the kiss, running his tongue lightly along her lips until she let him in.

Once again, she was lost to everything except his embrace. Her hands found his hard back, glorying in the strength and breadth of him. He left her mouth and began kissing her neck. His hot breath and his potent masculine scent overwhelmed her. She wanted to speak and tell him how wonderful he made her feel, but when she tried, the only sound she could make was a soft moan.

She could feel his hands cupping her breasts. She arched her back, offering her body to him, wanting. His wet kisses trailed across her chest to her breasts, bare now and aching for his attention. She squirmed when he took her nipple into his mouth, running her hands through his hair and holding him against her.

And then he stopped. Laying his head for a moment on her chest, he breathed deeply, before pulling back and looking at her. The bodice of her gown had somehow been pushed below her breasts. When he lowered his head once more to kiss each breast, she closed her eyes and absorbed every nuance of his mouth upon her body. Never had she experienced such intimacy. Her fiancée Robert had wooed her with flashy words. Until now, she had not realized that something was missing in the equation. Elliot gently pulled her gown up, covering her, then leaned forward once more and kissed her lips.

She opened her eyes and looked at him, disappointed that he had withdrawn from her. His hands gripped her shoulders as his blue eyes searched hers as though hoping to find something in their depths. She was still breathless, unable to stop her panting breaths. As though satisfied with what he saw, he gave a little half smile, one that made her heart ache. She wanted to pull him back into her arms.

With a final light squeeze on her shoulders, he removed his hands and shifted away from her. Giving her another lazy smile, he said softly, "I am afraid, my love, that if we continue, I will not be capable of stopping. And your disgruntled housekeeper might be in for a shock."

As if on cue Mrs. Bixby hustled into the room. "Would you like another cup, or can I take these out?" Eleanora felt her cheeks burn.

Elliot answered her. "Yes, another cup of tea is a fine idea, Mrs. Bixby. But you can remove these," he indicated the settings for Claudia and Mr. Peters, "they have left."

She looked at Eleanora as though wanting her confirmation, waiting for her nod before following his instructions. Eleanora cleared her throat. "Yes, yes, a cup of tea might be just the thing. And more gooseberry tarts if we have them."

Mrs. Bixby snorted her disapproval, making as much noise as possible gathering the teacups and clanging them together. They sat in silence until she tromped out of the room.

He grinned. "And that, my dear, is another of my reasons." For a second Eleanora was confused, wondering how her housekeeper could possibly affect his decision to marry, until she realized it was the kisses he spoke of. Her cheeks burned once more. He took her hand. "I shall put our announcement in the post tomorrow."

Elliot looked at her with a mischievous smile. "I shall apply for a special license, and the moment you weaken I will haul you to the altar." He pulled her close and kissed her lightly on the lips. "Enough for now. I know you are not interested in a courtship, but I am, and I must say I am looking forward to the challenge."

"You are?"

"Give yourself a little time to get to know me better Eleanora. Who knows? Perhaps in a week you will want to rethink the matter." He glanced down at the coffee table where the tattered address book lay discarded. "I think we need a distraction. Now may be a suitable time to go through Rose's little book together."

Eleanora agreed, "Excellent idea." She was eager to dismiss the topic. Tomorrow he would send a notice to the papers. At least one problem would be solved; she would have some relief from the constant barrage of suitors. She smiled at the thought of Mrs. Bixby, who would certainly be pleased to hear it.

She picked up the book, slid over beside him, and flipped it open to the first page, laying it on the table in front of them. "I thought we might go through it page by page. I will get a pen and paper. We can make notes of anything interesting." She left him for a moment, went to the sideboard, and retrieved the items.

Settling in beside him, she laid out the notebook. "Now then, I believe we had progressed to J, with no addresses and two names." She quickly flipped through the pages. "Here was one, Miss Emma Fairbanks." She jotted the name down while Elliot continued the search.

Mrs. Bixby cleared her throat to make her presence known. "Shall I pour ma'am?"

Eleanora answered without looking up from the book. "Yes. Thank you, Mrs. Bixby, that will be all."

A moment or two later they found the second full name. "Here we have Elizabeth or Beth Kipple, again with no address." Each time a name appeared she wrote it down. To her frustration, they had reached the letter R and still had found only two entries with both first and last names, and not a single address. There had been an Edith, a Sally, multiple Lizzies, even an

Anntonette, and not one of them with an ounce of information.

Eleanora leaned back for a moment and took a sip of her tea. She noticed her leg was pressed intimately against Elliot's. She did not move. There was something comfortable in his nearness.

She smiled to herself and went back to considering the task at hand. "I wonder about the lack of addresses. This book must be from her school days. Young ladies who have not yet set up their own residence."

Elliot frowned, still hovered over the notebook. "It could be. But why not at least scribble down the address of a parent. It could have given us somewhere to start. Surely one of them might have some information on her current whereabouts." He shook his head in frustration. "Most of these nonsensical writings have only a first name beneath them." Then he too took a break from the task, helping himself to a gooseberry tart.

"Why not indeed. You are right. Perhaps none of these girls have addresses." Eleanora set down her teacup, flipping the book closed while keeping her finger on the page. She examined the cover carefully, feeling her excitement grow.

"What do you mean, no address? Everyone has an address."

Eleanora ran her hand slowly over the cover. "Here it is! Feel this Elliot." She took his hand and laid it on the tattered cover. "There is an emblem embossed into the cover. I think this may be a gift of some kind. From a girls' school or orphanage of some sort! An orphanage! That must be it! None of the girls there would have a home of their own."

She flipped back to the page. "And this notebook contains no addresses, but rather a series of well wishes and childish poems. Take this for example." She opened the book to a random page. "Best of luck to you in the future Rosey." The wishes were followed by a picture of a bumble bee with the words 'be happy' scrawled beneath it in a childish hand, and signed, Emma.

"I think you may be right, my dear. It is certainly worth checking out. But let's finish, shall we? We are at R, almost done with it." He leaned forward once more and turned the page. A short poem was centered on a rainbow-colored page.

Eleanora read the entry aloud. "'Rosy Ormand dressed in yellow, all decked up to meet the fellows. How many kisses will she get—hopefully, a lot! Signed, your best friend Idelle Sewell.' Now that is interesting." She looked up at Elliot and raised her brows. "It seems Miss Rose Ingram is actually Miss Rosy Ormand. Oh, and we have another full name, an Idelle Sewell." She quickly jotted it down.

"Hmm. Interesting indeed." Elliot rubbed his chin thoughtfully. "The constables told Will that Rose Ingram appeared to have no past. And she does not. Rose Ingram never existed. It is little wonder no one has been able to find her."

"I am sure she is more than thankful now she used an alias. How perceptive of her. Though I suppose one might do exactly that if one were to take up the occupation of mistress." She flipped the little book closed. "The old connections in this address book may have given us little information, but at least now we know her real name."

Elliot mused, "With no photographs, if the woman kept to herself as she appears to have done, the law would have almost nothing with which to track her down. She could be identified only by her housekeeper if she had one. She could be living safely right under their noses."

"Her housekeeper! I don't know why I haven't thought of this before. I wonder if the police have been able to track her down. Mrs. Bixby told me she knew the cook at the neighbors! Do you suppose she may know anything? Rose must have employed a housekeeper or a cook of some sort. Afterall the kitchen was meticulously kept. Surely the employees would know something of each other."

"I would imagine the police have spoken to everyone in the vicinity. But it may be worth a try."

"When I first spoke to Mrs. Bixby, she was loath to share any information. It cost me several pounds just to get an address. It is in the best interests of people in service to avoid any business pertaining to their employer and the law. But I am sure there is much gossip among themselves."

She thought for a moment. Money had worked well with Mrs. Bixby. However, in the case of murder, a servant might want to stay completely out of the mess. "Maybe if we have a proper introduction, we could make some headway." She walked to the sideboard and pulled the lever to summon Mrs. Bixby.

Mrs. Bixby bustled into the room; her furrowed brows indicating her annoyance. "What is it you need?" she asked.

Eleanora took a seat next to Elliot on the sofa and indicated the chairs across from them. "Mrs. Bixby, I wonder if you could sit down with us for a moment. There is something we would like to speak to you about."

Mrs. Bixby eyed her suspiciously. She moved slowly across the room and sat carefully on the very edge of her chair. "What is it then? Is there some sort of problem?" she asked, tilting her head, and looking at her employer askance.

Eleanora was quick to reassure her. "No, no Mrs. Bixby. I have no problems with you or your service." Mrs. Bixby visibly relaxed. She pressed on. "I just need to ask you a few questions. I remember you telling me at our first meeting that you were good friends with the neighbor of Mr. Matheson's special friend. Mr. Sparks and I are inquiring into the death of Mr. Matheson, my former employee, and we are thinking of talking to the woman."

"Ah, Mrs. Yurek." Mrs. Bixby frowned. "I don't know that she will be wanting to speak to you. Besides, the police already questioned her, looking for the mistress' cook they were."

Elliot leaned forward. "And was she able to help them find her?"

"Oh aye. Miss O'Malley. She went back to the stews

she did. Gone to live with her sister in the Carmel building." Mrs. Bixby shook her head. "It is a sad case that. The Carmel building is just on the corner of Whitechapel, on Sidney Street, and not a place fit for man or beast. Mrs. Yurek was sad to see her go. But there is not much to be done about it, times being what they are and her being Irish. Hard for anyone to find work, worse for an Irisher."

Eleanora looked at Elliot and grinned, before turning to her housekeeper. "Thank you, Mrs. Bixby. You have been a great help. That will be all."

Eleanora could not contain her excitement. She rose from her seat. "Let's visit her Elliot! There is still time to hire a hansom cab and make it to Whitechapel before dark. The woman is bound to know something about Rosy's whereabouts."

Elliot leaned back on the sofa and contemplated her. "Not that this will dissuade you, Eleanora, but are you familiar with Whitechapel? It is a notorious slum, and not at all fit for a lady?"

"Oh Elliot. If you will not take me, I shall go on my own." She put her hands on her hips to emphasize her determination.

He groaned and rose to his feet. "Eleanora, you are a stubborn wretch."

She laughed. "Is that anyway to speak to your new fiancée? Besides, you will be there to protect me. And we won't be wandering around. We have the address. It will be just a quick visit, and then we will be safely out of the community."

Elliot looked grim. "Since I see no way of stopping

you, I will agree to take you. But I suggest you wear your oldest cloak, and one with a hood. There is no point in advertising your wealth or your beauty in that setting." He scowled. "And I won't even try to demand you stay in the coach. The last thing I need is you getting into mischief trying to follow me on your own. This time I ask that you stay close to me."

"I promise to stay close. And I have the perfect cloak. I used it to walk to work in Boston. You will be impressed with its shabbiness," she said and chuckled, pleased with his capitulation.

After donning her old woolen cloak, remembering to fill its pocket with a handful of banknotes, and wearing the stout boots Elliot insisted on, they were ready to depart. The fog had only begun to settle in. Thus, they were able to hail a hansom cab, without too much difficulty.

She looked across at Elliot. His frown, which had been evident since she first suggested the trip to the stews, made him even more unapproachable. He looked dangerous, with his tall frame and rugged features. Gray breeches were fitted taut across his powerful thighs and legs, tapering into his black riding boots. He had shifted in order to stretch them out across the breadth of the coach. His gray day jacket was tight over his massive shoulders and open to reveal a matching vest. He wore no cravat, only a white shirt, open casually at the neck. He did not look like a fellow someone would willingly tackle. Indeed, he looked like a man who could take on Tom Sayers, the famous prizefighter known worldwide.

And she was thankful for that. Although she did not want to admit it, she was a little apprehensive about the excursion. She had heard tales of the slums of London, even in faraway Boston. As the carriage lurched forward, she wondered if they should have waited until morning, or at least chosen a day without the promise of a smothering fog.

CHAPTER 14

The buildings grew taller and the streets narrower as they neared the Whitechapel district. Furthermore, their progress was impeded by constant stops to wait for pedestrians. Eleanora sat close to the window observing their surroundings as they traversed slowly down the busy streets.

The further they progressed into the neighborhood the more crowded it became. The streets may have been the same width, but the many lean-tos and makeshift structures propped against the walls of buildings made it appear even narrower. The smell was almost unbearable. Open sewers lined the streets and combined with the horse feces making the muddy lanes almost impassable.

Elliot handed her his handkerchief which she immediately used to cover her mouth and nose. "Do you still think this was a clever idea? We can turn back."

She ignored the suggestion. "Why are there so many people on the streets Elliot?"

"They are mostly Irish immigrants. They have been flocking to London since the start of the famine. Unfortunately, life here has not been much of an improvement for them. More and more of them are arriving every day, with no place for them to live and work. I have heard there are buildings with dozens of people crammed into one small room. The streets are the only place for them to move about."

Eleanora gazed out her window. More than half the occupants on the streets were children and all of them were skinny and dirty. But then it would have been impossible to be otherwise in such filthy surroundings. Her eyes began to burn with unshed tears. *How fortunate she was to have never experienced poverty, to never have been hungry*.

At last, the coach slowed to a stop. They had reached the Carmel building in the Whitechapel district. It rose five stories, and like the buildings around it had a series of makeshift tent-like structures braced against its sides. People in ragged clothing were lying about or huddled on crates to visit with neighbors. The late afternoon fog had dampened the streets, which saw little sunlight to begin with, thus many people pulled their clothing tight and crouched into themselves for warmth. Most of them looked like they could use a good hot meal. And a job, she added to herself.

To the side there was even a small pen, where a mother sow lay, nursing half a dozen piglets. It was guarded by a skinny urchin holding a thick club, too heavy for his small frame.

Elliot opened the door to the coach and hopped down. "Pull that hood up over your head, and wrap the cloak around yourself," he said, his expression grim. "I'd leave you here, but you will be safer with me. And for God's sake, stay close."

He helped her down and walked to the coachman. "We will only be a few minutes." Reaching into his pocket he pulled out a banknote. "Here is a tip for you. There will be another with your fare when you take us back."

The driver grinned and reached down to snatch up the bill. "Ye might want to hurry mister. I can't say I'm pleased to be sitting 'ere with only my club to fend 'em off." He reached down and lifted the long sturdy stick which lay across his lap.

Eliot pulled out a second bill. "We will double those tips then, but I expect you to be here when we come down."

The old man snatched the second bill from Elliot's hand with a toothless grin. "Ay, that'll do."

Elliot took her arm and led them to the main door of the building. He turned to an elderly woman with a thin gray scarf wrapped around her head and shoulders. "I am looking for a Miss O'Malley. She lives with her sister. Where might I find her?" He dropped a silver coin into her hand which she quickly pocketed.

"Aye, that'd be the widow Margaret's flat. Second floor, last door. She won't be there long, I hear," the woman muttered.

A heavy oaken door opened to the stairs which were situated immediately to the left of the entry. It was gloomy, and the air was thick with the smells of its inhabitants—wet wool, burnt grease, urine, and unwashed bodies. And even the stairwell was filled with people. They were sitting on the steps, or even sprawled out on the landing and all of them stared silently as they passed by. It was clear she and Elliot did not belong here. Elliot kept a firm grip on her arm as they passed. Eleanora breathed a sigh of relief when they finally reached the second floor and the door to the last apartment in the dark hall.

He rapped on the door. After what seemed like forever, but could only have been a few seconds, the door opened a crack.

"I am here to see Miss O'Malley, the cook who worked for Rosy Ingram," Elliot said, leaning into the shaft of light from the door.

"I suppose you are more constables," a woman's voice answered from within. "She has said all she is going to say on the matter."

Eleanora stepped closer to the doorframe. "We are not from the law, but we do have some questions. I also have a proposition for her that she will want to hear." She looked at Elliot who raised his eyebrows in an unspoken question.

The door swung open.

A woman of indeterminate age stood before them. She was big boned, but thin, wearing a worn house-dress covered with a faded apron. A tattered kerchief was knotted over her hair. The face beneath it was angular and hollowed, showing the strains of a life of poverty. Hard blue eyes looked back at them with a solid determined glare. This was a woman far different from the ragged folks they had seen huddled in the streets and shadowed halls. The streets of Whitechapel had not defeated her...yet.

Eleanora looked around the room. It was clean, with a set of bunkbeds against the far wall. Four little heads peaked out from the top bunk. A mattress was propped against the alternate wall, ready to be flipped down for sleeping. A small wooden table with two wooden crates for chairs sat in front of an oil stove and a rickety sideboard which held a dented tin basin. A bare window was open a crack to let in the fresh air.

Beside the stove another woman stood. Her clothing was less threadbare, and she was younger and plump when compared to her sister. She assumed this was Miss O'Malley, recently of Brightline Street.

"Miss O'Malley," Eleanora extended her hand. The girl nodded and took it.

The other woman stepped forward stating, "And I am Margaret O'Malley. She'll hear the proposition first, and then the questions."

Miss O'Malley blushed and indicated the crates for them to sit down. "You may call me Claire. Please, sit down."

Elliot remained leaning against the door. "I will stand if it is all right with you, you go ahead." Eleanora knew that with only two chairs, he was too well-mannered to take one.

Margaret interjected, eyeing them warily, "Let's hear this proposal then."

Eleanora settled carefully onto the crate while Claire took the one across from her. She glanced at Elliot who looked back at her, raising his brows, and tilting his head as though to say, I too would like to hear it.

Eleanora felt her cheeks begin to heat and cursed her tendency to blush. The only thing she could think of at the moment was the phrase that had been running through her head since she stepped from the cab—hot food and a job. She looked at Margaret. This was a woman who would be quick to set her in her place if she offered charity. She would have to tread carefully.

She cleared her throat. "I am the owner," she glanced at Elliot again and quickly amended, "part owner, of Pembroke Industries. We are looking to fund a charity in London and have decided upon opening a soup kitchen here in the Whitechapel district. I need a manager; someone who knows the area. It will be necessary to plan, purchase the food, and design hearty soups which can be distributed to high volumes of people daily. I will also need someone who can cook, and I assume, several servers and cleaners. My manager would oversee those details."

There was silence as both women stared at her with identical expressions of incredulity. Finally, Claire spoke. "I am a cook, and I can also help with the planning and purchasing of food. But I am not sure I would be able to manage. That might take a firm hand, and some experience, especially if it involves managing staff. But I do know someone who would excel at the job." She looked over at her sister and smiled.

Margaret narrowed her eyes. "And how much would a job such as this pay?"

Eleanora replied in the crisp tones she reserved for work. "Salary is negotiable. For now, we could begin with what I pay my housekeeper, doubled. I expect to pay a living wage, or more, but in return I will demand the best possible performance," she looked at Margaret, narrowed her eyes to match hers and added firmly, "or more."

There was a moment's silence again.

"I'd be interested. And Claire will make a fine cook." If Margaret was pleased, she did not show it, at least not with words. But Eleanora noticed her stiff form relaxed a little, and her eyes had a hopeful gleam.

"It is settled then. Your first task will be to find a shop. Something that can be converted easily into a kitchen and serving area. And mind, it must be in this neighborhood. Once that is done you will have to see that it is outfitted properly. I want it up and running as soon as possible." She reached into her pocket and pulled out the pound notes. "This should suffice for your first week's wages. There is also enough to take a hansom to Pembroke Industries once you have found a suitable location. We can then rent or purchase the place."

The money was a sure way of making the proposal a reality. Margaret stared at it for several seconds. For the briefest of moments her eyes shone with unshed tears. She blinked in rapid succession, carefully gathered up the notes, and tucked them into her apron pocket. When she met Eleanora's eyes again, she had regained her composure. "I already have one in mind, and it will be a purchase," she said, her voice betraying her by cracking slightly.

Eleanora instinctively ignored her emotional lapse. She was careful to keep her voice brisk and businesslike. "Perfect. When you get to Pembroke, you will speak to Miss Claudia Whitfell. And I warn you, she is exceptional at managing funds. She will be your contact person. Together you will lay out the plans for the endeavor."

Margaret nodded. There was the hint of a smile on her lips and her eyes sparkled.

"Now then, shall we get to the questions?"

"What is it you want to know?" Claire asked. "I will try my best to answer it."

"We are looking for the murderer of Mr. Matheson. We are not convinced it was Miss Ingram and are hoping to find her. She might have information about the culprit. She may have even seen him."

Claire sighed. "I tried to help the constables, but there is just not much I could tell them about where she could be. She kept to herself. The only guest was himself—Mr. Matheson."

"How were things with Mr. Matheson? Did they get along well?"

Miss O'Malley sighed. "Like I told the police, up until the end, they seemed to be on excellent terms. But the night of the murder they had a terrible row. When I left, they were shouting at each other. Yet I still cannot imagine Miss Ingram resorting to the violence."

"Were you able to determine the cause of the argument?"

"I only heard bits and snatches. I was on my way out, you see. I had been given a few days off to spend with my sister and was eager to be gone." She glanced up at Margaret. "It sounded as though Mr. Matheson had told her he was leaving. Miss Ingram was terribly upset." She shook her head. "But still, I had no idea she might do him in."

"Hmm..." Eleanora considered Claire's words for a moment. It was a motive for murder. Lovers' quarrels had certainly been the cause of many a death. She dismissed the thought for the time being and went back to their original objective. "Did she ever mention friends? Was there any time she talked of acquaintances?"

Claire knitted her brows. "Let me think. Hmm... There was one time that she talked of a friend. She had a strange name. I just can't seem to remember what it was."

"Could it have been Idelle?" Eleanora asked.

"That's it! I remember now! It was Idelle. She said something about hoping to visit Idelle." Claire grinned at her memory. "She said she hoped to sit with Idelle on the seashore once more."

Eleanora looked at Elliot and smiled triumphantly. He inclined his head and gave her a smile. He had said nothing during the meeting, content to lean against the door and silently watch the exchange. She turned back to Claire. "Is there anything else? Anything that might help us find her?"

"I can't think of anything. But if I do, I will send word."

Eleanora rose from her crate, "Thank you ladies. I look forward to doing business with you. It is going to be an exciting project."

Claire walked with her the few paces to the door. Eleanora looked back into the room. The children had remained quiet during the interview, hidden under a blanket in the bunk. This time only one peeked out at her from beneath the covers. Margaret, who was anchored in place by the stove, was looking teary once more. Eleanora turned to her, and said in her firmest voice, "I expect you at the office with an offer on our soup kitchen in the next few days. See that the matter is taken care of." Margaret responded with a nod.

Elliot swung the door open. When she stepped across the threshold into the hall, Claire followed her a pace, grasped her hand, and pulled her in close to whisper, "Thank you, thank you, thank you." Eleanora could only smile before Claire was gone and the door clicked shut.

They were silent until they reached the coach. Once settled and the carriage had begun to move forward, Elliot commented, "That was well done of you."

She smiled at him. "Pembroke should support a charity. This one is small indeed when weighed against the suffering in this community." She was looking out her window as she spoke, watching the misery of life on the damp streets pass by.

The words Miss O'Malley had spoken echoed in her mind, particularly the bits about the fight between the couple, on the night he was murdered. "Do you think Rose shot her lover?"

Elliot stretched out his long legs and leaned back into his seat. "It certainly appears that way. A rousing battle, followed by a shooting. It is a believable scenario, more believable than our theory about Lord Hargrove." He looked at her and shrugged. "We learned from Will's report that Hargrove is an unlikely suspect. He is living the life of the aristocrat, hanging with his peers while behaving in every way like the titled gentleman."

"But the man is arrogant. You saw him attempting to take control of Pembroke! Mr. Peters also said he is in dire financial straits."

Elliot gave a little snort of laughter. "Most of the elite spend beyond their means. And he certainly doesn't have the monopoly on aristocratic arrogance. Eleanora, you may have to accept the possibility that Matheson acted on his own. That he murdered Jem to cover his trail, then planned to leave town, abandoning his mistress, who ultimately took her revenge."

"I suppose that all makes sense." she replied, but she was not convinced.

Elliot continued, "And a sort of rough justice has been applied. Matheson was killed for his crimes."

"I still want to find Rose. We can at least hear her defense. I want to be certain before I pass judgement. Miss O'Malley did reinforce our theory on the possibility that Rose joined her old friend—she certainly made no new friends on Brightline Street."

Elliot sighed. "I too suspect our Rose Ingram may be sheltering with her friend Idelle. It is the only connection we have discovered so far. But finding them presents another problem."

"We do know this Idelle lives near the sea."

Elliot laughed. "Have you considered the fact that England is an Island? There are an infinite number of possibilities. Besides, it is more likely the women took a vacation together by the sea at some point."

"True. But there must be some way of locating her. This time we have a name, and we know she was at one time an orphan girl. I wonder..." she mused, "I wonder if her orphanage might know her whereabouts. Don't these places try to secure a spot for their girls when they come of age? If we are looking for this Idelle, surely the institution would have some inkling of where she can be found."

"It's possible. It may be worth our while to check the orphanages in the city." He looked out the window. "Perhaps tomorrow. It is growing dark, and if anything, the fog is thickening. Tonight, my dear, I just want to get you safely home."

He leaned forward, taking her hands in his and surprised her by kissing her lightly on the mouth. "And after finding this woman to satisfy whatever sense of justice you still harbor; we can concentrate on the courtship I spoke of."

Eleanora looked at his earnest expression. Before she could answer the cab slowed to a stop. "Bad timing," he said with a smile and opened the carriage door. He hopped down to assist her.

He walked her to her door and helped her open the lock. "I will bring around the company coach early tomorrow morning. We will check the orphanages," he said, setting the keys back into her hand. "Good night my love." He gave her a quick peck on the cheek.

Eleanora stood for a moment in the open doorway and watched him stride briskly down the walk, then swing up into the hansom cab. The fog swirled around the carriage as it moved slowly forward and disappeared into the darkening mists. It had gotten late. The sun would soon set.

She leaned against the open doorframe and considered him as a potential future husband. Elliot was all that was proper in a fiancée. He treated her with a gentlemanly deference that was certainly appealing. Touching the cheek where he had kissed her, she thought about his comment about wanting a courtship. His light kiss alone had her senses whirling. Maybe being courted by a man like Elliot would not be the unpleasant experience she hoped to avoid.

He could be her future husband, she thought. Her stomach did a flip at the prospect. For all her talk of the agreement they had made, she was finding it increasingly difficult to think of him in purely business terms. Just his touch was enough to leave her quivering. The image of his strong thighs sprawled across the narrow carriage came to mind, and she smiled to herself. Elliot was not a man who could be taken lightly. His very presence overwhelmed her senses.

She was distracted from her thoughts by Claudia's voice from within. "Eleanora, thank goodness you are home. I was beginning to worry, what with the fog rolling in."

Eleanora stepped into the house and pulled the door closed behind her. "Claudia, I have so much to tell you."

While taking off the old cloak, she began to fill her in on the day's events. By the time they had settled next to the warming fireplace in the sitting room she had described the little book's revelations and was beginning a description of their excursion to Whitechapel. Claudia would need to be completely informed on her vision of Pembroke's charity.

It was a relief to leave behind her thoughts of Elliot. She didn't want to analyze her feelings about him. She had her heart broken once. The painful experience of Robert's betrayal had left a taint on even the word love. She would not contemplate it.

CHAPTER 15

Elliot sat back in the coach, replaying his day with Eleanora. He was beginning to think he had been wrong about Hargrove's involvement in a murder plot. The argument between Rose and Matheson pointed towards a lovers' quarrel turned violent. It was a tidy end to a distressing situation.

He thought about his future wife and smiled to himself. Today she had proved herself to be a woman with a soft heart, and philanthropic goals. He could only admire the deftness with which she had presented her proposal to the proud Irish woman of Whitechapel. He could not have done as well.

It was all the more reason to take this woman as his wife. If he had his way, he would use the special license to marry her immediately.

"Not true," he said aloud, "I want more."

The business arrangement she proposed was not enough. He would somehow find a way to make this woman want him for more than just convenience.

Once again, he cursed his inability to easily flirt and charm a woman, a skill other men seemed to accomplish with ease. The idea of scribbling a love poem or giving her a flowery speech declaring his love was repugnant to him. He was sure it could only result in an awkward scene. He knew he wanted a courtship, and desperately wanted it to be successful; the problem was he had no idea how to go about the process.

She desired him; he was certain of that. Her response to him was obvious. Perhaps he could build on that to win her affection.

His thoughts were interrupted as the hansom coach rolled to a stop. Outside, the fog had obscured the street, leaving only the dark outline of his town house in the mists. There was an evil tinge to the mists today. The fog had turned a sickening shade of bile as it sometimes did, proving its namesake—a 'real peasouper.' He opened the door and hopped down to the street, walking to the coachman while digging in his pocket to produce the cab fare.

A figure leapt out at him from the fog, catching him unaware, with his right hand still deep in his pocket. He was slammed against the coach. The glint of a blade flashed before his eyes.

There was a loud crack as the coachman's stick came down, knocking the assailant's arm. A knife clattered onto the cobbles. Elliot had time to register only a slight figure wearing a hangman's cowl before the villain scrambled away into the mist.

Still sprawled against the coach, he took several deep breaths before he stepped forward and looked up at his savior. The whole incident had taken only a few seconds. He found himself still stunned by the attack.

"Bloody thieves," the man growled, "can' t stomach the likes of them bastards."

"That was well done." Elliot said, taking a steadying breath. He pulled out what money he had in his pocket and handed the whole of it to the man. "I cannot thank you enough. You are quick with that club."

"Oh aye." He was counting his money and did not look up. "I've had some practice, and mores the pity." He finally looked down at Elliot, chuckling. "I see you have made it worth my while. I thank you sir." His teeth gleamed a farewell, and he shook the reins. With a "Hup, hup," to the horses, the cab moved forward into the shrouded street.

Elliot stood for a moment listening to the sound of the horses' hooves on the cobbled street fade into the distance. When he turned to his gate and took a step, his boot collided with an object. Looking down, he saw the assailant's knife. He picked it up by its handle and strode to his door.

Once settled in his library, he examined the weapon. It was an officer's dirk, long and slender, with an ivory handle encased in polished bronze. It was not what he had expected. This was not the weapon of a street urchin, unless it was one recently snatched. A weapon such as this would be too valuable to keep, rather it would be quickly converted to cash.

He balanced it in his hand. It was well crafted. "Hmm," he considered. The attack could well have been a random one, but two circumstances suggested this was not the case. First, robberies in this neighborhood were rare. He was, after all, in one of the most prestigious parts of London. Incidents like the one he had just experienced were almost nonexistent. And second, the man who owned this knife was not your regular villain. This was an officer's dirk, one that had probably seen more parade dress than actual battle. The owner had to be someone of consequence, someone who could afford to keep the thing.

Whoever the attacker might be, the villain had very nearly been successful. He had been distracted, thinking only about Eleanora, with his right hand secured in his pocket. Had it not been for the coachman's quick actions, he would have been killed. He would have to be more careful from now on.

There were no enemies who might be interested in his death. He could think of no motive, outside of this business with Matheson, for the attempt on his life. And even then, there was no reason for Matheson's murderer to target him.

Unless, he considered, whoever murdered Matheson was aware of his investigations and hoped to put a stop to it. *That was a stretch.* It would mean they had been followed today—an unlikely scenario. And even if someone was aware of their investigation, they had learned nothing to incriminate anyone.

He sighed. His reasoning had come full circle. He was back to the idea of a random attack. This thief must have plucked the knife from someone recently and planned to use it a few times before selling it. He rose and placed the dirk carefully on his mantle. He decided to keep the incident to himself. There seemed no point in scaring Eleanora with this tale. Alerting the constables would have no effect. It was time to let the matter rest.

His butler stood in the doorway and cleared his throat. "The cook has prepared a light supper for you as requested sir."

"Thank you Flurry. I have another request. I wonder if you could ask below stairs if anyone knows the names and locations of orphanages here in town."

The man raised an eyebrow. "Orphanages sir?" he asked as though repeating blasphemy.

Elliot smiled. There was no one who less suited his name than Flurry. He could not imagine the elderly man moving in any way beyond the dignified, silent stride he practiced in his occupation. He had been in his employ for as long as he could remember, even accompanying him to India. Flurry was a firm believer in maintaining the formal reserve of a prestigious household. Even in the most cramped circumstances during his travels, Flurry remained steadfast. "Yes. Orphanages, either in London or nearby."

"Very good sir."

Elliot sat down to the multi-course meal considered a 'light supper.' He looked around the grand dining room. This house had been his mother's. It was far too big for a single man, but soon, he hoped, it would be filled with Eleanora and the family he longed to have. He had been on his own too long.

He thought about his plans to win his future wife's affections. He looked up to the portrait of his mother above the mantle, and wished she were here now to help him with his cause. She had loved his father, an extremely wealthy businessman who was nonetheless a step down in society's mind, without reserve. He too, had always hoped for such a marriage.

He wanted more than a temporary partnership with Eleanora. How strange it was that he was considered unromantic, when in fact he wanted a marriage based on love. With her business sense, he might be able to convince her of a marriage of convenience. But it simply was not enough, not with Eleanora.

So far, his plans to woo Eleanora involved using her attraction to him to seduce her. He was sure he could win her with a slow sensual lovemaking. She was to be his wife, after all. He smiled as he considered his strategy. It would certainly work to woo him—he was sure to be successful.

His mother's portrait seemed to stare down at him with disapproval. He peered back at her and said aloud, "I agree, it is not the best approach. Just what do you suggest?"

He looked at the beauty on the wall as though expecting an answer. In this portrait she leaned back in a wicker chair, young and relaxed against the backdrop of a flowered garden. She wore a light blue gown in the regency style, loose about her youthful body. Her jeweled hand held a single daisy. She gazed dreamily into the distance. There was a double strand of pearls, clasped together with a sparkling diamond pin at her neck, suggesting both her innocence and her status.

That is it! Elliot thought with excitement. I can give

her a jeweled gift, something which will express my regard for her.

He began making his plans for the morning. He would be off to Garrod's first thing, to purchase a trinket for Eleanora. And then he would enact both elements of his plan. They would spend time together, traversing the city, and visiting the various orphanages in town.

After a day in his company, where he planned to be most gracious and charming, he would invite her to his home for high tea. He could then give her his gift. He would have Flurry see to it that he and his fiancée had the privacy to enact part two of the plan. A gentle seduction played out in the comfort of his sitting room. He would be all that was romantic and loving—he would worship at the altar of her beauty. He laughed aloud at his poetic musings. Who said he could not be romantic?

He thought of serving a delicate champagne, but remembering the fiasco of her dinner party, decided against it.

He hopped up from his supper, pulling the lever to summon Flurry. He intended to share his stratagem with him. Everything had to be perfect. By this time tomorrow, Eleanora would be swept off her feet. She might even declare her undying love for him.

He smiled to himself while he waited for Flurry to attend him. He had the perfect plan. What could possibly go wrong?

CHAPTER 16

Elliot arrived while the ladies were still at breakfast. Claudia was quick to ask him to join them for the meal.

"I would like nothing better than to enjoy my breakfast with two such lovely ladies," he remarked with a grin. "I cannot think of a more splendid way to start my day."

Claudia looked at him with surprise. "You are in exceptionally good form this morning Mr. Sparks," she said, rising to hand him a plate and gesturing to the sideboard. "Please help yourself."

Eliot loaded half a dozen sausages onto a plate. "I am," he replied, before heaping scrambled eggs, kippers, and sliced tomatoes onto his dish. He set a couple of biscuits on top and took his place at the table. After taking a few forkfuls he continued, "How can I not be when I am looking forward to a fine day with my fiancée."

Eleanora returned his smile. "You will be happier

still when I tell you I was able to get the names and addresses of two orphanages here in town."

"Were you? I too have done a little sleuthing. We make a fine team." He grinned again, a boyish sort of smile she had not seen before and began to eat in earnest. She glanced at Claudia who smiled and shrugged her shoulders.

He spent the next few minutes eating a copious amount of food. Eleanora could not help but be impressed with his hearty appetite. The ladies let him eat in silence, sharing a look when he accepted another biscuit, then slathered it with red currant jelly.

After Mrs. Bixby had served coffee with heavy cream, they shared the names of the institutions they had discovered. Between them, they had three orphanages which took in only girls. Elliot then planned a circular route around the city, saving the furthest institution, St. Mary's, for last. It was located on the Great North Road on the Northern outskirts of London.

"Shall we, my love?" Eliot stood.

"I will just get my cloak."

Once in the coach Eleanora was disappointed to note that the fog from last night still lingered. It was another dreary overcast day. She had hoped to get a tour of the city, but it was not to be. The sites were blurred in a haze of yellow mist. Elliot seemed unaffected by the weather. He remained cheerful and endearing, an Elliot she had not seen.

Even the disappointing results at the first orphanage did not shake his optimistic mood. The headmistress was initially suspicious. She finally agreed to check her enrollment, but only after informing them it would be all the information she would share with them. No Idelle Sewell had ever been a resident of the place. At the second institution the head mistress was not in. Her assistant was an older woman who would not check the files, but insisted that no one of that name had ever been at the home.

"I think at the next orphanage we need a better cover, a credible purpose to be searching for Idelle," Eleanora said.

"Agreed. What do you suppose would be a common reason to find a former orphan? A long-lost family member? An inheritance?"

"Why not both? Hughes and Barnum were not keen to settle Jem's estate until all the heirs, myself included, could attend the reading. Maybe the same scenario could be happening here. We need to find Idelle so the will can be read, and the estate settled." She grinned. "That way we do not have to pretend a relationship with the girl. We can be frustrated with our need to locate her—which we are. And they in turn, will assume they are doing Idelle a service."

"I like it. My brilliant fiancée." He chuckled, still in a jovial mood. "You can be a cousin, and heiress to a portion of your great aunt's estate. I will be your impatient spouse, hoping to get my hands on the funds as soon as possible."

"And names?" Eleanora asked.

"Let's use mine. Mr. And Mrs. Elliot Sparks." He gave her a mischievous smile. "It's a name you will be needing to become accustomed to."

She laughed. "It works."

They were forced to travel back through the East End to the Great North Road. Earlier this morning there had been few people on the street. Now, even in this dreary weather, the streets had become clogged, especially here in the poorest districts.

Eleanora gazed out the window. At every corner, women stood, and when the carriage passed, they flashed their wares—a leg or a shoulder. She commented, "There are so many women plying their trade here, and the poorer the district, the older and more desperate they are. The East End is inundated with prostitutes."

"Prostitution is everywhere. It is in our community too, just less obvious. Rose, for instance, was paid for her services with her livelihood. There is even a higher level, the courtesan. Many who may be your neighbors, ladies who expect to be supported and to receive expensive baubles as a bonus. It is a profession, said to be the world's oldest."

She let the curtain fall back in place. "Speaking of occupations, how did you choose yours? You are well connected socially, comfortable financially, and most men of your class would live the life of the idle gentleman."

Elliot laughed. "I am not much for the life of the gentleman. I have been a disappointment to my poor aunt, Lady Mansfield, to be sure. She has quite given up on me I'm afraid. I think she fears I take after my father, a man of business. And I suppose she is right."

She watched Elliot as he talked about his passion

for business. He was animated and enthusiastic. Today, he had lost his usual reserve, emitting an exuberance she had not noticed before.

The journey flew by quickly. Only minutes had passed when the coach pulled up to a three story, gray building. Eleanora looked at its forbidding exterior and sighed. "Why do these buildings all look alike? Must they be so dreary?"

Elliot opened the coach door and helped her down. "When compared to Dorset Street in Whitechapel this place is a haven," he said taking her arm.

"Quite true." She looked up at the windows above her. A small face peered down at her from the bottom corner of a window, before a curtain fluttered back into place.

Elliot rang the knocker on the huge oak door. A lonely hollow sound echoed within. Moments later a maid in a dark uniform pulled the door open. Her face was stark, without an ounce of warmth. Dark eyes scrutinized them from beneath heavy furrowed eyebrows. "How can I help you?" she asked.

"We are Mr. and Mrs. Elliot Sparks. Could we speak to your headmistress? It is a matter of some importance." Eleanora answered.

The maid looked them over, taking in Elliot's finely cut coat and Eleanora's gray travelling cloak. Only when she was satisfied with her appraisal did she swing open the door. "Come in. I will see if Mrs. Haversham can see you."

The maid left them standing in the foyer, while she

went down a darkened hallway, her shoes echoing a brisk pace in the silence.

Eleanora found herself whispering, as though breaking the stillness was somehow a transgression. "How strange there is no evidence of children in an institution meant to house them."

Before Elliot could answer the maid returned. "Mrs. Haversham will see you. You can follow me."

Mrs. Haversham too was dressed in widow's black, her graying hair combed into a severe bun. But unlike her maid she exuded a friendly demeanor. Her face was pleasantly engaging, evidenced by the laugh lines around her mouth and soft gentle eyes. She stood behind a wide desk, with two chairs placed before it, and smiled. "Mr. and Mrs. Sparks, please sit down." She waited until they had settled. "How can I help you?" She had a large blank sheaf of paper in front of her on the desk, and a pen in her hand as though she was prepared to take notes.

Elliot cleared his throat. "We are looking for a girl, a young woman now, I suppose. Her name is Idelle Sewell."

Eleanora was sure she saw a spark of recognition in the woman's eyes, before she looked down at the quill in her hands and rotated it, as though considering their question. "May I inquire as to why?" she asked.

"My wife Eleanora has been informed of a substantial inheritance from her great aunt. It seems Miss Sewell is also a beneficiary. The lawyers refuse to settle the estate until Miss Sewell is found. You can imagine our frustration."

"Yes." Eleanora added. "We have searched endlessly for the girl. It was finally revealed to us that she may have attended a home for orphan girls here in London. We do so need to find her."

Mrs. Haversham looked up, with a twinkle in her eyes. "How very interesting. Miss Sewell is a fortunate young woman indeed. You are not the first people to come here with an inheritance for Idelle."

Eliot leaned forward and looked at her curiously. "She was here then? And someone else has been searching for her? Perhaps our lawyer—"

"No, no not recently, Mr. Sparks. Several years ago, just as Idelle was about to leave us, she received word of an inheritance. It was quite extraordinary actually. It is an orphan's dream, and never a reality. As you can imagine, every child here has the secret wish of being remembered by a long-lost relative. But it is never the case. And now, Idelle has had it happen not once, but twice."

Eleanora could not contain her excitement. "Do you have any idea of where we might find her?"

Mrs. Haversham smiled again. "I do," she said and rose from her desk to open her filing cabinet. "It is our goal to have all our girls decently situated when they leave us. Idelle was our most fortunate. She inherited a fine home near Reigate," she looked back at them and added, "a respectable estate, with an income. I have her address, and even a few notes giving directions to place." She pulled out a file and returned to her desk. "Let me see. Here it is. She scribbled the address and particulars onto her notepad, then tore it from the pad, and handed it to Elliot. "Miss Sewell has become the hope of all our girls here at St. Mary's. You will have added to her legend Mr. Sparks."

Elliot rose, tucking the paper into his jacket pocket. "My wife and I cannot thank you enough. It will be a boon to get this estate settled at last."

"Please send her my regards," Mrs. Haversham said. She too had risen to see them out.

"We will at that." Elliot reached for Eleanora's arm. "Shall we my dear."

It was difficult to remain silent as they traversed the gloomy hall back to the entry. Once in the coach she turned to Elliot. "We found her! And what better place for Rose to retreat to than a place in the country. I am sure she will be hiding there."

"She may be." He grinned at her. "Tomorrow is a fine day to take a daytrip. The community is not far from town, only eighteen miles." He looked down at the notes from the headmistress. "And according to the directions, the estate is a few miles this side of it. We could be there before noon."

"I love the idea! We can pack a picnic lunch. It would be lovely to get out of London's dreary fog."

Elliot laughed and reached across to take her hand, his eyes sparkling with merriment. "I have a date with my beautiful, intelligent fiancée. What could be finer?" He leaned forward to kiss her.

What began as a quick peck soon changed. The familiar wave of excitement rippled through her, as his kiss deepened. When he last kissed her, he had withdrawn. This time she was determined he continued.

She wanted to explore the feelings he had awoken in her. She put her arms around him, holding him close, and basked in his heady male scent. He began to kiss her neck, his breath hot and demanding as he struggled with her heavy cloak.

She needed him near her. Her hands left his back to untie the offending cloak secured at her neck. He pushed it off her shoulders, groaning his appreciation as his hot mouth trailed across her throat. She too wanted to touch him. She clutched the buttons on his jacket and fumbled to open them. He leaned back momentarily and removed the garment. But it was not enough. Her hands itched to feel his bare skin. She tugged on his shirt until it too was flung from his body.

In one quick motion he pulled her dress off her shoulders. Her arms were trapped at her sides as her breasts were bared. He leaned back again to survey her. "God…you are beautiful," he said, and pulled her to him.

The shocking sensation of skin against skin overwhelmed her. She wiggled about until her arms were freed and she was able to hold him tight against her. His back was wide; she could feel his strength as her fingers registered the ripples of his muscular form. His body was so different from hers—hard and exciting.

He laid her back on the coach seat. He suckled her breasts, while one warm hand found her stockinged legs and moved ever closer to her very center. Then suddenly he was stroking her, his hand using the same pulse as his lips and tongue. She wanted to tell him how wonderful she felt, and opened her lips to speak, but only moaned as his fingers entered her. Her body began to quiver in response. She dug her nails into his back, holding him against her, and willing him to continue making her body sing. She tossed her head back and forth as wave after wave of delicious euphoria coursed through her nether regions and shook her to her fingertips.

Finally, she lay back against the coach seat, panting to regain her breath, and reveling in the strange new experience. If this is what married couples do, it is no wonder men and women are so eager to wed. She was completely relaxed, giving Elliot a lazy smile to voice her appreciation. But Elliot appeared not to share the same languorous mood. His eyes glowed, with pupils so enlarged they seemed black in the soft coach light. Some of his hair had escaped its leather throng and fell in waves, framing his tanned face. You are beautiful too, she thought; rugged and manly and mine.

"You are so ready for me," Elliot muttered, and reared back. His hands left her to undo his breeches. She saw his organ spring free. A jolt of fear disrupted her feelings of languor. Surely the proportions were wrong; it would not fit.

"Elliot," She cautioned, but he was beyond hearing. It was as though he was lost in a fever. He leaned down and nuzzled her neck, his breath hot and desperate against her as he grabbed the hem of her dress, and petticoats, pushing them up until they were bunched around her waist. He then positioned himself between her thighs.

She held onto his shoulders as he began to push

into her. He seemed impossibly large, and she knew she had been right. Indeed, he was too big for her, because he appeared to hit an impasse. He was perspiring, his forehead was beaded with sweat. She assumed the task was as difficult for him as it was becoming for her. It felt like an intrusion.

"Elliot, this will never work. We do not fit." she said, voicing her concerns.

He leaned down and kissed her. "Hang on love. I promise it will only hurt for a minute." His words were anything but reassuring. She had time to grip his shoulders before he arched his back and plunged forward. A sharp pain startled her, and she let out a little squeal, instinctively attempting to squirm away from him.

"No Eleanora, lie still," he said, releasing a loud groan. And then his hips began to move. He began to withdraw from her slowly and she thought the ordeal was over, but instead he moaned and pushed back against her. "I am sorry love," he said as he arched over her once more. He pumped his body against hers in a series of quick thrusts, pushing hard into her a final time, impaling her into the coach seat. She could feel him throbbing inside her before he collapsed on top of her.

He lay sprawled against her, gasping his breath for several seconds. She was relieved when he used his arms to brace himself, taking some of the crushing weight from her.

She was unsure how she felt. The first part of the business of making love was marvelous, but the last bit was shocking and painful. She could do without repeating the process.

The sound of the horses' hooves, clattering against the cobbles reminded her where she was. Her cheeks began to burn. She had just been tumbled in a coach like a common prostitute. She pushed against Elliot's shoulders, to get him to move off her.

Elliot lifted himself and looked down at her. His face was serious now. "I am so sorry my dear. This is not at all what I had in mind."

His apology somehow made it worse, as though he was aware of the disrespect he had treated her with. It was too much. She squirmed away from him. This time she had the satisfaction of feeling him leaving her body. Sitting up caused a second humiliation. Her lower body was a sticky mess, and she looked down at herself with dismay.

Elliot pulled his trousers up over himself and reached for his jacket which had been tossed to the floor. He pulled a handkerchief from his pocket and silently offered it to her.

Snatching it from his hand without a word, she waited for him to busy himself with his shirt before wiping herself. The cloth came away red with her blood. She gasped.

"It is all right, Eleanora. It is normal to bleed the first time." He put his hand on her shoulder to reassure her. She wanted something from him, and she was not sure what it was. She had always pictured making love as an event enclosed between soft kisses and loving phrases. This scrambling about in a cramped carriage was not the romantic event she'd envisioned at all.

While buttoning up his shirt, his eyes followed her, as she tried to right herself. Her dress was in a terrible snarl. "Let me help," he said, and without waiting for a reply began to assist her. They had the gown back up over her bodice, and her arms in her sleeves.

She shook out her skirts. "I am fine now." The mood in the coach had deteriorated into an embarrassed awkwardness. She only wanted the coach to arrive at her door so she could be rid of the day. She needed time to digest what had happened between them.

He finished buttoning his shirt and pulled his jacket on. He looked no worse for wear; in fact, his appearance was perfect. She scowled at him; certain she looked a fine mess.

He sat across from her, giving her an apologetic half smile. To her relief the carriage came to a stop. She slid across the seat toward the door.

He put his hand on the lever, forcing her to pause for a moment, before turning the latch. "I have something for you." he said, reaching into his pocket, and pulling out a slim velvet box. "It is a gift to show my appreciation." He opened the box, revealing a diamond bracelet, which glittered, even in the orange glow of the coach lamps.

Her mouth dropped. "Your appreciation? Is this a payment of some sort?" The ladies of the street came to mind, lifting their dresses over their knees to entice.

"No! No! I wanted to get you a gift to express my gratitude—" He saw her outraged expression and quickly amended, "not gratitude, I meant my sincere feelings for you. Eleanora I—"

She gently pushed the hand holding the gift back towards him. "I am afraid I do not accept baubles in payment Mr. Sparks." She pulled down on the lever to open the coach door.

"Eleanora, that was not my intention." He scrambled from the coach and assisted her. He held her arm firmly in his. "I am sure you know that. I will come early tomorrow to fetch you for our trip to the countryside." he said as he walked her to the door.

She could only nod, unable to meet his gaze before slipping inside. For the moment, her thoughts were awhirl. She wanted to get to her room, have a hot bath, and contemplate the afternoon. There were no words for Elliot just yet. Perhaps tomorrow she could look at the events without feeling the embarrassment and confusion she was feeling now. The only thing she was certain of was her girlish daydreams of making love were far from reality. From her point of view, it was a painful, messy business she did not care to repeat.

Tomorrow she would explain to Elliot that they were not a good fit. It was clear they were not made for each other after all.

CHAPTER 17

It was a disaster, Elliot thought with a grimace. All his plans had come to naught. Somehow things had gotten out of hand. He cursed himself as he walked into his salon. Whatever had possessed him to seduce Eleanora in the carriage? And he had known too, she was a virgin. The only explanation was his intense desire for her. Even now the image of her pale skin in the amber glow of the carriage lamps was intoxicating. Somehow, she was everything he had ever wanted in a woman. They were made for each other.

The room was decorated as he and Flurry had planned. Bouquets of flowers graced the mantle and the end tables. *The place smells like a bloody green house.* He plopped down on the sofa. In a moment of disgust, he flung out his arm, sending the vase with its yellow roses and white baby's lace flying to the floor. The vase shattered with a satisfying crash.

Flurry came to the door with a tray of delicate sandwiches and delicious treats. He stood for a moment, taking in the sprawled young man, then the glass, water and flowers strewn across the hardwood floor. With a disapproving frown, he set the tray down as far from Elliot as possible on the tea table. He shot him a second stern look and began to silently pick up the pieces of shattered glass.

"My apologies Flurry," Elliot muttered.

But for a grunt to emphasize his disapproval, Flurry ignored him. A footman came to assist and in moments there was no evidence of his burst of temper.

"Can I assume there will be no guest for tea?" Flurry was all politeness, but his manner reflected a silent accusation.

Well, if you think I have blown the whole business of this courtship you would be correct, he thought grimly. He said aloud, "You assume correctly." Elliot was finding it difficult to keep his anger in check. Flurry sighed, before he silently withdrew.

Elliot groaned. He mentally reviewed the fiasco in the carriage. He had behaved like a schoolboy, unable to manage his desires. It was not a common occurrence for him. Even as a young man, he had been able to exercise control. But today, he had lost all sense. He shook his head.

Then there was the gift. He had picked a perfectly ridiculous time to give her a token of his appreciation. He scowled, adding the unfortunate phrase, 'and gratitude' to his memory of the event. Not his finest moment, he decided.

Perhaps his friend Will was right, and he was best

suited to a time when the mate of your choice could be flung over your shoulder and hauled into a cave.

He ran his hand through his hair, pulled the leather thong which held it secure at the nape of his neck, tossed it aside, and shook his head. His hair fell freely around his face, dark and thick. Selecting a sandwich from the tray, he devoured it in two bites. If I behave like a barbarian, I might as well look like one, he thought to himself.

There was little he could do to rectify the situation until tomorrow. He decided to spend the rest of the afternoon attending to some of the personal business he had been neglecting of late. He piled several more delicate sandwiches onto a serving plate and retreated to his library.

THE NEXT MORNING Elliot arrived early at Eleanora's door. He had decided to use the buggy today, rather than his coach. He would be able to take the reins himself, without the need for a coachman, and even more importantly, Eleanora could ride up beside him. Flurry had packed a huge basket for a picnic lunch. He only hoped the weather would cooperate. March was unpredictable. It could be a lovely spring day, or the weather could turn on a dime, and they would be huddled under coach blankets in freezing rain.

But he was willing to take the chance. Once out of London, he was sure this infernal fog would lift, and they could enjoy the sights on their journey to Reigate.

But just in case, Flurry had tossed in a couple of coach blankets and a kerosene warming lamp.

Once again, he had been invited to breakfast, which pleased him—he had only had time to grab a couple of biscuits on his way out the door this morning.

Mrs. Bixby glowered at him as she laid out a place setting. "Mayhap we should keep a third plate on the sideboard since you're making this a habit," she growled.

"Why thank you Mrs. Bixby," he grinned at her, "how thoughtful of you."

"Hmph," she snorted and returned to the kitchen. He caught Eleanora's eyes and the two of them shared an amused smile. It was a good start, he decided.

He filled his plate at the sideboard, and sat down, comfortable listening to the ladies' conversation while he enjoyed his breakfast.

"Before you arrived, Mr. Sparks, I was informing Eleanora on the progress being made in your new charity," Claudia said. "It seems Margaret O'Malley has found a suitable building. And what's more the place has two stories. You may be able to cover some of your expenses by renting the rooms above."

"How many rooms?" Eleanora asked.

"Four, not counting the kitchen and a bathing room. Three bedrooms and a small salon which could be converted into a rentable space or left for the tenants to share."

"Hmm," Eleanora considered, "I think not. Make the apartment an extra bonus in the wage contract for Mrs. O'Malley. The one-room space she had was far too small for four little ones and a sister. Besides..." she added, "I have no intention of becoming a landlord in the Whitechapel district. And furthermore, having someone near the place in that neighborhood is probably best." She took a bite of her toast and considered. "Be sure to state it to her in those terms. Remind her that it comes with the responsibility of looking after the place."

Elliot thought of the four little heads peeking out from the covers of their top bunk. Eleanora had made a fine decision. He realized that one of the aspects of her personality that so attracted him was the difference in her role of a lady compared to others he had met and even courted in the past. Eleanora was a working woman. She saw the world differently than the upper-class women around her. Most women of her status lived their entire lives without seeing or considering the plight of the lower classes. To them the unfortunate were nonexistent.

But Eleanora, like him, had lived and worked with people from all levels of society. As a manager she must have learned to respect individuals for their talents and skills as opposed to their social position.

She was nonchalant about the fripperies and laws of etiquette which so bound the other women of her class. It was a freedom of sorts for her, and for him it was refreshing and enticing. He smiled to himself at his insights.

He went back to tackling his eggs and kippers, letting his thoughts and the ladies' conversation fade from his consciousness.

When he finished his meal, he sat back and sipped his coffee—one American habit he had come to enjoy. He looked at his fiancée once more. His Eleanora was a lady in the true sense of the word. Today he would prove he could be the perfect gentleman. Under no circumstances would he make any advances toward her. He aimed to prove he could treat her with the respect she was entitled to.

And absolutely no kisses—he was obviously unable to control his passions when he was near the woman. He had no intention of destroying his opportunity to redeem himself. This time he would not stray from his plan. It promised to be a fine day, he thought, firm in his resolve. By nightfall, his fiancée was sure to consider him the model of gentlemanly conduct.

CHAPTER 18

Eleanora allowed Elliot to assist her up onto the buggy seat and wrap the coach blanket around her skirts. He lit the coach warmer, and a second blanket was draped across their laps to hold the heat. The night's fog had left the morning with a damp chill. She had dressed in a warm light gray travelling suit, with a full-length woolen cloak, and together with the blanket and warmer she was sure the trip would be comfortable enough. She only hoped the skies would clear when they got out of the city limits.

She glanced at the skyline with its maze of chimneys spewing black smoke into the air, which sunk slowly to the streets below in the chill air. London sat on the banks of the Thames, nestled into a low-lying flood plain, protected from the winds. It made for a circumstance of constant dreary fog, even without the thousands of coal chimneys puffing relentlessly. It would be a relief to breathe the fresh air of the countryside.

Once they had left the congested streets, she had her wish. The skies cleared. Initially the countryside was agricultural, with fields of grain and pastures where cattle and sheep grazed. As they progressed the land became wooded, with rolling hills. At times, the branches of towering oaks leaned over the road, wrapping them in tunnels of lush green foliage.

Elliot seemed determined to avoid any reference to yesterday's incident in the carriage, which was a relief. Eleanora was pleased to keep the conversation light. Instead, he pointed out the sights along the way, and regaled her with stories of how as a child he had been determined to be a farmer.

Eleanora laughed. "Somehow, I cannot picture you as a farmer. You are so much the man about town."

"Yes well, I spent some time with my paternal grandmother, who lived quite simply in a rural community, despite my father's constant attempts to persuade her into more comfortable quarters with us in London. It seemed a fine life to the boy I was."

The buggy had reached the crest of a massive hill. From here the land stretched out before them, a magnificent expanse of green fields, tucked between darker plots of wooded regions.

"It's beautiful."

"It is," Elliot agreed, "And just over there, in the copse of trees is the manor house we are seeking." He pointed to a location on this side of a distant village. Though the estate was still far away, the sun reflected off a white building snuggled in the trees. "It might be wise for us to pause here and concoct some kind of story. If Rose is there, I am certain Idelle will be loath to give her up."

"True." Eleanora considered the problem. "But the truth of the matter is we can only be of help to Rose. Her chance to live a life free of this murder charge rests with having her name cleared. And we are trying to do just that."

Elliot was skeptical. "Hmm. You are right, but it may take some convincing."

"I think we have no choice but to share what we suspect. If Rose is innocent, she may well leap at the opportunity to help with the investigation."

Elliot snapped the reins, and they proceeded down the hill. The manor was accessed by a long lane of oaks ending in a clearing where the house stood. It was white brick, not the grand structures inhabited by the wealthy aristocrats, but respectable. It rose two stories, to a red tiled roof, with windows in a two, three, two, formation on each side of the entry. To the right, down a gentle slope the outbuildings were sitting against a wooded background. The home and grounds were well kept, with manicured grass and shrubs anchoring the building at its ends. The entire impression was one of charm. Idelle had certainly inherited a fine piece of property.

The door was answered immediately by a young maid. They asked to see Miss Sewell. Elliot handed her a card, which the girl looked at suspiciously. After a long wait in the entry, the maid returned. "Miss Sewell will see you. If you could come this way." Eleanora released a breath. At least they had gained entry.

They were led into a small sitting room with windows facing the drive. It was comfortable, with furnishings that spoke of an earlier era, but clean and smelling of lemon. Eleanora noticed the curtains and cushions had been updated. Again, the overall effect was one of comfort and charm.

A moment later a woman, who she assumed to be Idelle came into the room. "How can I help you..." she glanced down at the card in her hand, "Mr. Sparks?" She had red hair, pulled back into a loose braid. Her most interesting feature was her large green eyes, almost too big for her small face. A scattering of freckles across her nose gave her a girlish appearance.

Elliot cleared his throat. "I am Elliot Sparks, and this is my fiancée, Miss Eleanora Pembroke. Together we own Pembroke Industries in London. Have you heard of the company?"

"I have, though I am not sure how this is connected to me." Eleanora was sure she saw relief in Idelle's wide eyes, as she gestured to an arrangement of furniture by the fireplace. "Please sit down." She waited until they were settled before she added, "How can I help you?"

Eleanora thought it would be best to simply pour out the entire story. She began with the death of Jem. "My manager, Mr. Briggs, was murdered under suspicious circumstances," she said. She then related the entire story of the embezzlement. When she came to the part of Matheson's murder, she paused to let Elliot take over the tale. She noticed Idelle's eyes nervously darting to the open door of the salon.

Leaving Elliot to complete the tale she lowered her

eyelashes and glanced surreptitiously at the open door. The ruffled hem of a gown spilled into the room, at the base of the door frame. A jolt of excitement rippled through her body. Rose was here, and she was listening.

When Elliot completed the tale, she added, "We are convinced of Rose's innocence. What we need is some help to prove it. We have a former runner working on the task, but we desperately need more information about the true killer."

Eleanora resisted the urge to glance back at the open door, adding, "Anything Rose knows about that evening or even about Matheson's business deals could be the key to finding the true murderer. If we are successful, Rose will be cleared and able to resume her life without the constant fear of being discovered."

Idelle said nothing. Instead, she looked at the open door. Again, Elenora forced herself not to follow her gaze.

A tall young woman walked into the room. "I am Rose Ingram, or should I say Rosy Ormond. I can try to answer your questions."

There was a moment's stunned silence. "I will see about getting us a spot of tea," Idelle said and left the room.

"Thank you Rose for speaking to us. I can assure you that whatever happens, we will keep your location in the strictest confidence."

"I would appreciate that," she said. She was a beauty, and despite her slender frame, not girlish like her friend, but stunning with thick dark hair rolled into a bun, and perfect classical features. It was easy to see why she had been able to snag a rich man as her keeper.

"I will tell you what I can, and only hope there is something to help you." Her voice was calm with a note of determination. Eleanora sensed this was a person not easily victimized.

"Let's start at the beginning, with anything you know about Mr. Matheson. Any details might help." Elliot asked.

Rose sighed. "I met Matheson when I applied for the role of under-clerk at Pembroke. I had always been good with figures and hoped to find a position, even though those jobs were exclusively for men. He didn't give me the position. But he began to court me. I believed he would marry me, naïve girl that I was." She paused and closed her eyes briefly. "Needless to say, the proposal never came. I was taken in. By the time I realized my mistake, it was too late. I had given up my former position and seemed to have been left with few choices. At any rate I chose to be his mistress."

She looked down for a moment, then met their eyes once more, as though looking for any condemnation. Seeing none, she continued. "I was determined to be smart about the whole affair. I made a business deal with the man. I would be his in exchange for the title to my home and an income. I made sure it was enough for me to put money aside in case the whole enterprise collapsed." She gave a little half smile. "I am good with figures as I said.

"At any rate that was how matters stood until the

night of the murder. Matheson came to me in a panic that night. He wanted all the jewels he had gifted me, and there were plenty of those. He had been generous. I refused. I knew what this meant. I knew he was planning to leave, and I would need my pension fund now more than ever. I was furious to learn he would so callously leave me and outraged that he expected to take his gifts with him. We argued..."

She looked down once more, taking a breath. "Finally, he confided to me he was in trouble, that he was being forced to leave town with only what liquid assets he could carry. He then offered to take me with him, declaring me the love of his life. We reconciled. I went into the spare room, one I used to keep my wardrobe in, to change into a night gown he had recently purchased for me." She took another deep breath.

The young maid came in with a tea tray and began to serve. "Miss Idelle said she would join you in a bit," she said. Rose nodded, pausing in her story until the girl had left.

"I was about to join Matheson in the bedroom when I heard someone on the stairs. Thankfully, I stayed where I was. Then there was shouting."

"Did you hear what was being said?" Eliot asked.

"Some of it. Matheson said, 'I am leaving town. What more can you want?' I did not hear the man's reply, only his muffled voice. But it was a man's voice. I heard him laugh." Rose closed her eyes once more and took a deep breath. "Then Matheson screamed. I don't think I will ever forget it. He yelled, 'I have done everything you asked of me and more—for God's sake mercy.' That was when the shots were fired." She paused and took a sip of her tea. Eleanora noticed that her fingers trembled as she raised the cup to her lips.

She looked at Eleanora. "I did care for the man you see," she said quietly.

"But how did you escape the murderer? He must have known you were there. It was your house after all," Eleanora asked.

"I am still not sure why the killer left me alive. I hid, and not in the best of spots. The only place in the room there was to get out of sight was the closet. And I am sure it was obvious to the killer where I would be found. I heard him come into the room. And he laughed again. I will never forget that laugh. I thought for certain I was dead, but he did not even search the room. He said, 'I will leave you to it.' Then I heard him going down the stairs. I left after that. I packed up all my valuables and called a hansom to take me to the train station."

"You never saw him then? Could not identify him?"

Rose shook her head. "No. I wish I could, but no. I had never heard the voice before, of that I am certain."

"Just one more thing. What did he tell you about his troubles? About why he had decided to leave?"

"He said he had been caught with his hands in the cookie jar—those were his words. He also said his bloody partners had left him to take the fall. But that was all I could get out of him."

"He said partners? Plural?" Elliot asked, "You're sure?"

"That is what he said. I am afraid that is all I can tell you. He made a point to never discuss his work. I forever wanted to be a part of his life, but he kept our relationship separate; I had never even been to his home. Other than that last evening together, I don't think he ever spoke of his work or his home life."

Elliot took a final drink of his tea and set it down. He rose to his feet. "Thank you for your help, Miss Ormond, and you have indeed been of help to us. At the very least we know our suspicions are correct."

"Yes." Eleanora added. "And rest assured your location is safe with us. We have no intention of seeing you wrongly charged with this murder."

Rose showed them to the door. Elliot handed her a card. "If you think of anything else, anything at all, please contact me."

She took it and slid it into her skirt pocket. "I certainly wish you all the luck in finding the culprit." Rose said with a wry smile. "It will be in my best interest that you succeed."

Once back in the carriage and on their way, Eleanora said, "I found the woman to be straight forward and truthful. I believe her. What was your impression?"

"I agree. I think we can now assume we were correct in our theory about Matheson's murder. There would be no way Rose would have known about the embezzling otherwise. We can also begin to look for a partner. Rose was adamant about Matheson saying partners. It means there are at least two people involved."

Elliot snapped the reins and the horses moved forward at a brisk trot. He added, "It was worth our while to follow this lead, though I have no idea how we might catch the perpetrators at this point. Hargrove may have gotten away with the perfect murders. He has motive, but there is no proof whatsoever of his guilt. Our only hope may be in one of the two betraying the other. Will is tailing Hargrove. With any luck he will meet with his partner at some point."

They rode for some time in silence. Eleanora contemplated the situation. There was something she was missing, some connection she hadn't made. She mentally went over the conversation at the manor one more time but could not determine what it was that nagged at her.

It was frustrating to think they might never catch the villains who orchestrated the crime. True, Matheson had met his just reward, and if they placed a claim against the man's estate, they might even recoup the money he had stolen. He had owned a valuable property; it would be more than enough to pay for his theft.

Still the idea of the people responsible, and she was sure one was Hargrove, getting away with their crimes was frustrating.

A flash of tan and white interrupted her thoughts. A deer streaked across the road and leapt into the woods. "A deer! How lovely! Did you see him, Elliot?"

Elliot laughed. "I did. I cannot help but think this is one of the most beautiful parts of England."

Eleanora silently agreed. She banished all the thoughts of the murder and leaned back in her seat to enjoy the views. Though the spring air was still crisp, the sun was higher in the sky now and it had begun to warm considerably. She looked at Elliot and smiled. He balanced the reins in one hand and reached down to squeeze her hand as though he too appreciated the journey.

After more than an hour on the road, he turned the horses onto a trail, leading off into a bluff of trees next to a creek. "I thought we might find a place here for our picnic. We will want to have it before reaching the open fields near London," he said.

They found the perfect place just a hundred yards down the trail. It was a grassy knoll, next to the creek, protected from the winds by the trees which circled it.

Elliot watered the horses, while she laid out the coach blankets and the picnic basket. Once she had everything set up to her satisfaction, she opened the basket to see what had been packed. There was a plate of sandwiches wrapped in paper, a jar of pickled vegetables, cheese, biscuits, strawberries, and grapes. There was even a bottle of red wine with two tumblers. It was a feast.

She laid it out, pleased with the picture. When Elliot approached, she smiled at him. "You certainly thought of everything."

"I did no such thing. Flurry packed it." He sat down on the blanket, choosing a sandwich, peeking inside to see what it contained before eating it. He grinned and exclaimed, "Thank goodness for Flurry; I am famished."

Eleanora found she too was hungry after all the

fresh air. The two of them ate silently for a few minutes. It was wonderfully comfortable with the sun, the sound of the stream beside them, and Elliot enjoying his meal.

After eating her fill, she took a handful of grapes, popped one in her mouth, and smiled at him. “This is a lovely picnic, in the most beautiful of spots.”

Elliot opened the wine and poured each of them a glass. “I am pleased you like it.” He set his glass down and gestured toward the food. “Would you care for more?”

“No, I am quite done, thank you Elliot.”

He smiled and repacked the basket, leaving out only the grapes and the wine, then shifting the lot to the side of the blanket.

“You are a very handy man to have around," she teased.

“I have ulterior motives,” he grinned. She thought for a moment he would reach for her and kiss her. But instead, he took off his jacket, rolled it up and lay down, using it as a pillow. “We can take a few minutes to enjoy the sun, before getting back on the road.” He loosened his collar and closed his eyes.

She was surprised to discover she was disappointed. However much she had disliked the finale of yesterday’s fiasco, she still enjoyed his touch.

He opened his eyes again, held out his arms and said, "Come, lay next to me.” He smiled and added, “No shenanigans this time.”

Eleanora took off her travelling jacket, rolling it up as he had done, placed it beside him and lay down on her back. She stole a quick glance at Elliot and caught a glimmer of his smile, though his eyes remained closed.

She looked up at the leaves of the trees above her, gently turning in the breeze, sparkling each time they faced the sun. It was peaceful here. She was glad Elliot had taken a few minutes to enjoy it.

The sun was warm. She was feeling lazy and satisfied from eating a delicious meal, and Elliot lay beside her, his shoulder touching hers.

She thought about the problem they had in their relationship—the fact they did not fit. Now might be the perfect time to address her concerns. It was a delicate topic, too intimate to speak of in a normal setting. But here, with him relaxed beside her, she thought she may be brave enough to bring it up. Besides, his eyes were closed. She was convinced not having to look at him while she broached the whole embarrassing difficulty would be an extra boon.

"Elliot," she began, watching the leaves as a gust of wind had them twirling about above her.

"Hmm," he responded.

"About yesterday afternoon, in the coach." She paused while she considered her approach. She decided there was no route to take except directly forward. "I think it was rather apparent to both of us that we have a problem. We do not fit well together. It is not your fault really. You are just... anyway it will never work."

She felt Elliot's strong arm against her stiffen, and knew he was listening. After a moment or two he said, "You think not?"

She hurried on before she lost her courage, "I know you must have noticed it too. We are just not a good match in that way. It is never going to work."

"Hmm."

"It was a huge disappointment for me. I thought about it last night for a long while. I had always heard such thrilling things about the experience you see. And the books—they hint at the metaphysical aspect of the whole endeavor. I am sure it is something we can never achieve together. I mean, it is an issue of dimensions." She could feel her face burning and was thankful she did not have to face him.

"Dimensions?"

"Exactly. We simply will not fit together. It is an engineering problem really. I mean I loved the first part, the touching and all of that, but it seems our bodies are not right for each other." She was pleased with her explanations, thinking she had done rather well with the difficult topic.

Eliot shifted abruptly, rolling toward her, placing one hand on the other side of her to encompass her in his arms. He looked directly into her eyes. "Then we are fortunate my dear."

His sudden nearness startled her. She stared up at him, unable to think of anything except that he had flecks of gold running through his blue eyes. He seemed to want a response. She stuttered, "W-why is that?"

"Because I have been dealing with engineering problems recently. This is one I think I can solve."

He leaned down and kissed her. Again, her body

immediately responded, and she put her arms around him. He was warm, and she relished the feel of his broad back beneath her hands. As his kiss deepened, she lost all thought and could only hold onto him, never wanting it to end.

He paused and looked down at her, pleased with her reaction to him. And then he began to unbutton her blouse, slowly. "Yes," he said when she arched her back to assist him in removing the garment. "I have a few theories in mind to rectify this little problem."

When he had removed her blouse, he began to work on her skirts, leaning down to kiss periodically—on her lips, neck, and breasts. When he had stripped her to her chemise, he said, "I need to see the whole picture, before I can enact my plans," and pulled the garment over her head, tossing it aside.

She was naked before him. He knelt between her thighs. She held her arms out, wanting him to lean in and rain her with kisses again, but instead he looked down at her for a long moment. Then his hands found her breasts and at last he was close to her once more. He kissed her long and hard, pressing his lower body into hers so that she could feel his manhood hard against her. His trousers chafed against her nether regions, and there was an ache, a powerful need to pull him close to her. She found herself arching against him, burying her head into the warm place where his neck met his shoulders to take in his scent.

"Elliot," she murmured when he lifted from her and began to ease down her body. He kissed and suckled her breasts, then her flat belly and finally the very center of her. She was taut and swollen. In moments, her body reacted, rising to a crescendo. Just when she was certain she would burst, she felt the familiar euphoria ripple through her body. She could not stop herself from crying out, overwhelmed with the intensity of the experience.

Before she could fall into the lassitude she remembered from the afternoon in the coach, he was slipping inside her. She braced herself, waiting for the pain, but it did not come. There was only a fullness. This time he did not move, instead he stayed still inside her and began to kiss her.

He lifted for a brief second and yanked his shirt over his head. Her hands found his bare back and she held on tight. He rubbed against her, rocking, and pushing gently until she began to feel the aching sensation once more. It was a wanting, a need to move, and to feel him move within her. She arched against him, hearing him groan in response.

Finally, he began to move slowly back and forth inside her. She needed more. Putting her hands on his buttocks, she pulled him down hard against her and rotated towards him taking him deep inside her and wrapping her legs around his body. He grunted in response, a deep guttural sound, then gradually increased his speed, until he was thrusting powerfully into her.

And then she lost all thought. It was as though nothing existed except the feelings inside her. When Elliot reared up, grabbed her hips, and arched back, the first pulse of his body sent a shock wave through her.

She hung on tight to him, unable to stop herself from crying out, as the waves washed over her.

Elliot collapsed against her, letting her take the full weight of his body for several seconds as he panted against her, before bracing himself on his elbows, and tucking his head against her neck where she could feel his warm breath.

For the longest time they lay tangled on the blanket. When Elliot lifted his head to kiss her lightly on the lips, she realized she may actually have dozed. She gave him a sleepy smile, which he returned.

He kissed her again, a playful kiss this time. "I think we solved our little engineering problem, don't you?"

"Oh Elliot, it was marvelous! So much more than I thought it could be."

He laughed; it was a happy, joyful sound. Then he rolled them onto their sides, looking into her eyes with grin. "A truly metaphysical experience?"

This time she laughed. "It was."

"And now we best get on our way. It is beginning to cloud over, and we'll not want to do the rest of the journey in a downpour."

She looked up at the sky, which had indeed clouded over. "Oh dear."

He rose, reached for his jacket, handing her his handkerchief with a smile, then shrugged into his shirt.

She held the soft cotton handkerchief in her hands and smiled. "I'll let you put away the picnic while I clean up." She bundled up her clothes, walked to the stream, and set them on the bank. The soft grass felt good against her feet. It was strangely exhilarating to be naked in the natural surroundings, she thought as she stepped into the water. She was sure she had never experienced it before. She smiled to herself, glancing back at Elliot, who had paused in his work to watch her.

She put her hand on her hip and raised her eyebrows as if to say, leave me my privacy. He grinned at her and went back to folding the coach blanket.

The water was cool against her skin. This time she felt no embarrassment as she wiped the traces of their lovemaking from her body. She stepped from the stream and pulled on her chemise, thankful that she had forgone the usual corset this morning. She donned the blouse and pulled on her skirt, smoothing them out as best she could. When she had buttoned the travelling jacket, she looked down at herself, satisfied with the results. No one would know she had just had a romp in the woods. She could not help but giggle at the thought.

Elliot had brought the horses around and stood ready to assist her into the buggy. She smiled at him and took her seat. In moments they were leaving the clearing. Eleanora turned and looked back. The only evidence of their presence, and all the joy she had experienced there was a square of flattened grass where the blanket had lain.

The rest of the journey passed quickly. She sat quietly beside him, content to simply enjoy his presence, even as the sky clouded, and the familiar cold mist rolled in. It was as though the sky had cleared only for them, giving them a window of time to enjoy the day. And now they were back to the status quo, the land had flattened, and the houses of a gray London came into view.

Elliot interrupted the silence as they neared her home. "Tomorrow we will meet with Will Peters to tell him what we found out. As I said we at least have confirmation that our suspicions are correct. I will send you a message, and this time perhaps, we can gather at my home." He turned and smiled at her. "I want you to see the house. It will soon be your home."

Eleanora did not want to think about commitment just yet. The business of their engagement, and the bargain they had struck was foreign to this new feeling she had for him. She focused on the investigation instead of acknowledging his comment. "Yes. That is an excellent idea. We can only hope he also has discovered something of value."

If he noticed her hedging, he did not comment, and she was thankful for it. They pulled up to her house. Elliot jumped down to secure the horses, then reached up to assist her.

At her door, he made a formal short bow. "Thank you for a lovely day, my dear. It has been one of my best."

She could not resist smiling at him, "And mine," she said as she let herself in.

She leaned against the door for a moment listening to the sound of the horses as he left. It had indeed been a good day. And it truly was one of the best.

But her thoughts returned to his comment about his home, and she frowned. How absurd that she had never thought about the changes a marriage would make to her life. She had not even considered the fact that it would mean moving—she had just made a move. The momentousness of such a decision was gradually dawning on her.

Claudia's protests when she had discussed the plan with her, took on a whole new significance. As a business deal, she was pleased with the choice. It made sense. But now it was beginning to feel as though her heart was involved, and that scared her. She did not ever want to feel the pain she had experienced with her last betrothal.

She wondered if it was already too late to change her mind, to retreat into the safety of her career once more. Or if she even wanted to.

CHAPTER 19

When Elliot opened his door, Flurry was there to greet him and take his coat. "Thank you for the picnic lunch, Flurry. It was appreciated," he said and smiled at the man.

"The outing was a success then?" Flurry asked, not betraying his satisfaction.

"It was. An astounding success indeed. And tomorrow we will have the pleasure of having her, Miss Claudia, and Mr. Peters, for tea. It is a business meeting of sorts, but because it is the first time my fiancée will see her future home, I want everything perfect." He gave his butler a stern look. "Leave nothing untouched. Everything from the lights to the uniforms of the staff must be at their best."

Flurry was undaunted. "Very good sir," he replied. "While you were out a packet arrived for you from your work. I set it on your desk."

"Ah," he responded, and headed to his library. He was correct in assuming the blueprints for their new ship had arrived. He sat down to examine them. Hours passed, with only the occasional interruption of Flurry silently serving tea and snacks. The ship would be a beauty; sleek, with the new steam propulsion and plenty of room for passengers and cargo. There were a few questions for the designers which he jotted in the margins, but overall, he was impressed with their work.

He rotated his neck, flipped the oversized packet to its cover page, and relaxed, leaning back in his chair. Glancing at the window, he saw the sun was setting, and dark shadows stretched across the gloomy layers of fog. Not the most pleasant of evenings, he thought, wondering if he should bother to take his usual brisk walk to clear his head before sitting down to a late dinner.

Deciding some exercise would be the only cure for the stiffness from hours of slumping over his work, he grabbed his jacket and pulled it on over his crumpled shirt. At the door, Flurry as usual anticipated his needs, holding out his black domino and beaver hat.

The park was deserted this time in the evening. Any brave souls who had ventured out during this dreary day had long since retreated to the comfort and warmth of their home. There was a stillness tonight. Had he not known he was in a district of London, he could well imagine he was in the wilds of Yorkshire. It suited him perfectly. The only sound was the distant clopping of hooves from a carriage on one of the streets nearby.

The fog swirled around him, obliterating the lush

trees and shrubs which made the trek so pleasing on a clear summer's day. It was becoming too dark to venture from the path. Thus, he followed along the trail, keeping a brisk pace. He went over the events of the day; his thoughts returning again and again to Eleanora. The image of her standing naked at the brook in the woods came to mind. The picture was burned into his memory.

And then there was her passionate nature. He smiled as he recalled her soft cries, and the look on her face when she reached her pleasure. He squashed the thought. It was too enticing, much too distracting for this cool spring night.

The damp air chilled him. He paused and pulled his cloak together. There was a rustle from the bushes next to him. It was too loud to be one of the small animals which sometimes frequented the park. Perhaps a stray dog, he thought, but he felt the hair on his arms prickle in warning.

When he began walking forward, he was sure he heard footsteps. He stopped again. Whoever, or whatever was behind him also stopped. He deliberately softened his step, all his senses entuned to hear any sound behind him. But there was nothing. He decided he was overreacting. The swirling fog and the intense dark must have triggered his imagination.

Ahead of him the cenotaph commemorating the fallen soldiers of the Spanish War emerged out of the fog, signaling he had reached the perimeter of the park, near Eleanora's home. He paused for a moment, resting his hand on the cool cement of the structure.

The distinct sound of the scrape of a shoe on the trail behind him alerted his senses once more. This time he was sure he was being followed, and not by a stray dog. He turned, peering into the dark, but could see nothing. Again, he felt the hair on the back of his neck bristle in warning. Someone was out there, following him. Whoever it was, they had stopped when he had, and now remained still. Elliot strained his eyes, attempting to see the danger. But it was too dark, and with the fog it was impossible to see more than a few feet.

Then, for the briefest of seconds, the fog parted, and a shadowy figure took shape. A man stood not twenty paces behind him; his arm raised to shoot. He flung himself towards the safety of the cenotaph as a shot exploded into the night.

He felt a sting in his left arm, as he slid across the rear face of the monument. A second shot rang out and he rolled into the shrubs behind him.

Damn! he thought. I have been hit. He used his right arm to touch the spot on his upper arm which was already damp with his blood. Damn, he cursed again silently. He used his right arm to hold it against his chest, hoping to stop the bleeding.

And then he heard a scuttle of footsteps as the villain came to search for his prey. He froze, not daring to even twitch as the footsteps echoed in the stillness.

"I know I hit you, Sparks," a voice reverberated in the silence. "Show yourself."

The shooter rustled about in the darkness, rooting through the shrubbery where he lay only a few paces away. He had to get away. He thought the man would naturally expect him to continue moving to his left, therefore he moved slowly to the right. He would have run, but in this blackness, he would have had to stay on the path, lest he fall and be easy prey once more. And on a straight path, a couple of shots from the man would be sure to score a hit, even in this darkness. He could not take the chance.

At one point a whiff of breeze thinned the heavy mist, and he could make out the form of a man, his hand still clutching his gun which he used to part the bushes on the edge of the trail. Elliot eased himself toward the backside of the shrubs, which in turn were banked against a hedge separating the park from the cobbled street. He calculated his movements to his pursuer's, hoping he would not be heard. Gradually the distance between them widened.

But he was bleeding profusely now. He could feel himself weakening and knew it would only be a matter of time before the man found him—helpless, perhaps even unconscious from the loss of blood. He pressed his useless arm across his chest once more. He would have liked to rip a piece of clothing to make a tourniquet, but the process would have been a noisy one.

He continued to ease himself along the ground, away from the sounds of his attacker's search. Pressing his back against the hedge behind him, he hoped for a break large enough for him to squeeze through. He was thankful for the man's frantic rooting about. If the villain had only stood still and listened, he would surely have been discovered already. Finally, his back found an open section between the gnarled branches of the hedge. It was just wide enough for him to squeeze through. He waited, listening until the man began to beat the bushes with renewed vigor, cursing as he worked. Elliot pushed himself through the narrow break in the hedge. Then he lay silent, again waiting with his heart pounding in his breast for the fellow to discover him.

But all was silent. His attacker had stopped. Perhaps the man had heard branches snap as Elliot had forced his way through the hedge. Or hopefully he had simply changed his strategy too late to locate him. Elliot desperately hoped the latter was the case.

He was now on the grass facing the street. He rolled silently forward until he reached the curb, staying low, knowing the thick fog would shroud him from sight.

The clatter and rattle of a coach could be heard coming down the street. This may be my only opportunity, he thought to himself. He hooked one boot onto the other, and levered it off, then did the same to the second boot, using his right arm to assist. His left arm hung uselessly by his side.

Knowing the epitaph was directly across the street from Eleanora's town house, he strained his eyes attempting to identify her home. But the thick fog made his search useless. *No matter, he thought, I know where I am. It might be my only advantage over this man who is out to kill me.*

He would have to make a silent run for it, using the coach for what cover it could provide. At best the noise would cloak his movements, leaving the man still searching the bushes. He prayed Eleanora's door would be answered quickly or they would find him dead on their threshold in the morning. Nudging his discarded boots aside, he crouched into position, and waited for the carriage.

He smiled as the grunting and thrashing sounds behind him to his left indicated the man had resumed his search and was still intent on finding him huddled in the shrubbery.

The vehicle approached. When he could make out the looming shapes of the horses, he moved quickly into the street, careful to touch the ground only with the balls of his feet. Spinning around the back side of the carriage, he was able to open Eleanora's gate and latch it silently before the coach disappeared into the fog. He leaned against her gate, listening. Nothing—only the clacking of hooves fading into the distance.

A wave of dizziness overwhelmed him. He was tempted to sink down onto the walk and simply rest. He touched his left arm. His jacket was saturated; he was losing a lot of blood. A steady stream dripped from the fingers of his left hand. He forced himself to move forward, intent now on reaching her door.

The entry seemed to fade into the distance even as he moved forward. Finally, his stocking feet hit the cement of her step, and he stretched out his hand to her railing, using all his remaining strength to hoist himself up and fling himself against her door.

He reached up and lifted the knocker managing to clump it down twice before the darkness overcame him.

CHAPTER 20

Eleanora was halfway down the stairs when the thump at the door was followed by the knocker being struck.

"For the love of God," Mrs. Bixby muttered as she trudged into the foyer, "some straggler just in time for dinner no doubt." She swung the door open, her mouth gaping as Elliot fell into the room.

Eleanora let out a squeal as she rushed down the stairs to his side.

"Close the door, close the door," he gasped, bracing himself up with one arm, the other side of his body red with blood. "Now. And lock it."

Before she could fully grasp what he was saying, or why he was saying it, Mrs. Bixby pushed his legs aside, closed the door firmly, and threw the bolt. Elliot slumped back to the floor and closed his eyes.

"But what has happened! My God he is covered in blood! Claudia!" Eleanora shouted. Claudia hurried in from the dining room. “Claudia! The Blood! Oh, my word!”

“Stop that nonsense.” Mrs. Bixby snapped. “Get Ned to go for the doctor. He is in the kitchen having his supper.” She put her hands on Eleanora’s shoulders and turned her in the right direction. Once she had moved to follow her instructions Mrs. Bixby added, “And while you're there bring me a basin of hot water and a pair of good shears. Help me get him up Miss Claudia. We’ll take him into the salon.”

Eleanora ran to the kitchen with her head in a whirl. By the time she had sent Ned, the gardener, to fetch the doctor, and together with the cook prepared a basin of boiled water, some shears, and a pack of white cloths, she had forced herself to calm down. She carried the lot of it into the salon, putting it on the tea table.

Claudia and Mrs. Bixby had already laid Elliot on the sofa. They had somehow removed his jacket. The left side of his white shirt was saturated in blood. She gasped. Mrs. Bixby shot her a glare, then finding a hole near the shoulder of his shirt, ripped the fabric wide in one quick motion.

His chest and shoulder, now exposed, were covered in blood and a wound on his upper arm still seeped in a gentle pulsing rhythm. Without speaking, Claudia handed Mrs. Bixby a towel and she pressed it into the wound. Elliot groaned.

“He’s a lucky man, he is. It’s in his arm and not his chest like I first thought. That’s a good thing.” Mrs.

Bixby made a tut-tutting sound. "That's if he hasn't bled out. I've the feeling the shot's gone clean through."

Eleanora released a breath she had not been aware of holding, almost dizzy with relief. He was injured, but not fatally.

Elliot winced as Mrs. Bixby lifted his arm. "Just as I thought," she muttered. "Clean through." Claudia handed Mrs. Bixby another wadded towel and she shoved it under his arm, then took another, and pressed it against the wound.

"We will need to keep him warm," Eleanora said. "I'll fetch a blanket."

By the time she returned, Mrs. Bixby had cut the remainder of his shirt away and was wiping him with a wet cloth. Claudia must have tossed more coal on the fire because it raged. The room would soon be too warm. She tucked the blanket in around him anyway.

His blue eyes watched her from beneath heavy lids. She reached forward, stroked his cheek, and murmured, "Oh my love..."

He gave her a lobsided smile. "I hope it is not too late for a visit."

"Oh Elliot, what happened?"

"It seems I will do anything to gain your attention," he said, then grimaced when Mrs. Bixby pressed harder against his wound.

"I'm thinking the doctor will want to stitch him up. Until then we can try to stop the bleeding," said Mrs. Bixby, still holding a folded towel into the wound.

"I'll do that Mrs. Bixby," Claudia said, and carefully replaced Mrs. Bixby's hand to put pressure on the arm.

Mrs. Bixby gathered up the ruined clothing and soiled towels. “I’ll have cook make up some more boiled water.” She looked at Eleanora. “Still a bit of cleaning to be done around the wound,” she said as she bustled from the room.

Eleanora eased carefully onto the sofa next to Elliot and began using the now pink cloth to wipe his chest where the blood had soaked through. He was hairless, his body tanned and strong. She could not help but appreciate the firm manliness of his shoulders and thick upper arms. An image of his bare chest pressed against hers in the woods intruded into her thoughts, and she stole a look into his eyes.

He raised his eyebrows at her, flashing a cheeky smile as though he knew what she was thinking. She quickly looked away, feeling her face burn as she resumed her task. Forcing herself to take a more professional approach, she rinsed the cloth out in the basin, now red with blood, and squeezed it out. She then wiped the area closest to his wound with brisk strokes, only relenting when she heard him grunt in pain.

“Now then, who did this to you and why?” she asked.

Elliot closed his eyes for a moment. “I have no idea who or why. I was attacked in the park, just across the street. I was fortunate to be so near your home.”

He shifted and made as if to sit up, but Claudia was quick to intervene, pushing him back onto the couch with her free hand. “Oh no you don’t.” she said. You’ll not move until the doctor arrives and stitches you up. And even then, you have lost a lot of blood."

"I think he just grazed me," Elliot protested.

Eleanora gave him a stern look. "The bullet has gone through your upper arm. The doctor will assess the damage. Until then you'll stay put as Claudia said."

"The doctor has arrived." Mrs. Bixby said, balancing a fresh basin of water and an armload of towels. Behind her a frail elderly man, carrying a worn case came into the room. Initially she was dismayed. The last thing they needed was an inept old man, performing some sort of dangerous quackery on Elliot. But on closer inspection, the doctor had an intelligent face and shrewd eyes which brooked no arguments.

"Ah, Elliot Sparks," he said looking down at his patient, "It has been a while, but always a pleasure to handle your scrapes. It is good to see you."

Eliot groaned. "I am not sure I can say the same."

The doctor surveyed the room, pausing to assess each of the ladies in turn. "I'll have you stay," he said to Mrs. Bixby. "You other ladies can wait outside the room. The last thing this man needs is an audience."

"I think a bracing cup of tea may be in order," Claudia announced, leaving Elliot to their care.

"I rather thought I would have a brandy," Eleanora muttered, evoking a smirk from the patient and a forbidding glare from Mrs. Bixby.

The ladies settled in the dining room, where they compromised with a glass of wine. Miss Anne served them a cold cotillion. Their dinner, according to the cook, was not salvageable.

Eleanora was surprised to find she was hungry. The two ladies ate in silence, both thinking about the events of the evening.

Miss Anne removed their plates and refreshed their wine.

"What do you suppose happened?" Claudia asked.

"When I asked Elliot, he had no idea. He had apparently just been out for a walk. One shudders to think we have such dangerous villains in our neighborhood."

The doctor cleared his throat from the doorway. He held his case in his hand. "I have finished with the man. He required a few stitches, but he is a lucky young man. The bullet passed through without hitting the bone. Very lucky indeed."

"He will be all right then?" Eleanora asked.

"He has lost a lot of blood and will need rest, but other than that, he will come out of this intact. I gave him a dose of laudanum for the pain which will have him out for the night. I suggest you leave him where he is. He is quite comfortable." He turned to go.

Claudia rose. "What do we owe you doctor?"

The doctor paused and answered. "Mr. Sparks insisted I stop at his home tonight to be reimbursed." He chuckled. "Along with a list of other instructions for me. Which reminds me. You can expect his man to arrive some time tonight with a few necessaries." He raised his hand when Claudia approached to walk him to the door. "Sit down. Enjoy your meal. I will find my way out."

Sometime later Eleanora tiptoed into the salon for one final check on Elliot. All the lamps but the one on the end table had been extinguished. It and the fire provided a soft light. She sat on the side of the sofa, careful not to wake him.

After the doctor had left, a stoic fellow had arrived and took control of the sickroom. Elliot was now outfitted in a clean night shirt. A change of clothes and a pitcher of water with a glass sat on the end table. The fellow had announced he would be returning first thing in the morning, 'to see to his man.'

A strand of Elliot's long dark hair had escaped its tie and she brushed it back, her hand lingering on his rugged cheek. He stirred, opening his eyes briefly, and smiled before falling back asleep.

In that moment she knew with certainty she loved this man. She was not sure when it had happened. It could even have been the first day when he had so easily accepted the role of partner she had forced on him—but love him she did. Tonight, she learned she could never have borne losing him.

She let her hand trail down to his warm chest, leaning forward to place a chaste kiss on his forehead. "Goodnight my love," she whispered.

She sighed, rising to slip from the room. It was time to go to bed and spend the night sorting out her thoughts. Today's discoveries were a confusing mixture of elation and distress. First there had been the wonder of the afternoon in the woods, then Elliot's getting shot, and now this unsettling recognition of her feelings for Elliot. She scowled. Her plans to create a proper engagement of convenience lay in ruins. All the pains she had taken to protect her heart in this affair had been for naught.

The last time she had declared her love for someone, it had been an unmitigated disaster. It was not comforting to know she had opened her heart once more, that again she was vulnerable to the pain of heartbreak. For now, it might be best to keep her secret.

CHAPTER 21

When Eleanora came down for breakfast, she expected to see Elliot still laid out on their couch. She hurried into the salon. Other than Mrs. Bixby, who was scrubbing the stains from the sofa, there was no sign of the man.

"He left. That snooty man of his was over early this morning and had him in a coach at dawn." Mrs. Bixby said, without looking up from her work. "It has been a bloody mess to clean and that's certain. I've already spent an hour on the walkway and stoop. The goings on in this house!" She dunked her cloth in the basin beside her, and deftly squeezed it out. "He left you a note. I set it on the mantle."

Eleanora snatched up the letter and went to the breakfast room, where Claudia already sat, a cup of coffee in her hand. "Elliot has left. Mrs. Bixby says he was gone at dawn," Eleanora said, pulling back her chair to join her.

Claudia laughed. "Not quite at dawn. He left an hour ago."

"Did you see him? How was he this morning?" Eleanora asked.

"I saw him, and he was much improved. However, his man Flurry said there would be no meeting today or tomorrow. He made it clear that no visitors will be allowed past the threshold. Elliot will be resting."

"That is a relief. And a rest will no doubt be needed." She flipped open the note Elliot had left and smiled grimly as she read, finally tossing it onto the table. "The nerve of the man." She had thought Elliot would write something to allay her worries and the letter would contain some sort of endearment, if only in the closing. She was completely wrong. "He has left us a list of orders. First, on no account are we to leave the house today." She looked up at Claudia. "Even you Claudia. He insists that if you wish to work you are to send for a packet from the office."

"Yes, I know," she smiled wryly, "he told me this morning."

"And we are to allow no one in the house. Finally, he insists we say nothing about the shooting—though how he thinks we could manage to speak to anyone under these conditions is beyond me. Apparently, he has already spoken to Mrs. Bixby about it and would have us address it again, with her and the rest of the staff. He says he will explain all of it when we meet with Mr. Peters. I wonder what he could be thinking?"

"This morning he told me the man who hunted him last night, knew him," Claudia said, "called out to him by name. I am not sure what all of this means, but I agree with Mr. Sparks. We will need to take precautions." She grimaced. "At least until we can determine what this person's motives are."

"Knew him? You mean someone intended to kill him? But why?"

"He is convinced it has something to do with our investigation. Someone may be concerned that we will discover the truth. "

Eleanora filled her plate at the sideboard while she considered Claudia's words. "But who knows we are even suspicious of foul play?" Eleanora took her seat at the table and poured herself a cup of coffee from the carafe. "Besides the two of us, Elliot, and Mr. Peters, and perhaps Inspector Mcgowan, who else would know?" She considered for a minute. "Mr. Wicket at the office may have pieced it together, but it seems unlikely he would be involved. It makes no sense to me."

"I know, nor to me. But do not forget Rose. What did you discover yesterday about our Rose? Perhaps it is somehow connected?"

Eleanora filled her in on the revelations of yesterday, while selecting her toast, then returned to the sideboard to retrieve a jar of jam.

"There is the possibility Rose had second thoughts after you left. That you know her whereabouts puts her very life in jeopardy, after all," Claudia said.

"Hmm...I cannot see it. First, she was most agreeable. She seemed hopeful when she discovered we had chosen to pursue the case. And then, she is too far from town to have arranged such a thing only hours after our return." She dismissed the idea with the wave of her hand, buttered her toast, and liberally applied gooseberry jam. "And why the secrecy? Why has Elliot not reported this outrage?"

An image of Elliot with his torn shirt open to the bleeding wound and his face pale from loss of blood intruded into her consciousness. She tossed the toast down onto her plate. "I think we should be calling in the constables, and alerting Mr. Peters. We could even hire a second agency to track down this fiend. Everything should be done to stop this villain." She trembled a little when she thought of the peril Elliot faced. Never again did she want to see him saturated in blood and worry for his life. It was not to be borne.

"Elliot thought the man might return this morning, looking for a body, or evidence that he was fatally wounded. It is why he had poor Mrs. Bixby out scrubbing the walk first thing. I believe he planned to have Mr. Peters send out men to watch for any suspicious characters this morning."

Eleanora shivered. "I hope they catch the man." She tried to eat her meal, but somehow everything tasted like dried oatmeal. She gave up and sipped her coffee. Coffee was a new favorite, a habit they had picked up in America. Glancing across the table she spied a stack of letters next to Claudia's plate. "Has the post arrived?"

"It has. And there is a cable here from Arabella." She handed her the missive.

Eleanora ripped it open, sure what it would

contain. She had sent a wire to inform her grandmother of the engagement. Arabella would be more than satisfied with her announcement. She read aloud, "Dearest Eleanora. Much pleased with the news. I was certain Elliot Sparks was the right man for you. You may thank Claudia for her part. Much love to you both. Always yours, Grandmother."

Eleanora laid the message down carefully next to her plate and looked across at her friend. Claudia had the grace to flush. "Well?" She raised her brows, "What is this? Did the two of you set me up?"

"It wasn't like that. Arabella had met Elliot when the governor of India visited. She spent a bit of time with him when he toured the business. Elliot was and is very enthusiastic about the role and function of the shipping industry, especially the developments in steam..." She paused.

"And?" Eleanora was not about to let Claudia off the hook too easily. She was more than happy with her choice of Elliot as a husband, but it irked her to know that as always, her grandmother could not resist interfering in her life. "And," she repeated, "just how did she manage to get you in on her scheme?"

Claudia sighed. "I told her no, that I had no intention of getting involved in her machinations. But she insisted. She said all I had to do was deliver the advertisement into Mr. Sparks' hands. And that in no way was I plotting anything. It seemed a small favor to ask."

"I am sure she called it just that, the smallest of favors." She laughed. "The woman is impossible. Even here in England she has somehow managed to get her claws into my affairs." She looked at Claudia, "I cannot believe you were so easily taken in. Why did you not tell me?"

"Oh Eleanora. All I said when he applied was that he was almost over-qualified. No one was more surprised than I when you actually hired him." She rolled eyes and looked up with a sigh. "Then you were determined to propose to him. It shocked me. And you must admit I did all I could at that point to discourage you."

"You did."

Claudia shook her head. "What irritates me is Arabella was so certain he was the man for you. Then, as it turned out, she was not far off. The two of you sizzled together since your first meeting. For all your talk of a fake engagement, I am certain Elliot will be the husband you choose."

Eleanora sighed. "I suppose it is water under the bridge." She smiled as a thought occurred to her. "But I warn you, the very first opportunity I get to interfere in your love life I shall do so."

"Oh Eleanora, I have no love life. I have been so focused on my career there hasn't been time. I am not an heiress like you, no one will pursue me for my fortune. I simply have not given the prospect any of my energies."

"You are not beggarly that is certain. You have an income of at least 2000 pounds from your father. I also know Arabella granted you a fund which I am sure you more than doubled given your financial prowess. Hmm..." she considered, "I am sure there will be plenty of suitors who would want your fortune." She laughed when Claudia made a face. "But there is one, I think, who would take you without it. What do you think of Mr. Peters?"

When Claudia flushed, she knew the attraction went both ways. "I wonder if the man needs a little nudge to begin his courting. Sometimes a little competition does the trick."

"Eleanora, you cannot think to interfere—"

"Interfere?" she laughed again. "I wouldn't think of it."

ELEANORA SPENT the rest of the morning, and a good part of the early afternoon, perched on a chair, in the small sitting room upstairs. The room had a window which overlooked the park. Beside her on the floor was a basket of mending, and in her lap a blouse lay with its missing button ignored.

So far, she had been able to identify nothing unusual. Thankfully, the weather had cleared, due in part to a brisk westerly wind. There was a gap in the trees along the path where she had a clear view, and it was there where she focused her attention.

The park had been occupied for the most part with women pushing prams or hurrying to follow behind a running toddler. Occasionally ladies hoisting a parasol strolled by in colorful, frilled day dresses which rippled in the breeze. Some of them were accompanied by men, but they seemed unlikely suspects. Who would take a woman courting while searching for a body? There had been several men. Eleanora had stiffened to attention as they passed, but there was no telling whether they were there to enjoy the day or if they were the culprits she sought. Overall, it had been a frustrating and fruitless endeavor.

She was about to give up and go down to tea when a coach pulled up in front of the house. The footman hopped down and assisted Amelia to the walk. The wind caught the rows of flounces in her light green gown, and she shimmered like a great oak in a windstorm. Crystabel followed, looking more sedate in a pale day dress.

She sighed. There was not much to do but have them in for tea. She was sure Elliot's warnings did not apply to two women arriving for a visit with tea and cakes. Besides, the task of monitoring the park had become tedious. A distraction was needed.

She hurried down the stairs to answer the door. Mrs. Bixby had not been in the most pleasant of moods today and greeting guests might be a challenge for her.

Claudia had beat her to it. "Why Mrs. Brigg, and Lady Hargrove," she turned back to Eleanora, as if to ask if they should be allowed in. Eleanora shrugged, then nodded. "Do come in, we were just sitting down to afternoon tea."

"Ah Eleanora. We were doing our rounds today and simply had to stop and visit my niece." Amelia bustled in, took her hands, and kissed her cheeks. "There is so much to talk about, and a wedding to plan. Very exciting."

Mrs. Bixby stood with her hands on her hips and watched as Claudia and Eleanora took their parasols and cloaks. She caught Eleanora's eye and gave her a warning look. It was clear she had embraced the 'no guests' rule.

Eleanora ignored her glare. "Mrs. Bixby, we will have tea in the salon," she said firmly.

The ladies settled in the room, with Amelia spread out comfortably in a sea of green ruffles on the sofa, and the ladies in chairs.

"Now then, you must tell me if you have set a date. It is the talk of the town you know. Everywhere we went today people wanted to know the details and I had nothing to say. Imagine. I could not give a word of explanation." Amelia waited for her response. "I am all ears my dear. What have the two of you decided?"

"We have not set a date just yet. Elliot suggested, and I agree, to spend a little more time enjoying each other's company before the marriage. We have spent so brief a time together as of yet." Eleanora responded.

"You mustn't wait too long. Get it down in writing, our Jem would always say, and I quite agree. I am loath to bring this up, my dear Eleanora, but it seems to me you were engaged before. As I recall, the fellow managed to slip the noose. One would think you had learned your lesson. No, it is best to get it all wrapped up nice and tight, and as soon as possible. We do not want this fine catch to somehow slip away." She accepted a cup and saucer with her tea and raised it to her lips to take a sip before setting it down on the tea table.

"Oh, mother really. Eleanora is right to spend some time before planning a wedding. Many couples spend a year as an affianced couple." Crystabel chimed in. She turned to Eleanora. "There is no need to rush into things. And truly, to plan a proper wedding one must have time. I would delay it until next season. Only think of the event you could plan. It could be the highlight of the social scene next year."

Amelia shook her head. "Nonsense," she said with a snort, "you give the man that much rope he will shy off."

Claudia snatched up the tray of dainties and offered them. "You must try the gooseberry tarts. Our cook has outdone herself with this new recipe."

Amelia was distracted only long enough to choose a tart. "No. The wedding definitely must proceed this season. Now then, once again, what plans have you made for the affair?"

"I intend to have a simple ceremony. No event at all really. In fact, he has already secured a special license, and we thought to marry with just our witnesses."

Eleanora expected Amelia to loudly protest this arrangement, but to her surprise the woman only raised her eyebrows and smiled, saying, "Very wise. You are a shrewder girl than I suspected."

It was Crystabel who found her plans unacceptable. "Oh, but you cannot! Your wedding should be an elaborate affair. It is a once in a lifetime occurrence. You should not even consider a tawdry affair. Why you are an heiress! You are entitled to a grand celebration." She reached for Eleanora's hand and gave it a gentle squeeze. “No, no. If it is all the preparations which worry you, mother and I could certainly help. Is that not so mother?”

“Of course, we could,” Amelia said, which Crystabel rewarded with a smile. “But I do like the idea of a quick affair. Do it up right and tight as I said,” she added, which prompted a glare from her daughter.

“Let’s leave the matter to rest for now." Eleanora said, hoping to end the argument.

Crystabel was not done with the topic. “I will simply state my case for a grand affair to Mr. Sparks.” She looked around the room as though expecting to find Elliot there. “Where is the man? I would have thought an ardent suitor would present himself for tea.”

“I believe he is working today.” Eleanora said without hesitation, although she could not resist a quick glance at Claudia.

“Yes,” Claudia added. “He just received the specs for a new ship. I dare say he will be going over them.”

“Oh ships, always ships,” Amelia waved her hand as though tossing the subject aside. “The topic bores me. I miss Jem, but I can’t say I miss the nightly conversations.”

Eleanora smiled mischievously. “I do have something more interesting to talk to you about Aunt Amelia. In fact, I need your help.”

“My help? Anything my dear.”

“My friend Claudia, like me, is reaching an age—”

“Eleanora!” Claudia tried to interrupt. “Do not—”

“An age where she is considering a husband.”

Eleanora quickly continued before Claudia could protest. "She has a decent portion, two thousand pounds a year, and a sizable investment portfolio."

"Really? I had no idea you were so flush my dear." Amelia put her hands together and smiled. This was a topic she adored. "But how wonderful! There are those who would consider two thousand pounds a year as a worthwhile stipend indeed. And an investment you say? Even better my dear." She gave Claudia a wide smile. "Now then, what is your family history Miss Claudia?" Amelia leaned forward, clearly eager to begin her next campaign. "If we can put it about that you have strong connections, a family in good standing, then it is all the better."

"Claudia's father was the commander of a ship. Captain Whitfell was the name." Eleanora said.

Claudia flushed a deep red. "Mrs. Brigg, Eleanora is wrong minded in this. I have no intentions—"

But Amelia had already warmed to the topic. "Whitfell is your name. Hmm... if I remember correctly the Whitfells are a family in Scotland. We could certainly claim a connection there. And the title of captain is a boon to be sure. How wonderful!" She looked at Eleanora and smiled once more. "And then there is your connection to Miss Pembroke. That too is an asset. After all the Earl of Pembroke is no small family tie, and finally there is Miss Pembroke herself. Yes, I think something can be done with all of this. Oh, it is so very exciting!"

She leaned forward and patted Claudia's hand. "Not to worry my dear, I will take you in hand. A husband will be found for you in no time at all. Why the social season has only just begun."

Claudia could only look at Eleanora and glare. Eleanora gave her the sweetest smile in response.

"We had best move on." Crystabel announced. "We do not want to overstay our welcome," she said rising to assist her mother to her feet. "But on the topic of your wedding Eleanora, I am almost tempted to drop in on Mr. Sparks and press him to agree to host a decent affair for the occasion."

Claudia was quick to object. "Oh, I would not do so today. I know for certain Mr. Sparks is heavily engaged in the new plans for the ship."

Amelia frowned. "Heavens no, Crystabel. It has been a long afternoon. I fear I am ready to retire to my room for a nap. Besides, calling on a gentleman is not done." She turned back to Claudia when they had reached the door. "Do not fear my dear, I will take on this little project for you. Why in no time I shall have some prospective suitors lined up at your door. I am the very best at this sort of thing. And I will begin immediately spreading this information about to the interested parties."

Claudia colored again and said nothing in response.

Amelia set her cup on the tea tray. "Now I believe it is time we took our leave. Come Crystabel, help your mother up."

The ladies made their way to the door. Eleanora followed in their wake. "Miss Claudia is understandably shy when we speak of this, but let me assure you, she is more than pleased, and so looking forward to your assistance." Eleanora said with a smile.

She could hear Amelia chuckle in response as she closed the door. She had clearly made her day. Not so Claudia. She was glaring at her with such a look of outrage that Eleanora had to laugh.

"How could you Eleanora? To set that woman on me is outrageous. It is not well done of you at all."

"But only think of it, Claudia. Mr. Peters is attracted to you; of this I am certain. If he sees a little competition, he will surely spring into action." Eleanora assured her.

"I think this is your revenge for my interference in your love life." Claudia accused.

"A small part perhaps," she laughed. "But it is a plan which will spur Mr. Peters into action. And then my dear, we will both be young wives, starting the next part of our lives together." She took her arm as they returned to the sitting room.

"Eleanora, your schemes always go awry." Claudia objected.

"Nonsense. Look how well it has turned out for me. You must admit my plan to marry Elliot is a success." She squeezed her arm before letting her go to take a seat on the sofa. "Besides we both could use a happy distraction from this worry about Elliot. I wonder if there is any progress in finding his assailant?" She grimaced. "My surveillance from the upper window this morning accomplished nothing. I only learned that mornings are a prime time for nannies and their charges."

"We have no option but to wait until our meeting with Mr. Peters tomorrow. Perhaps he has discovered something." Claudia said.

"If Elliot is being targeted, we simply must get to the bottom of it. I do not think I will be able to bear the worry. Tomorrow our focus must be to find a way to catch the villains." Eleanora frowned. Finding the murderer seemed an impossible task.

She sat for a moment, frustrated by her inability to think of a way to find Elliot's pursuer. "I suppose there is no point in returning to the upper window for me. I wonder if I missed identifying the assailant. Elliot was sure they would come by today." Eleanora grimaced. "If someone was searching for evidence of Elliot's condition, I certainly did not see them."

CHAPTER 22

After a day spent quietly at home, with Mrs. Bixby strictly adhering to Elliot's rules governing guests, the day for the meeting with Mr. Peters finally arrived. The ladies ordered the company coach to arrive early. Claudia wanted Eleanora to stop by the office to sign papers pertaining to the purchase of Pembroke's new soup kitchen, before attending the meeting with Mr. Sparks and Mr. Peters. The ladies waited in the salon for their ride to arrive.

"I do hope you have not assigned too much responsibility to this Margaret O'Malley." Claudia said as she pulled on her gloves. "You have given the woman a great deal of your trust in its management."

"I have every confidence in Mrs. O'Malley. And if I am wrong, and it does not work out, we will simply have to look for a new manager." She smiled. "But in this instance, I am sure that will not be the case." The clatter of a carriage interrupted her thoughts. "Ah, that must be our coach now."

The ladies reached the foyer and were pulling on their cloaks when the knocker sounded. Eleanora paused in securing her bonnet to reach out and open the door, surprised that the coachman would alight to ring the bell. Claudia nudged in beside her, as the door was swung wide.

To her astonishment, an East India woman in bright orange and blue regalia stood on the stoop. The woman wore a thin patterned veil of sorts, held to her head with a ribbon adorned with cut glass crystals across her forehead, framing her cheeks and falling to the hem of her gown. The jeweled tones, with the elaborate headdress, were exotic and foreign. She held an infant to her chest, and two small faces, half shrouded by her veil, peered out from the folds of her sari. The children could not have been more than three or four years old. The woman looked at them with large kohled eyes, widened as though afraid.

Eleanora and Claudia were momentarily stunned into silence. They stood with mouths agape for a moment before remembering their manners.

Claudia was the first to break the silence. “Good day. How may we help you?”

The woman’s expression flashed with what Eleanora thought was surely panic. It was very strange. “Miss Pembroke please, I wish to speak.”

Eleanora pulled the door wide. “I am Miss Pembroke. Won't you come in.”

To her surprise the woman quickly answered, “No. No. I only come to show you these children.” She paused, her eyes flitting between Claudia and her, and then back to the open carriage. For a minute it seemed as though she was prepared to dart back to the hansom cab.

She took a breath and continued in broken English. "These babies, they are mine. Lovely babies, born in my homeland." She reached down and set her hand on a small girl's face, smoothing back a strand of ebony hair. The child shyly tucked her face back into the cloth of her skirt. The woman raised her head and cleared her throat, not quite making eye contact. She took another deep breath and began talking rapidly, "My children and Mister Sparks' children. All his children they are. He is a very bad man, this Mister Sparks, not good. He brings me here to this country and leaves me now with these babies. He promised marriage, but it is not with me. I am alone. I only come to tell you this. Mister Sparks is a bad man."

The woman turned and hurried down the steps to the waiting carriage.

Eleanora was frozen in place, stunned for a few seconds by the woman's words. Had she heard correctly? Was this foreign woman claiming to be Elliot's abandoned mistress? The woman had spoken so quickly, and her message was so bizarre, it took a while to process. She looked at Claudia, tilting her head in an unspoken question, but Claudia was staring open-mouthed at the departing woman.

And then she knew this drama was a ruse of some sort. Elliot would never abandon three of his children. It was unthinkable.

"Wait!" She hollered, hustling down the step toward

the hired hack. But it was too late. The woman slammed the carriage door shut and the conveyance moved hurriedly down the street.

Turning the corner from the opposite direction was their company coach. She looked back to Claudia who stood on the stoop. "Hurry Claudia, we must follow her." Their coach had barely rolled to a stop before the ladies quickly levered themselves in and Eleanora shouted her orders to follow the vehicle.

The coach sped off. Eleanora stood at the trap door, giving further instructions to the driver. "Keep the carriage in view but try to stay back enough that we are not detected."

"Yes ma'am," he answered.

Eleanora sat back down and slid the window open, leaning out to look ahead into the street. She had to reassure herself the woman was still in sight. And sure enough, when they turned a corner, she spotted the hired hack up ahead. She could not take her eyes off it as it moved through the busy streets ahead. "I hope we don't lose her." she muttered.

"What exactly do you hope to accomplish Eleanora?" Claudia asked.

Eleanora reluctantly pulled herself back from the window. "We must follow her and speak to her. Someone had to have hired the woman to deliver this message."

"Have you considered the possibility it may be true?" Claudia asked. "She is East Indian. Mr. Sparks just returned from an assignment in India."

"Don't be ridiculous. Elliot would never do such a

thing. To abandon his mistress is one thing, but three children? Never." Eleanora looked out the window once more. They were heading to the East End. The streets narrowed as they approached an area near the docks.

It was still early in the day. Here the streets were quiet as though the occupants slept after a busy night. Tall tenement buildings rose on each side of the street, blocking the morning sun, leaving the area in damp shadow. The gutters were clogged with rubbish and discarded gin bottles. Only occasionally a pedestrian was seen plodding along, hunched in a heavy cloak.

Up ahead the hired cab rolled to a stop, and they quickly followed suit. The hansom cab had stopped at a two-story building on the very end of the street. Eleanora peered nervously out the window hoping the woman would not see them parked at the end of the lane. But the woman was intent on helping her children from the carriage and paid no mind. She gathered her children close to her, then approached the driver. The driver handed her a small leather bag, which she tucked into her pocket before entering what looked to be a lean-to on the side of the building nearest to them.

Once the hansom cab left, and the woman had disappeared into the lean-to, Eleanora stood and opened the trap door to instruct the coachman to move forward. They came to a stop outside the ramshackle house. It appeared to be a lean-to pieced together with bits of lumber salvaged from the streets and braced up against the gray wall of the corner building. It was difficult to believe such poverty could exist only a short distance from their comfortable townhouse. It was as though this was an entirely different city.

Eleanora waited for the coachman to get her door and set out the little step before helping them down.

"This cannot possibly be a residence, can it?" Claudia said as she stepped onto the street, scanning her surroundings with a mixture of shock and disbelief. Eleanora realized this was Claudia's first glimpse into the lives of the poor. Even in Boston she would have been sheltered from the realities of the destitute.

"I believe it is." Eleanora replied, ignoring Claudia's stunned expression. There was no time at present to lecture her on the conditions of the poor. She walked briskly to a door hanging slightly ajar, from the height of the lean-to. "And from what I saw in Whitechapel with Elliot she is lucky to have it."

The sound of a voice speaking in another language could be heard through the door. When Eleanora rapped all went silent. After a pause, the rickety door opened a crack, revealing the kohled eyes of the woman who had stood on their stoop only a few minutes ago.

The woman's eyes widened with fear. She attempted to quickly pull the door shut once more. But Eleanora managed to slide her boot into the gap, and gripping the door with both hands said, "Please, please. I just want to speak with you. I mean you no harm."

The women stared at each other for long seconds. Eleanora continued to hold the door with one hand while reaching into her reticule with the other to pull out a wad of bills. "I will pay you for your time."

The woman glanced down at the handful of bills. The sound of an infant crying from within interrupted them. She turned back into her hovel, then looked down at the money once more and snatched it from Eleanora's hand.

"Come," she said. The door slowly creaked open.

The interior of the home was a pleasant surprise. The first thing that struck you upon entering was the smell—a blend of incense and curry which left an impression of both comfort and the exotic. It was one room, not more than ten feet wide but twice as long, with a roof that sloped from a height of just over six feet to a meagre four feet, right to left. Halfway down the length of it, the patterned veil the woman had worn earlier was draped across the room with a string, creating a back compartment which appeared to serve as a bedroom. Behind the veil the floor was covered with cushions where the two children were buried beneath a blanket. The plank floors in the foreroom were insulated by a handwoven straw mat. Along the high wall a row of cushions served as chairs. The dwelling reminded Eleanora of a painting she had seen of the interior of a Bedouin tent, colorful and comfortable, even in the dim light.

And the room was dim; its only light coming from two small windows on the low exterior wall. An oil heater with a pot sitting on its grill sat beneath one of the windows on a wooden crate. A second crate beside it served as a cupboard and a countertop. Despite the meagre furnishings the lean-to was a home. Eleanora was struck again by the resourcefulness and the determination of the women who made life bearable in the extreme conditions of London's poor.

The woman reached behind the curtain to pick up the whimpering baby and comfort it against her chest.

When the infant quieted, Eleanora began speaking. "Again, I want to reassure you that I only want information. I know you were paid to come to my home with this tale of Mr. Sparks."

The woman nodded, then gestured to the cushions, sitting down only after Eleanora settled herself on a cushion. She glanced up at Claudia, who waved away her silent invite and remained standing by the door. The baby fussed again, and it was a few minutes before the woman looked up from comforting her.

"My children hungry," she said, carefully pronouncing each word, "I make money how I can."

Eleanora nodded. "I understand."

"Bharthi...husband, bring me here. He worked the ships. Then died." She looked at Eleanora who nodded once more.

"I know what you said about Mr. Sparks is untrue. I want to know who paid you to give me this message."

The woman shifted her child to her shoulder and used her free hand to reach into her pocket and pull out a crumpled note. She handed it to Eleanora. The note had her address scrawled in heavy letters across the top. Below that was the name Elliot Sparks underlined twice.

"The note was given to me by a man I know not. He told me what to say. So very sorry."

"What did he look like? Can you describe him?" Eleanora could feel her heart thumping in her chest.

The woman shook her head no. "It was evening. Very dark. He wore a..." she gestured to her head.

"A hat?"

"Yes. A hat. Low, low on his face." She mimed a hat pulled down over the brow. "Very dark here at night. I could not see much. He had a..." she touched her upper lip.

"A moustache!"

The woman nodded. "He pay me well. He says, bring the children with you and for more money, I do. Part now, part from the driver when we come." She looked at her apologetically. "I need much money to come home to India."

The baby had gone to sleep, and she rose to settle her in the back before sitting down once more. "I knew it would not work. No good woman would believe, but I say yes. It was good money. So sorry." She lifted her hands outward in a shrug. "I cannot tell you more. It is all."

"Thank-you. Mrs. B...Bharthi?"

The woman smiled. "No. Mrs. Shan."

Eleanora rose to her feet. "Thank you, Mrs. Shan." She turned to Claudia. "When do we have a ship leaving for India?"

"I believe the steamship Commadore is being loaded now. She will depart in three days."

"Mrs. Shan, I have a ship leaving for India in three days' time, the Commadore. It will take you and your children home to India. You must be at the dock at dawn in three days. Do you understand?"

"You? You have a ship? And I can go?" Mrs. Shan stared at her with disbelief.

Eleanora laughed. "I do and I will send you home. Do you understand me? There will be passage there for you and the children. Just be there in three days at dawn. I will tell them you are coming." She turned to Claudia. "Do you have any cash? I seem to have spent mine."

Claudia raised her eyebrows and saying nothing, dug into her purse to retrieve a billfold.

"I will need it all," she said, holding out her hand.

Claudia reluctantly pulled the mass of bills from her folder. "It is a lot. I had planned to make a few purchases."

"Excellent. Mrs. Shan will need it for her journey and to settle in, once home. I will reimburse you," Eleanora took the bills and handed them to the woman. "This is extra for your journey. Your passage is already paid."

The woman fingered the money lovingly, her eyes filling with tears. She slowly pocketed the bills, then looked Eleanora squarely in the eyes. "I will send you much karma. May you and your loves be blessed." Then she grasped her by the shoulders and hugged her. "Many, many thanks," she whispered before releasing her.

Claudia pulled the door open and the two of them were hustled into the coach by the driver who seemed eager to leave the neighborhood.

Eleanora slid open the window and looked back. Mrs. Shan stood on the threshold of her modest home. She waved at her, and the woman held up her arm in response as they turned the corner.

Claudia cleared her throat. "You gave the woman my fifty pounds, plus whatever you handed her at the door. It is a bit much Eleanora."

In response Eleanora stood and slid open the trap door, instructing the driver to stop at the bank before proceeding to Pembroke. She seated herself and smoothed out her skirts. "There. I will collect some cash to reimburse you immediately." She smiled at Claudia. Her friend was always a stickler with money. "I know how it bothers you to spend frivolously. But only think of Mrs. Shan, a widow far from her home, alone and destitute. And we, my dear, have helped to make it all better." She leaned forward and squeezed her hand.

"You have always been a soft touch, Eleanora. I suppose you are right. We could not leave those poor children in those conditions." Claudia was quiet for a moment. "How were you so sure Mrs. Shan was not Elliot's former lover?"

Eleanora laughed. "If you recall you once called Eliot a dragon. Dragons may be fierce, but they are always honorable," Eleanora said, then added in a more serious tone, "but the more important question is who and why is someone determined to malign Elliot and end our engagement?"

CHAPTER 23

When they stopped at Pembroke industries, Eleanora decided to stay in the coach. They were already late for the meeting with Elliot and Mr. Peters. She pulled back the curtain from the coach window and gazed into the street, her mind on the young woman and her three children. She hoped the woman's journey would be an easy one and wondered if the cash was enough to see her settled in her own country.

The streets were wider here in the business section, and regularly cleaned. The brick walkways on each side of the road were quiet this time of day when most employees were already at their work. Her gaze landed on a gentleman who stood across the street. He was noticeable in that he was still. He stood in his cloak pulled over a business suit with a bowler hat and simply stared at Pembroke Industries. He was a heavy-set man, impeccably dressed.

Eleanora gave a gasp as she realized his identity. It was Lord Manford. And then, as though aware he had been identified, he swung about, walking briskly to the corner and out of her sight.

Lord Manford would certainly have read the announcement of their engagement. His plans for a merger would have been dashed. Perhaps he was here today mourning his loss.

Eleanora's thoughts were interrupted by the return of Claudia. "That was quick," she said as Claudia settled into her seat.

"Yes. I didn't want to keep the men waiting too long. They are never good at it." Claudia said as the coach lurched forward.

Elliot's townhouse was a prestigious red brick set back from its treed street. It sported a columned entry, which provided a shaded front step running the length of the house. To her surprise when Flurry opened the double doors, he, and several staff, were lined up at the entry.

"Lady Pembroke, welcome." Flurry did his short bow, before he took her cloak. Each of the maids and several footmen, all in uniform, formally greeted her. It was a surprise and a little disconcerting. She glanced at Claudia, who raised her eyebrows and shrugged.

"Mr. Sparks has requested you join him in the library ma'am. If you could come this way." The ladies were led through the elaborate entry, its focal point a curved staircase leading to the balconies on the second floor. The polished wood of its railing and stairs gleamed, reflecting the light from the windows opposing them; the whole area saturated in the rich odor of old wood and lemon. To the left, they glimpsed an expansive parlor, behind a wide arched wall, one that could be used for massive entertainments.

Flurry took them to the right, opening a set of double doors with a flourish, then formally announcing their arrival.

"Ah, there you are. We had begun to lose hope that you would join us," Elliot said as he rose to show them to their chairs. Eleanora took in his appearance, scrutinizing his left arm and face for any signs of his injury. Outside of holding the injured arm carefully against his body, there was no outward sign he had been injured. His face had regained its tanned hue. If one had not seen him covered in blood and weak in her home just two days ago, it would have been impossible to notice he had been hurt. She returned his smile in greeting, satisfied with his recovery.

She took a moment to survey the room. Like the foyer and front parlor, it rose two stories. Books lined two walls and a narrow balcony accessed the two-story height with circular stairs on the far wall. Centered in front of the bookshelves on the far wall sat a huge mahogany desk, its top busy with neatly stacked files, quill, and ink. The area nearest the double doors contained a fireplace and a cluster of furniture. There were two red sofas intimately facing each other with a low serving table between them. A pair of stuffed Queen Anne chairs were placed comfortably by the fire. The entire room spoke of old wealth and style.

“We had an unexpected delay,” Claudia said, as she settled herself on a cushioned sofa next to Mr. Peters and accepted a cup and saucer from Flurry. "You will not believe our morning. I will let you tell the story Eleanora.”

Eleanora arranged herself next to Elliot on the sofa. She then waited until Flurry had poured her tea and discreetly retired, closing the double doors behind him, before relating the tale. Elliot remained quiet while she related the incident, his face betraying little of his thoughts.

“How bizarre.” Mr. Peters commented. “Whoever hired the woman was obviously intent on destroying the relationship between you and Elliot. A sweet little ploy, which by the way, should have worked.”

“Well, it did not. I was not convinced for one moment that Elliot was capable of such a thing. Three children indeed!” She glanced at Elliot, who was looking at her with a strange speculative expression.

Mr. Peters quipped, “That is three attacks on you Elliot, and all of them within a few short days. You are being targeted my friend.”

“Three? I count two.” She looked at Elliot who scowled at his friend. “Was there a third?”

Elliot sighed and rose, walked to the mantle, picked up an ivory handled dagger and set it on the table before them. “The other night after our visit with the O’Malley household, I was attacked in front of my home. The man thought to knife me and if not for the intervention of the driver, who knocked this weapon,” he indicated the knife, "out of the culprit’s hand, he would have succeeded. At the time I brushed it off as an attempted robbery. But now, given the events of the last few days, I am certain the assailant meant to do me harm."

"Oh Elliot! Why did you not tell us?" Eleanora could not take her eyes off the knife, its long narrow blade glittering ominously against the white linen tablecloth.

"I thought not to worry you. Had it been an isolated incident, you would not have been bothered with the tale."

"Someone certainly is intent on getting you out of the way," Mr. Peters mused, picking up the knife and examining it carefully as he talked. "All of this is starting to take a new twist. Keeping in mind the attacks began with the engagement, the whole business appears to be tied together. More than anything else, this incident with Mrs. Shan tells us someone is desperate to remove Elliot as a potential husband."

He held the knife closer for inspection. "There is an inscription here on the blade. 'Presented on the field of honor, August 10, 1808. 4th Battalion, Spanish Campaign'. Interesting. I will take this knife if I may. I may be able to trace it." He carefully slid it into his inside pocket.

"Do you think the murderer of Matheson is the same person who is pursuing Elliot?" Eleanora asked.

Mr. Peters nodded. "From the information gathered from Rose Ingram—" Eleanora opened her mouth to comment, and Mr. Peters raised his hand as though to ward off her words. "And no, Elliot did not tell me how you were able to locate her or where she is, though I am certain the little notebook held the key. We can be certain Matheson's murder is tied to the embezzlement at the firm. It is unlikely there would be two separate sets of fiends intent on murder, both connected to Pembroke."

"But why target Elliot?" Eleanora asked.

"I would assume there are two reasons removing me from the equation would suit our villains," Elliot said. "The first is to get me out of the office, where I might discover the discrepancies and do an investigation. The second is that once you have a husband, Eleanora, whatever chance they had of acquiring Pembroke is forever lost to them." He scowled. "Whoever you marry controls Pembroke, in their minds at least," he added when he noted her frown. "Part of their strategy must be to acquire the business through marriage."

"But our main suspect, Lord Hargrove, is already married. He could not pursue Eleanora." Claudia interjected.

"His partner is obviously not." Eleanora pointed out. "Rose Ormond was firm in her statement that Matheson's murderer had referred to an accomplice. Though why either of them would think I might so easily be coerced into a marriage is beyond me."

Claudia frowned. "True, but let's not forget Amelia announced to all and sundry you would be choosing a mate this season. That would surely add an element of desperate aspiration to the killers' plans."

Flurry chose that moment to open wide the library

doors, addressing Elliot. "Excuse me sir. Shall I serve a few delicacies for high tea?"

Elliot motioned him in. "I think a morsel of food may be an excellent notion."

Flurry entered followed by two maids in crisp starched uniforms. All of them carried trays of food. Eleanora's mouth was slightly agape at the abundance of dainties served. Trays of small sandwiches, each with the crusts removed and in a variety of fillers took center stage on the table, followed by a variety of sweets, arranged on layered trays, and elaborately garnished. Flurry stepped back to supervise as the young maids refreshed their tea, serving it precisely.

When all was accomplished, Elliot stole a look at her before saying, "Thank you Flurry, that will do."

"Well Elliot, in all the times I have visited your home, I've never been treated to a spread such as this." Mr. Peters said, plucking a small sandwich from a tray and taking a bite.

"My staff hope to impress their new Mistress," he replied with a quick wink in her direction.

"And you may tell them I am suitably impressed. This is lovely." Eleanora smiled back at him. "I am convinced Queen Victoria herself could not have enjoyed such a wonderful luncheon." Eleanora noticed Claudia and Mr. Peters share an amused glance.

"But back to the business at hand." Mr. Peters interjected. "We can assume someone is targeting Elliot. Whoever it is, the ultimate goal must be to acquire Pembroke Industries. Because certainly, if a marriage takes place, whatever chance they may have had at the firm would be lost. They have tried hard to remove him from the picture, even resorting to this recent ploy with Mrs. Shan."

Mr. Peters paused to select one of the canapés from the tray. "Whoever this man is, he will be single and one of your suitors of late, Eleanora. He will have made his presence known. That should narrow the field considerably."

"I can certainly list those." Eleanora grimaced. "I have not been in England long enough to have acquired many. The first set were those introduced to me by Amelia: Lords Farrow, Brambury, Manford, and Mr. Weins. Then there was Charles, Lord Mansfield, Salsbury, and, oh dear, a host of other gentlemen at the ball."

"I think we can safely eliminate Charles." Elliot said.

"And Farrow," Eleanora added, "It is impossible to imagine so meek a fellow involved in all of this. Mr. Weins has certainly been a strong suitor; he has even approached Hargrove with a proposal. Manford is also persistent. And there is the rumor about the death of his first wife to consider."

Mr. Peters pulled a small black notebook from his pocket and flipped through its pages to find an entry. "Manford, you say? Lord Manford is a connection of Hargrove's. We have him with Hargrove at his club several times this week. Very interesting indeed."

The four of them went through the suitors, with Will Peters jotting notes into his little black book. At the end of the ordeal, Eleanora was disappointed. For all the discussion, they had accomplished little in way of finding the murderers. And Elliot was still a target.

She sighed. "Where do we go from here? We have few leads."

"Not true. We have a narrow list, and if this knife is connected to any of them, we have our first confirmed suspect, and our first concrete proof." Mr. Peters patted his jacket where the knife rested inside. He looked at Elliot. "I will be sharing this information with my friend Inspector Mcgowan. He will need to be informed. But until we catch the culprits, you will have to exercise extreme care. I will send a man down to be a protector and I suggest you keep him close. Indeed, I would suggest you keep to your house for a few days, especially with your injury. You are still a target."

"I agree. You mustn't leave the house, Elliot." Eleanora said in her firmest voice. "At least not until you have completely healed."

"There is work to be done at the office—"

Eleanora interrupted. "Claudia and I will go in tomorrow. Anything you need we can have delivered to you." She leaned towards him and placed her hand on his thigh. "Please Elliot. If nothing else, it will relieve me of this terrible worry."

Elliot reached down and took her hand in his. "If it will please you, I suppose a day or two at home cannot be too difficult. But I warn you I will not be confined longer than that."

Eleanora nodded, aware that it would be a small window of opportunity to find and capture Elliot's attackers. She had no idea how to proceed. A shiver of dread rippled through her with the realization that the next move was likely to come from the villains themselves. They would have no choice but to strike before she married. And with Amelia announcing their plans for a quick wedding to all who would listen, they were sure to act soon.

CHAPTER 24

The next morning Eleanora joined Claudia and went into Pembroke to catch up on some of the work. It had been a few days since she had been in. The year-end reports were completed, and she found herself engrossed in the accounts well into the afternoon. Then there was payroll which required a parcel of signatures. It was almost five when she pulled the specs for the new steamship onto her desk and began looking it over, paying careful attention to Elliot's notes.

"I am ready to leave for the day, Eleanora," Claudia said from the doorway. "The company coach has been brought around and waits for us at the entry."

"Why don't you go on ahead Claudia. I want to spend a few minutes finishing what I started. There is no point in waiting, you can send the coach back for me."

"Are you sure?"

"I see myself with another half hour for certain. Go on ahead."

Eleanora lost herself in the plans for the new ship. It promised to be a beauty. Finally, she lifted her brooch watch from her jacket and checked the time. It was long past the half hour she had blocked to look over the blueprints. She reluctantly set them aside.

When she walked to her doorway to pull on her cloak, and tie her bonnet, she noticed the office was eerily quiet. Everyone had left for the night, even the security man, usually parked outside her office had finished his shift and retired for the evening. The hallway to the stairwell was dark, no lights had been left burning. Her stomach twisted with a flash of fear, and she shook it off, striding purposely down the stairs to the main entry.

It was too early yet to be so dark outside, she thought as she paused to lock the door. *The blasted fog!* It swirled around the coach and smothered the quiet street. All was still, which was not unusual for this time of night on a street housing office workers, most of whom had left for the evening. Again, she experienced a queasy premonition, as though evil lurked around her. *It is just the infernal fog,* she assured herself.

The horses snorted, billowing steam into the cool air, while shuffling their front hooves against the cobbles, impatient with the wait. She wondered how long the coachman had been parked at the door.

Without glancing at the poor man, she opened the coach door and was about to pull herself in without his assistance. In a burst of movement, he leapt down from his perch, grabbed her by the waist, and shoved her forward into the coach, following in behind her. It had all happened so fast; she had no time to do anything except sputter in indignation as she was slammed against the far interior wall of the coach.

She straightened in her seat and pushed back the bonnet which had been forced over her eyes. To her surprise Crystabel sat primly in the seat opposite her, her blue silk dress cascading in a perfect sea of ruffles around her, shimmering in the soft coach light.

Before she could speak, an arm was roughly flung across her chest, pinning her to the seat. Mr. Weins, in the uniform of her coachman, leaned into her line of vision. "Do not make a sound," he snarled, his arm sliding upward to press against her throat. Convinced she was about to be murdered; she was temporarily frozen.

"Hello darling," Crystabel said, her voice casual, as if they had gathered for tea.

"Why Crystabel? What will you accomplish by killing me?" Eleanora asked. Arthur Weins pushed down hard on her throat, warning her to hold her tongue.

"Kill you? Nonsense, my dear." She smiled at her. "We have only snatched you to bring that man of yours to us. He is a bit slippery as you know. It is he we will be killing. We have better plans for you my dear."

Eleanora could not answer. The arm against her throat was now too tight for her to even breathe and she struggled against the pressure.

"I have a little something to make this trip more

comfortable. She reached into her reticule and pulled out a brown bottle and a handkerchief. When she twisted the cap, Eleanora immediately smelled the sweet deadly scent of chloroform. She instinctively pressed her body back into the seat behind her. Arthur Weins laughed; a loud evil guffaw, and momentarily slackened the force on her throat. Rose's words came to mind—the murderer's laugh, and she closed her eyes, taking a breath to forestall the panic.

Before she reopened them, the chloroform saturated cloth was pressed against her face. She tried to squirm, tossing her head back and forth, but it was of little use. Eleanora saw only the dark eyes of Arthur Weins as blackness closed in on her.

ELEANORA'S HEAD was thick and heavy. She seemed to be secured to a chair, her arms pulled behind her and tied to the rails of the chair's back. She shifted her ankles, discovering her feet too were bound. She could hear a faded conversation in the distance. And then panic began to set in as a flood of memories returned to her. She took several deep breaths to calm herself. She suppressed a moan, remaining still until she could make sense of her surroundings.

She concentrated on the conversation, steadfastly keeping her eyes closed and remaining still.

Crystabel's voice invaded her consciousness. "I have no idea how much time will pass until she awakens. I am not a doctor. I used as little as possible. She is of no use to us dead." Her voice seemed to echo, and Eleanora wondered if it was the acoustics or the condition of her head, which pounded worse than the morning after the brandy incident.

"She won't be a threat to you while I'm gone, trussed up as she is. I'll not be away more than an hour. We cannot risk sending a delivery boy, who could be a witness later. It's a task best done by me. I will simply ring the bell and slide it under the door. Be patient my love. All will work out as we planned."

Eleanora risked opening her eyes a crack. She was in a warehouse of sorts. It was a high-ceilinged space, with stacks of crates piled twenty or more feet in high rows on her left. A loft of sorts, which she knew would contain more cargo circled about the perimeter. There was a lantern turned up on a desk beside the wall near Crystabel and Weins, but other than that the cavernous room was steeped in shadows. The building would be down at the docks, used for ships to unload and store their cargo.

I have been in many such buildings, she thought, and the idea somehow comforted her. But never at night, she added ruefully, and never strapped to a chair.

She heard footsteps and assumed Weins was leaving. A door slamming in the distance confirmed her suspicions. Then Crystabel's soft step as she walked around the chair. She could feel eyes watching her and forced herself to breathe evenly. After a minute, which dragged into years, her soft steps receded.

Eleanora was not sure what assistance her secret

wakefulness would be, but for now it was the only advantage she had, and she was unwilling to give it up.

The room had been silent for several minutes. She risked opening her eyes the tiniest sliver. Crystabel sat in a chair behind the rickety desk, some ten feet away, her face illuminated in the lantern. The desk appeared to be central to the length of the warehouse, pushed up against an exterior wall, with the cargo stacked in looming heaps opposite it. They were in a circle of dim light produced by the single lantern. The rest of the warehouse was shrouded in darkness.

She had taken a piece of paper from the desk and appeared to be writing or sketching to pass the time.

Eleanora began to work her hands. The ropes were tied tightly, and it seemed a hopeless endeavor. She shifted her feet. There was play in the rope, so much that she almost smiled. She continued to work her feet, slowly gaining slack. Twice Crystabel rose and walked around Eleanora's chair, and once she felt her wrist for a pulse. Eleanora concentrated on keeping her breathing even, replaying Crystabel's words in her mind to ease the tension. Crystabel had no idea how much chloroform she had given her or how long she would remain unconscious.

By slowly shifting, and gradually working her right foot higher, she was able to work it from the ties. It was free. She kept her feet together, as though she was still tied and peeked again at her captor.

Crystabel had tossed her papers aside and began to pace. Eleanora pressed her feet together and prayed she would not check the bindings. She worked her hands trying to keep her fears at bay.

But her thoughts persisted. Elliot would come, of that she was certain. And when he did, they would kill him. Her heart ached. She could not lose Eliot, not now when she knew he was her only true love. Whatever fate was in store for her was inconsequential. Without Elliot, it didn't matter what was done to her.

CHAPTER 25

Flurry opened the library doors and cleared his throat. "A Mr. Peters and Mr. Mcgowan to see you sir."

Elliot slid the spread sheets back into the folder and pushed them to the corner of his desk. "Send them in Flurry." He rose to greet the men as they entered.

Will Peters strode into the room. "It's late I know, but we have learned something I knew you'd want to hear immediately." He gestured to Mcgowan. "You remember Inspector Mcgowan of course."

"Yes. Come in. Sit down. Can I get you a brandy?"

Mcgowan settled himself on the sofa, with his back against the armrest and his body turned into the room, folding his hands comfortably on his rounded belly. "I could do with a good brandy," he said. "Quite the place you have here."

"Yes." Elliot answered, preparing three glasses, and handing one to each of his guests before taking a seat.

"It has been in the family for a few generations. What news have you?"

Will reached into his pocket and pulled out the dagger, "We have managed to trace the knife. You might be surprised with the connection we've found."

"Brilliant, I don't suppose it's Hargrove's?"

"The knife was awarded to a Major Henry Weins, for outstanding service on the Spanish Peninsula." The inspector announced. "We have spent the day checking in to the man." He paused and sipped his brandy, giving a satisfied grunt before continuing. "Seems the fellow has a grandson named Arthur Weins, one of Miss Pembroke's suitors I'm told. Quite the coincidence given the events of the last few days, eh?" he took another sip of his brandy.

"Coincidence indeed."

"Ah," the inspector took another sip of brandy. "Very fine brandy. I like a good blend." He held his glass to the light and swirled it about. Will caught his eye and grinned, content to let Mcgowan share the information. "It seems young Mr. Weins is in shipping. A good friend of the Hargrove's and often a guest at their home. Another coincidence, eh?" He sighed. "We will be bringing the man in for questioning. Shake him up a bit."

Flurry stood at the library doors. "A letter for you sir. Most unusual. The knocker sounded and the thing was slid under the front door. I checked the street, and no one was about. Whoever delivered it appears to have run off," he said as he entered the room and handed Elliot the envelope. "I assumed you would want it immediately."

"Quite right, thank you Flurry."

Elliot ripped the envelope open and read, while the room remained silent. He tossed the paper at Mr. Peters and leapt to his feet. "Good God, they have Eleanora. I have to go to her."

Mcgowan too, rose to his feet and moving quickly for a big man, grasped Elliot's shoulder. "Wait. We will need a plan. Sit down sir." He put firm pressure on his shoulder until Elliot returned to his seat. "Wait," he repeated. He looked at Will, who had read the missive and was sitting wide-eyed. "Let me see the thing," he said, snatching it out of Will's hands.

Mcgowan sat down on the sofa, this time perched on the edge of his seat, while he scanned the note. "Hmm, they have taken Miss Pembroke. And they don't want a ransom, they want you. A handy location too. Down at the docks, looks to be the warehouse district, down by the old wharfs. Of course, you are to tell no one and come alone." He looked up at Elliot. "If you rush in sir, you'll give them what they want, and that looks to be your life."

He handed the note back to Elliot, and leaned back on the sofa, rubbing his heavy sideburns. "No. We need a plan. I'm thinking the young lady will be fine. It's not in their best interest to take out their bargaining chip. If we're smart, and a little lucky, we will have these culprits before the night's over."

Elliot took a calming breath. Mcgowan was right. Running off to the docks might get both Eleanora and him killed. He fought back his desire to gallop to her rescue, forcing some semblance of calm into his shattered being.

Eleanora was his woman, his fiancée, and the love of his life. The sniveling Mr. Weins would never take her away from him. He would stake his life on it.

CHAPTER 26

Eleanora held her feet closely together, feeling the loose rope draped around her ankles. She wished she could look down and be sure they at least appeared to be still bound, but to do so would give away all. She was sure it was well over an hour since Weins had left. Her neck was stiff, from holding her head slumped to the side. She was not sure how much longer she could continue the ruse, or even if it were worth maintaining.

Crystabel was back at the desk, humming to herself as she wrote on the papers in front of her, and looking for all the world like a princess, without a single concern. She cursed herself for not recognizing Crystabel as the villain she truly was. The clues were there. She now knew what had bothered her with Rose's statement. Rose had said she had never been to Matheson's home. Yet Mrs. Bixby, Matheson's former housekeeper, had told them a veiled woman frequently visited. That woman, a fancy piece, according to Mrs. Bixby, must have been Crystabel.

And the close relationship between Arthur Weins and Crystabel had been apparent throughout. It was Mr. Weins himself who had told her they were childhood friends in Yorkshire. Furthermore, it was Crystabel who had checked to see if Elliot had been injured or killed at the park. Eleanora had been too blind to see it.

Eleanora's thoughts were interrupted by the slightest sound from the balcony above. It was a rub, like the scratch of shoe leather on a dirty floor. Her eyes darted to Crystabel, who was unfazed. Her humming must have disguised the sound. Perhaps she was imagining it, or possibly it was a rat, scuttling about. She heard it again. This time she was sure someone lurked above.

A door slammed in the distance. Eleanora could not resist peeking once more. She strained her eyes attempting to peer into the dark recesses of the warehouse. It took a moment for Mr. Weins to emerge out of the darkness and join Crystabel near the lantern.

She closed her eyes and breathed once more.

"The note has been delivered. I waited outside his door as long as I could and saw him enter his coach before I left. Took Sparks long enough to make his move. Typical of the lazy nobs. But the man has taken the bait. It will not be long now love, he can only be minutes behind me."

"I hope so. It is bloody dreary in this shed of a building. Eleanora is still out, which is too bad for her. I could have at least had some pleasure in tormenting her."

"Still out you say." Eleanora heard Weins step towards her. There was a moment's silence. And then she felt the man's warm breath on her cheeks. It took all her strength not to cringe away from him.

"Boo!" he shouted into her face. Eleanora jumped; her eyes open wide. He laughed, the same horrible rasping sound she had heard earlier. She lifted her head to glare at him.

"No, my dear she is quite lucid." He laughed again.

"Hello Eleanora," Crystabel said. "How naughty of you to pretend to sleep. And we could have had a little girl time."

"What is it you hope to gain by this Crystabel?"

"Why everything love. I want what you take so lightly—Pembroke, the money, and the right to marry the man I love." She leaned back into Arthur Weins. He put an arm around her, pulling her towards him, and kissing her neck from behind before she stepped away from him and smiled at Eleanora. "It is not too much to ask, after all I have as much right to it as you do."

"I cannot see myself handing it to you, Crystabel. And if I die, certainly my grandmother won't be giving it to you either."

Weins took several steps forward, until he stood directly in front of her. "Oh, but you will. That is the beauty of our little plan. You are going to marry me sweetheart. Then by law, everything you own becomes mine. Handy that."

"Never." Eleanora spat.

Crystabel smiled. "You could have made it so much easier for all concerned if you had just accepted

Arthur as your husband. Now you will have no choice." She gave an odd little giggle. "It is rather like the situation I faced with Stephen, who was my only option for a title. The idea of us switching places pleases me." She walked closer to Eleanora's chair and peered down at her. "We have the perfect little dungeon room in Yorkshire prepared for you my dear. All we need is a signature, and by the time we are done with you, you will beg us to let you sign." Crystabel shrugged. "And who is to help you? Your champion will be dead, and that old woman in American will be no threat to us."

"That gives Weins my fortune, not you. You have a husband, Lord Hargrove, or have you forgotten him?"

Crystabel laughed. "Stephen? He is a brainless little man, easily controlled. Sadly, he will soon have an accident."

"But what of your daughter? Would you truly take away her father?"

Weins leaned toward her and hissed, "She is my daughter. It is my family the idiot Hargrove claims." He walked back to Crystabel, raised his voice once more and said, "But not for long. His days are numbered."

Crystabel placed a hand on Weins' shoulder. "Arthur and I are one. We have been since we played together as children. It has been a long journey, building the life we dreamed of, but we are almost there. We will have it all…a title, money, and the place in society I deserve. You are just the final hurdle in our path, my dear."

The creak of a door opening ended the conversation. All eyes peered into the darkness. There was no sound of approaching footsteps.

"Sparks, it must be you. Show yourself!" Weins voice echoed in the warehouse. He pulled a pistol from his belt and hurried to Eleanora, grabbing her shoulder roughly and bracing the gun against her head. "Show yourself or I'll shoot her."

Elliot's voice sounded eerily from the blackness, "Mr. Weins. Nice little warehouse you have here. Nothing compared to Pembroke's enterprises. In fact, it looks a trifle grim, but that is to be expected, given the size and age of your little operation."

Weins frantically searched the shadows. "Come forward you bastard or I'll shoot!" Eleanora could not suppress a shudder as the cold steel was pressed into her neck. Weins stepped around behind the chair.

"Relax Weins." Eliot's voice was calm now, almost soft. "I will come forward for you. But first I want a few answers. I am entitled to them, don't you think?" There was the soft scrape of footsteps. Straining her eyes to peer into the dark, Eleanora was thankful she could not make out Elliot' s form.

The gun began to tremble beneath Weins' hands. He crouched behind her chair, using her to shield his body. Crystabel had backed slowly away from the scene and stood braced against the wall. Eleanora realized they had badly miscalculated. Elliot had not rushed forward to where she was tied to the chair. Instead, the two of them were glowing targets in the dark of the warehouse. It could not have been what they had envisioned when they concocted their plan.

"Let's start with the embezzlement. It was an impressive piece of work. I estimate you managed to get yourself at least five thousand pounds." Eleanora wondered why Elliot had purposely undervalued the theft.

"You're a fool Sparks." Weins laughed. His hand relaxed, and the pressure on her neck decreased slightly. "We got more than double that. And if those steamships had come off their run before the old man came into the office, it would have been triple." Weins laughed again, clearly enjoying the opportunity to brag.

"Too bad Brigg had to come in and spoil it then. Is that why you shot him?"

"The old man had one foot in the grave anyway. He was hardly worth the effort. The bastard had been on my back since he found out about Crystabel and me. Old bugger couldn't mind his own business—and worse, he had Matheson and I figured out in days. He did a more accurate job than you Sparks." Weins snorted.

"And what about Hargrove? I suspect he is the mastermind in all this."

Weins was indignant. "Hargrove a mastermind? Ha! The man is a fool. He knew nothing. He is nothing but a puppet! The man has no right to everything that should have been mine. A title! Bah." Weins was angry now, spitting out his words. "He was such a complete failure in Pembroke, even Matheson could mislead him."

"Ah yes, Matheson. I suppose he had to go." Elliot said from the dark.

"That was Crystabel's idea. I was content with him leaving. Not saying I didn't like the job." Weins chuckled. "He was waiting in his bed for a surprise from his lover, and I gave it to him, right in the chest." Weins laughed again. "Not what he was expecting at all."

"And what plan have the two of you cooked up for tonight?" Elliot asked, his voice soft.

"Step into the light and you'll find out. As much as I've enjoyed this little chit chat, I am getting impatient to see your face." He rose, slid the gun forward and pointed it down at her body. "I suppose I could start with a few shots to the legs, then the arms."

"Don't shoot." For the first time Eliot's voice had a note of panic. "I'm coming."

Eleanora listened to the sound of Elliot's footsteps moving closer. She knew the moment Weins could make out the shape of Elliot's body, he would shoot without hesitation. Already the barrel of the gun was inching outward. Weins was prepared.

But so was she. Eleanora slowly moved her feet, bracing them. When Elliot stepped into the light, she was going to use her feet to spring up and throw her body into Weins. If she could knock him off balance before he had an opportunity to shoot, Elliot would have a chance.

Nothing could be heard except the scratch of Elliot's boots on the dusty oak floors. Her eyes strained into the darkness, her heart pounding in her throat with each of his steps. Beside her Weins' arm trembled as the barrel of his pistol turned, pointing away from her and toward the darkness.

And then it happened. Elliot stepped into the light. She used every ounce of strength she had to rear up and knock into Weins. A roar of gunshots echoed through the warehouse.

Eleanora hit the planked floor, helplessly turtled by the chair strapped to her back. Her cheek was pressed to the rough planks, and still the shots rang out. Beside her she witnessed Weins fall to the floor. She twisted her body to search for Elliot, desperate to see if he had survived unscathed.

The space was somehow bathed in light. There were lanterns all around her. The shots had stilled, and the smell of gun powder, mixed with the screams of Crystabel filled the air.

And then Elliot was beside her, lifting her, chair and all into the air, setting her to rights and kneeling beside her. "Are you hurt? Are you injured?" He smoothed back her hair, his blue eyes close to hers. "Tell me you all right my love."

"Oh Elliot. I am fine. I am more than fine now that you are here." She leaned forward in the chair resting her head on his shoulder, unable to suppress a sob. "I love you, Elliot."

He brushed the hair back from her face and kissed her forehead before going behind the chair to release her hands.

Eleanora looked at her surroundings for the first time since hitting the floor. She had not imagined the lanterns. The warehouse was illuminated by at least half a dozen of them. A circle of constables had appeared from between the gaps in the stacks of cargo, and even the balcony above was glowing with light.

Will Peters walked towards her and tipped his bowler hat. "It's all over ma'am." he said. He turned to Crystabel who was still braced against the wall, her eyes wild. Inspector Mcgowan too, came forward from between the piles of cargo.

Eleanora rose stiffly to her feet. A loud moan from Crystabel drew her attention.

Crystabel stood, alternately turning to Mr. Peters, then Mcgowan, her beautiful face twisted with shock and horror. She pushed off the wall in a flurry of blue silk, brushed past Eleanora and ran toward the rear of the building, and the stairs to the balcony.

"Halt!" Mcgowan yelled. "Stop or I'll shoot!" But he did not fire. Instead, several constables ran after her, their shouts and footfalls echoing in the warehouse.

Crystabel reached the circular stair and scurried upward. She raced along the balcony, her ice blue gown shimmering behind her. Too late she saw the cluster of lanterns in front of her.

"Don't move!" a constable hollered. Facing a wall of police with guns drawn, Crystabel paused and turned, but behind her Mcgowan's men had already negotiated the stairs. She was surrounded.

She stood at the rail. A moment later she was hoisting herself over the side.

"Crystabel no!" Eleanora yelled.

A loud crack resonated through the warehouse as the railing gave way. Crystabel was flung forward. For a moment she dangled precariously from the balcony, a piece of her dress snagged on a shard of wood. Her blue gown caught the lights and glittered as she swung above them, looking like a ballerina in perfect flight before the material gave way with a dreadful ripping sound and she fell to the floor below.

Eleanora turned her face into Elliot's chest, hoping to dispel the image which would be forever etched onto her mind. There was an awful silence, broken only by the sound of footsteps approaching the body.

"Neck's broken." Mcgowan announced into the quiet.

ELEANORA SAT HUDDLED in the corner of the sofa, a blanket wrapped around her, and Elliot nestled beside her. She held a cup of tea in both hands and sipped it as Mr. Peters and Elliot described the ordeal at the warehouse to Claudia.

"I don't understand. Why did you not just shoot the man when you arrived in the warehouse?" Claudia said.

Elliot answered. "Two reasons actually. The first is Eleanora was too close. We could not risk it unless there was no other option. And the second, if we wanted the pair of them at the Bailey facing murder charges for Jem Brigg and Matheson, we needed a confession."

"Somehow Elliot managed to get one in front of swarms of officers," Mr. Peters interjected. "Had events gone more to plan, we would have arrested them. But when Weins opened fire that option was off the table."

"I knew he would shoot before you had the opportunity to defend yourself. Spineless scoundrel of a man! It was the reason I pushed into him."

"You did well, my dear." Elliot said, putting his arm around her shoulders and holding her snug against him. Eleanora was surprised with his show of affection, especially in front of others. Despite that she took advantage of his nearness, leaning her head on his shoulder and relishing the close warmth of him.

Mr. Peters finished his portrayal of the scene and set his teacup back on the tray. "Mcgowan's boys will be breaking the news to Amelia and Lord Hargrove as we speak. I'm sure the family will be devastated by the news. I talked to Mcgowan about the possibility of leaving Crystabel's role out of the news reels. There is the daughter to consider after all, and this scandal will not be easily forgotten. Hard to be the child of a murderess I would think."

"And did he agree?' Claudia asked.

Will chuckled. "Only after Elliot negotiated a rather large stipend." He paused at Claudia's gasp. "Don't be so surprised, my dear. It is how it is done. Inspectors make little money, as do the constables who work beneath them. They take what they can, especially when it does no harm…just like their predecessors, the Bow Street Runners, did in the past." He laughed again. "With the amount Elliot doled out, I'm guessing Crystabel will be made the tragic heroine of this story."

"Oh Elliot, that was so good of you. Anna need not

ever know of her mother's part in all this. And poor Amelia will be spared the scandal." Eleanora said, thinking of the harmless old woman. She would be devastated, but she would have her granddaughter. And little Anna would have Amelia, she added silently. She was glad no one else had heard Weins claim Anna as his daughter. The child would at least be left with a father who loved her dearly. The one positive attribute Hargrove had was his dedication to his daughter. Eleanora was the only one left knowing the damning secret, and she would never tell.

Mr. Peters rose, "I must be off. I promised Mcgowan I would make a formal statement. He will be closing the case today and releasing the news to the press. I imagine it will be a pleasant surprise for your friend Rose."

Eleanora smiled, thinking of the beautiful woman tucked away in the country. "I should think so. I will send a note to inform her."

"Thank you for your work, Will. You produced a sound plan. I will settle the bill with you this week," Elliot said.

"Let me walk you to the door," Claudia said taking Mr. Peter's arm and smiling at him.

Eleanora watched them leave the room. Mr. Peters said something to Claudia, and she laughed, pulling him close. "Those two are meant to be together," Eleanora observed.

"As are we." Elliot said, slipping his good arm around her. "I want to hear the words you spoke to me in the warehouse one more time."

"What words?"

"You said you loved me. I want to hear it again."

"Oh, Eliot I—"

Elliot cut her off before she could protest. "You already said it, and you may not take it back."

She laughed. "I do love you, Elliot. With all my heart...I love you." Leaning forward she kissed his cheek.

"Ah, this is good. I have been waiting to hear it." He sat back with a satisfied smile on his face, taking her hand in his. "And now, I think, we can use that special license to marry. I want the woman I love, the woman of my dreams to be at my side." He leaned forward once more and kissed her. His touch was sweetly tender. She marveled again that a man so large and strong could be so gentle.

"How does tomorrow sound?" he murmured against her lips.

"Perfect," she muttered and deepened the kiss.

THE END

IF YOU ENJOYED THIS BOOK, please leave a review with Amazon.

There is a prequel to this story, featuring Arabella, Eleanora's grandmother. It can be found in my novel, The Smuggler, also available on Amazon.

If you wish you may visit my Facebook page under Cynthia Keyes. You will find updates and information on my latest novels there. I am currently setting up a website where you will be able to access more information, get the first chance at sales or giveaways and contact me. I look forward to hearing from you.

AND NOW, turn the page for a peek at the first draft of my next book. It has developed into a bit of a gothic, one that has quickly become my favorite.

CYNTHIA KEYES

Lord Montrose selects his bride

Lord Montrose stood in the shadows, gripping the balcony rail. "She is the one. I will make the offer tomorrow," he said, his eyes not straying from the scene below. His darkly handsome face was in profile. It was comfortable for him to present such a stance, even with Hamish, who certainly was familiar with his disfigurement.

The musicians began to play a country dance. He watched as the young woman maneuvered through the dance steps, smiling each time she came together with her partner, and exchanged a brief word. She wasn't too young, nor was she too beautiful. She had acceptable looks. Her auburn hair was done up in braids around her head and garnished with small buds of flowers. They were her only accessory. Her gown was not the latest fashion and looked as though it had been recycled many times. She was exactly what one could expect from a woman who was impoverished, but genteel.

"You're sure?" his man asked, shaking his head. "I can't say I like this scheme, Jules. Why not meet her, let her get to know you before you decide. She might just choose you as her husband without all the bribery."

"Do you honestly think that would work Hamish?" He turned to his man, letting him see the disaster that was the left side of his face. A thick scar ran from his chin to the corner of his left eye. Stark and almost white against his swarthy complexion, it pulled his skin into puckered ridges across his cheek. When he grinned as he did now, the left side of his face did not respond, leaving him with a permanent half smile, a sort of sarcastic grimace, which he thought suited him well enough.

"It might. If you at least tried to be a little charming."

Julian laughed. It was a dry joyless sound. "Hamish, you overestimate my charms. No. I have what the woman needs. I don't think she will have much choice, given the family's financial situation—a turn of events which suits my plans perfectly. My money will make the decision. It will be a bargain that benefits the both of us; I save her family from ruin, and she provides me with the heir I need."

"I think you may have misjudged this woman. From all our reports, she appears to be a sensible and intelligent person. You might be surprised by her reaction to you."

"The only reaction I need from her is her agreement," he said, his gaze back on the dancers below. Lady Madelyn Guilford, his quarry, threw back her head and laughed at something her partner said. From this distance he could not hear the sound, but her merriment was obvious. For a moment, his heart yearned for a scenario where that joy would be directed his way.

He quickly squashed the thought. He knew well the expression of revulsion in the eyes of those he met, though most were quick to hide it behind polite exchanges. The love of a woman could not ever be for him. If she agreed to be his wife, and produced an heir, it would be enough.

~

A bargain is struck

"You must get up my girl. Your mama wishes to speak to you. Come on, up up."

Madelyn groaned. "Heavens. What time is it? Why would she want to see me so early this morning when she knows the ball went until almost dawn last night. Surely whatever it is can wait a few hours." Madelyn pulled the pillow from beneath her head and flopped it over her face. "Tell her no," she muttered.

"She insists," said Milly. When this pronouncement had no effect on her charge, she added slyly, "There are men here. I think you may have an offer."

Madelyn peeked out from under the pillow. "Men?"

"Men. Two of them, or so Grimes said. They arrived early this morning and have been with your mama for two hours now."

"Oh goodness." Madelyn tossed the pillow aside and sat up. "I doubt it's an offer, Milly. I am guessing they are here to evict us." She sighed. Life was about to take a bitter turn. There would be no stopping the misery that would befall them now. She trudged across the room, where Milly waited by the washstand, facecloth in hand.

Last night, she knew the ball was likely to be her last. She had been determined to enjoy it. And indeed, this morning the time for retribution had come. There was no help for it but to dress and face the day.

Her father, may he rest in peace, had always managed to find the worst possible investments. His last venture had left them with no money, and a mortgaged home. When he died two years ago, the family was left destitute. There was her mother, Lady Guilford, and four daughters to support: Madelyn, Beth, MaryAnn, and Clarice. They had been forced to apply to their father's brother, Uncle William, for assistance. He had reluctantly agreed to pay their expenses on the meagerest possible budget.

But just last week they had received word from Uncle William that he was no longer able to carry the cost of maintaining their household. In fact, he had quit paying the mortgage some time ago. Their house was about to be foreclosed. Mother had been frantically making arrangements to move in with her estranged sister, Margaret. Only yesterday they had received word that the woman would grudgingly accept the destitute family into her home, on the condition the girls work for their board. Not the best of prospects for all concerned.

Mother was convinced the arrangement was an act of brutal vengeance on her sister's part and had been distressed since receiving the letter.

For the past two years, her mama, and no doubt her Uncle William, had hoped Madelyn would alleviate some of the pressure by making a decent match. She was the only girl of marriageable age, being eight years older than her next sibling, Beth, who had only just turned sixteen.

But those efforts had failed. No one had been interested enough, or wealthy enough to take on the burden of supporting a household with four unmarried girls. To make matters worse, Madelyn herself was not the ideal young woman most men of her class strived for. She was too intellectual, and too brash to hide that quality, forever putting forth her opinion when it was least wanted or appreciated. Despite her best effort to be the gracious young woman most men expected, she was unable to curb her tongue and portray the model of decorum her mother so hoped she would be. Madelyn knew she was a bitter disappointment to the family.

Milly fastened the bow on her best dress. Madelyn was too tired to wonder about the choice of gowns.

"Your mama asked that you meet her in the library." She handed her a cup of lukewarm tea, laced with cream and sugar as she liked it. "Drink this. It will wake you up." Milly looked at her charge and scowled. "There is no time to do up your hair. We'll leave it down. It is your best quality." She pulled a piece of hair from each side of her head and secured it with a clip at the back, letting it fall in waves past her shoulders, then looked at her critically. "It will have to do." She reached over and pinched Madelyn's cheeks for color before taking the cup from her hands and pushing her to the door. "Off you go."

On the landing of the stairs, her eight-year-old sister Clarice met her with teary eyes. Clarice grasped her arm and walked down with her a few steps, patting her reassuringly as they progressed. Madelyn paused, tugging her arm away. "Whatever is wrong with you Clarice? Have you lost the blasted puppy again?"

Clarice shook her head no, while biting her bottom lip. Staring at her with mournful eyes, she pushed past her and scurried back up the stairs.

At the bottom of the staircase her two other sisters stood and waited. They too behaved as though doom and gloom had descended. Maryann's face was red and puffy as it always looked after she had shed tears. The eviction process must have begun, she thought grimly.

Beth stepped forward and squeezed her hand. "You don't have to say yes," she whispered.

Madelyn only had time to glance at her with confusion before the library door opened and mama gestured for her to enter. Her mother turned to her sisters. "You may go to your room girls," she said with a stern look, "and stay there until I send for you."

Mother stepped back, to let her pass, closing the door briskly behind them. "Sit down Madelyn. You and I must have a chat," she said, pulling back a chair in front of her father's massive desk and taking a seat in his leather chair behind it. Her formality was disconcerting.

Never in all the years she had known her mother had she seen this side of her. She sat across from her now with a face so serious Madelyn shivered with dread. Something terrible must have happened. Perhaps her Aunt Margaret had turned them down and they faced the poor house, or life on the streets. She braced herself for what was to come.

Mama took a breath and began in a business-like tone. "I have had an offer for your hand in marriage. The Lord of Montrose has proposed a marriage settlement where he would provide a proper dowery for each of the girls. Furthermore, he has agreed to purchase our home, in your name, and take on the expenses of this household. There will also be an allowance which will allow us to live decently, at least until all the girls are married. It is the answer to our prayers."

Madelyn was struck dumb. Her heart was beating wildly. She forced herself to take a calming breath. A proposal? The house purchased in her name? Even doweries! It was too much to take in.

She looked at her mother's face. Her mouth was set in a firm line, and the jubilation she would have expected from her under these circumstances was not evident. "Do I know a Lord Montrose? And why are you so glum?" she asked.

Her mother colored slightly. "No. I do not believe you have met. He, however, has seen you. He finds you acceptable both in appearance and social standing."

She waited for her mother to continue. There was something odd in this proposal, something her mother was hesitant to share with her. "Again mother, why are you so glum? I would think you would celebrate this event. It is exactly what you hoped for, is it not?" When Lady Guilford still did not reply she asked, "Is he ancient? I suppose he is sixty or some such thing?"

Lady Guilford cleared her throat. "No, he is not ancient. He is thirty. But there are some difficulties." She raised her eyes to gaze directly into her daughter's face. "I will not deny I want this marriage. It solves all the financial problems, and it gives your sisters their only chance of a respectable future. As for you, there will be a life of comfort, beyond anything we could have hoped for. I will say now that I expect you to do your duty for the family."

Madelyn swallowed. "What is this difficulty?" Her imagination had gone wild. Whatever it was, the longer her mother delayed the more nervous she became. She had every intention of accepting this offer. There was no choice. Nothing could be worse than the future Aunt Margaret proposed, relegating her and her sisters to the life of indentured servants.

Her mother answered bluntly. "First, he intends to take you North, to Yorkshire, far away from the family. He warned that it will be unlikely you will spend much time in London in the future." Her mother looked at her and paused, a hint of sadness in her eyes. But then she straightened her shoulders and continued in her no-nonsense voice. "Lord Montrose is a widower. His wife died at least ten years ago. There were no children. After her death he enlisted in the British army for a time. He was injured while in service on the Spanish peninsula. The left side of his face is badly scarred. He told me he also has an injury to his left hip, but it is not noticeable, or at least I was unable to discern it, though he does carry a walking stick as many fashionable gentlemen do."

"Oh." Madelyn could think of no response. There would have to be some gross impairment for the man to make such a settlement. So, she was to marry a scarred and crippled man, and be secluded in the wilds of Yorkshire, she thought numbly. She grimaced. Well, it could have been worse. He could have been over four hundred pounds and a bloody tyrant. Or he could have come with a packet of unruly children.

"I have every confidence you will do your duty and accept the man. You more than anyone know the position we find ourselves in." Lady Guilford set her hands on the table in front of her and waited for her reply.

Madelyn's stomach churned. She cleared her throat, forcing out her words, "I will do what I must. May I meet this Lord Montrose before I make my final decision?"

Her mother smiled for the first time in the interview. "Of course. He and his man are waiting for you in the parlor. I will introduce you."

The house was oddly silent as they left the library and crossed the hall to the parlor. Madelyn glanced up to the balcony above and was not surprised to see three dark heads at floor level, peering through the banister above. She smiled.

When she walked into the parlor, two men rose to greet them. Each of them did a formal bow.

Her mother announced, "Lord Montrose, Mr. Macgowan, let me present my daughter, Lady Madelyn Guilford."

She lowered her head to do a graceful curtsy. When she rose, her gaze settled on the taller man on the left.

He faced her, raising his chin slightly as though to guarantee she would examine his scarred face.

She was careful to keep her expression impassive as she took in this man who would be her husband. The left side of his face had a long-puckered scar. It ran the length of his cheek. It was a shock of white against a swarthy complexion, made somehow worse by the fact that the other side of his face was darkly handsome. He had dark long hair pulled back and secured with a leather throng, and blue gray eyes, over chiseled classical features. His scarring was a painful sight, but not horrific, and she dismissed it as irrelevant to her circumstances. In truth the man was handsome.

She let her gaze wander to his board shoulders, down his body to his fashionable trousers, stretched tight across thick thighs and legs tucked in to riding boots. He was tall and strong. She was reminded of the mythical warriors of old.

That is it, she thought to herself, this man is a warrior. Even the ghastly scar fit her definition. She smiled, thinking he would have suited well the blue war paint worn by the fierce tribesmen of the past. She could picture him riding on a massive steed, brandishing a mighty sword, as he charged the enemy. Her whimsy made her smile wider.

After slowly appraising his body, she looked again into his eyes. She realized with a start that he had been aware of her appraisal. His eyes sparkled with what she thought might be curiosity or amusement, and something else. Her cheeks began to burn, and her heart pounded in her chest.

Her mother was speaking, but she had missed entirely what was said. Everyone was looking at her as though waiting for her to speak. "I am pleased to make your acquaintance sir," she stuttered, hoping it was the appropriate response. Mr. Macgowan chuckled, and she realized she must have said the wrong thing. She was beyond embarrassed now.

Her mother quickly intervened. "And as I was saying it is such a lovely day, I thought the two of you might take a stroll in the garden. It will give you a chance to talk." She walked to the double doors, which opened to the back patio and flung them wide.

"An excellent idea." Lord Montrose held out his arm. "Shall we?"

She took his arm. There was a warm strength emanating from him. He wordlessly led her from the room. Once outside she took a deep breath and straightened her shoulders. She glanced at him from beneath her lashes. She faced his right side. He looked outrageously handsome.

He led her to the garden bench, and the two of them sat down. It was a short bench, forcing them to sit closely together, her shoulders and hips touching him intimately. Again, there was a sense of comfort and safety in his nearness, and she wondered if it was her imagination.

His right side faced her, his classical features looking for all the world like drawings she had seen of Roman statues. He did not turn to her, but instead held his head stiffly forward. She was unsure if it was shyness, distaste for her, or an attempt to hide his ravaged cheek.

When he spoke, his voice was low and soft. It sent a shiver down her spine. "I know this proposal is a surprise for you. I must first apologize for the lack of a courtship. Under the circumstances, I thought it best to keep our negotiations on a strictly business level." His voice was steady, quiet but forceful. She ruled shyness out as a possibility.

"A business level?" She looked up at him, surprised. She had not expected romantic words—or perhaps she had, at least a few. "Do you not want children then?" She realized the improper nature of her question and cringed. It was exactly this bluntness which had turned away potential suitors in the past.

"I do want children. It is the very reason I hope to marry." She looked at him and noted that this time it was he who colored ever so slightly.

There was a minute of awkward silence. He still refused to look in her direction. "I see no point in drawing out the whole endeavor," he said, "I am sure your mother will have laid out the bargain clearly for you. Will you accept me as your husband, or no?"

She glared at him, willing him to face her. He did not. But his arm held hers gently, his body still felt safe and comfortable against hers, and his words were spoken softly. She took a calming breath.

"If you wish to refuse me, I would that you said so now."

"I would be honored and pleased to be your wife," she blurted, surprising herself with the quick admission. The words had just spilled out, without her having analyzed for even a moment the ramifications of them. She felt her cheeks redden again and wondered if she would forever be blushing like a girl fresh out of short dresses in his presence.

He smiled for the first time.

"But only if you look at me," she added recklessly.

The smile died on his lips. He turned ever so slowly toward her, his face serious, and his eyes unreadable. She looked directly into their depths, realizing they were more gray than blue. He leaned toward her. She could feel his warm breath on her cheeks. She thought for a second he would kiss her, and her heart began to beat wildly in her chest.

But he did not. Instead, he leaned back suddenly, staring straight ahead once more. She sighed her disappointment, and he glanced at her sharply.

He cleared his throat, not acknowledging the moment they had just shared. "I have a special license. If you have no objection, I wish to be married the day after tomorrow. There are papers to be signed, and titles to be transferred, but all should be accomplished by then."

"So soon?" The reality of the situation set in. In just two days she would leave everything she had ever known. A ripple of panic flipped her belly. She wanted to object, then run to the safety of her room, where she could bury herself in the covers and will this scenario and her uncertain future away. She stood up abruptly.

He too rose to his feet, and must have sensed her rising hysteria because he took her hands in his and squeezed them gently. For once he turned toward her. Again, she found herself gazing into the clear depths of his eyes. "It will be all right. Whatever the future is between us, you will always have my protection and loyalty."

His declaration had the ring of a vow to it. It calmed her. She wanted to give him something in return. "And for your generosity to me and my family, I will give you my respect and loyalty."

He laughed. It was a joyful sound. He looked at her once more. "I believe I have chosen well. You will make a fine mistress of Montrose Manor." Together they walked back to the house and the open doors to the parlor.

The phrase 'mistress of the manor' set off another wave of panic. "Oh dear. I just realized I am quite possibly the worst choice you could have made for household management. I fear I tend to become lost in my books, and I... I--"

He laughed again, taking her hand as they entered the parlor. "You are all that I require in a wife," he said.

Mr. Macgowan looked at them quizzically, his head tilted to the side, as they entered the room. "Is it settled then?"

"It is. We wed the day after tomorrow. After which we will return home to Yorkshire," Lord Montrose answered.

Her mother could not be happier. "How wonderful!" Lady Guilford clapped her hands together. "I know it is morning, but I think a toast may be in order. She turned to Grimes who stood quietly by the door.

"We have one bottle of champagne hidden in the cellar for just such an occasion. Please fetch it for us."

Madelyn was feeling as though she had been taken up in a whirlwind and was being spun about. In two days, everything about her life would change. She realized she was still gripping Lord Montrose's hand. It took an effort to loosen her hold.

For better or worse, she had made her choice. It was the right decision for her sisters. But would it be the right choice for her?

~

Lady Montrose hears three tall tales

Leaving London was a relief after a wedding breakfast punctuated with tears and even the occasional wail from her younger sisters. Outside of Hamish Macgowan, the guests had been restricted to family; the only notices sent beyond the household were to Uncle William, and Aunt Margaret. The latter invitation was sent purely out of a need to gloat, with a note attached, thanking Amelia for her generous hospitality, now no longer needed.

It took three exhausting days to reach York. The weather, a miserable combination of intermittent showers and howling wind, made the roads a slippery mess. Her husband and Mr. Macgowan had purchased half a dozen horses and two carts full of goods in London, thus their party made a bit of a train as it crawled Northward.

For the most part she had been left to herself; the gentlemen riding their horses and only joining her in the coach to escape the worst of the rain. It gave her plenty of time to contemplate her future. Mr. Julian Stallridge, Lord Montrose, was now her husband, which made her Madelyn Stallridge, Lady Montrose. She spent the first part of her journey practicing this new name and title.

The hours of jostling about in the coach, trying to sort out her future, had begun to wear. She tried to avoid thinking about the challenges she would face as a mistress; managing a household, or building a relationship with the husband who had largely ignored her the past few days. Instead, she spent hours reviewing her history of Yorkshire, using the battles of Marston Moor, during the republican years and Battle of Towton in the War of the Roses as benchmarks to guide her. She managed in this way to keep her growing apprehension at bay.

Upon their arrival in York, Lord Montrose announced he had business to conduct, and thus they would spend two nights at a coaching inn. She was allotted a room of her own, a generous purse, and a lad named Jimmy, who would accompany her on any shopping excursions she might take. It was a welcome relief to leave the jarring coach, and even enjoy a proper bath.

She had hoped her husband would at least take her to dinner in the public dining room that evening, but it was not to be. The first night in the inn, she saw nothing of the man, and ate a lonely supper, in the sitting room of her suite.

Part curiosity and part petty retribution for the lack of interest shown in her by her new husband drove her onto Coney Street the next day for a whirlwind of shopping. The streets were wider in the market district, and to her delight, paved and tidy—a recent change much bragged about by the various shopkeepers.

A variety of shops lined each side of the street, with broad windows displaying their wares. The stretch of business fronts was more of a promenade than a purely shopping experience. It was populated by the upper classes in afternoon finery; a kaleidoscope of colored parasols punctuating the brick walkways. But loitering was not for her today. She was bullishly determined to spend every pence allotted to her.

She managed a pair of ready-made sturdy boots, and three books; a massive tome on British architecture of the seventeenth century, and for light reading, two penny dreadfuls. She also splurged on several bolts of cloth, two hats, and various fripperies for her own selfish adornment. Poor Jimmy was quite loaded down by the end of the afternoon. In the end, they had to have some of the purchases delivered.

Once back in her room she decided to take matters into her own hands, sending Jimmy with an invitation to her husband to dine with her. It was her honeymoon trip after all. She received an immediate reply: Lord Montrose regretted he would be otherwise engaged for the evening.

His response left her pacing her rooms in frustration. It was clear the marriage would be a difficult one. Her first reaction was to plan a subtle revenge and return his indifference with her own. It took her the good part of the evening for a more practical approach to prevail. Her life would be a lonely one if she alienated her partner and husband. She had certainly had a taste of that loneliness the last few days.

With three sisters, moments of quiet and privacy in her home had been rare. She had treasured any time spent alone. Tonight, she would gladly have accepted intervening in a battle between Clarice and Maryann or chasing a mischievous Beth to retrieve her private journals.

She sighed. There was little she could do at the moment to improve relations with her new husband. She could hardly force him to spend time with her. But once in her new home, she decided she would embark on a campaign to get to know the man. Surely there would be a way to bridge the gap between them.

She dug through her things to find the penny dreadful she had purchased. The story she chose involved a young woman sent as punishment to the wilds of Yorkshire, where she ultimately took bloody vengeance on her brutal keepers. A perfect novel for this night's reading!

~

They began their trek north early the next day. It was during this final leg of their journey that Madelyn was to hear three legends.

She kept her coach window open, relishing the rough Dale country with its views of rocky cliffs and moors covered with purple heather. She began to realize the sheltered existence she had lived, never leaving the well-known streets of her neighborhood in London. Yorkshire was to her a foreign land, unpopulated and mysterious---the land of myths and fairy creatures.

The sky had become an ominous dark blue, shrouding the wild landscape in shadows. A burst of thunder rocked the carriage. It was immediately followed by a gusting downpour, forcing her to tug the window closed before she got drenched. The coach came to a stop. Moments later the carriage door swung open, and Montrose and Mr. Macgowan climbed in, shaking off their brimmed hats and cloaks as they settled.

Her husband lit the coach lamp, basking the dark interior in a soft warm light. It felt safe and comfortable there in the carriage, with the rain pouring down outside. Madelyn felt sorry for the poor coachman out in the storm, and hoped the fellow had something to protect him from the driving rain, as the coach lurched forward.

"Oh. It's a bitter brawl that one. Sorry to invade your space ma'am, but it's not to be endured out there," Mr. Macgowan said with an apologetic smile.

"No apologies necessary, Mr. Macgowan." She gave

him her best smile. "I am pleased with the company. There has been naught to do but enjoy the sights. And I have enjoyed them. It is a strange and beautiful land."

"You must call me Hamish ma'am. Mr. Macgowan is too formal now that we are so close to home."

She glanced at her husband. "Are we nearing your home now?"

Julian pulled his hat down and turned in her direction. "Our home," he said with a quirk of his lips. "And it is not far now. We should reach Montrose Manor just after dark if we aren't laid up by the storm."

"I'll be glad when we get there," Hamish growled. A flash of lightning lit up the skies, followed almost instantly by a crash of thunder. "It is a powerful storm, that is for certain. We will want to be out of it before night."

Madelyn looked out the window. Even in the downpour the moors were darkly romantic. "It is awe inspiring, this land," she said.

"You like it, do you? It's rough country, but it gets in your blood." He too looked out the window. "Do you see those two boulders just there?"

Madelyn peered through the glass, seeing two huge stones about forty yards apart, just off the road and scarcely visible in the rain. She nodded.

"Well, there is a legend about those stones, and some of the wild country you have seen today. It is said they're the grave markers for the giant Wade; one's his head stone, the other's his feet."

Madelyn estimated the stones to be at least forty yards apart. She looked at Julian who raised his eyebrows and smiled. She knew she was about to get a tall tale.

"See Wade the giant lived in these hills with his wife, the giantess Bess. They each built a castle: Old Mulgrave and Pickering. But they only had one hammer see, and so they tossed it back and forth, giving a holler to warn its approach. And the thunder you are hearing now is the echo of those very shouts." He paused. As if on cue a clap of thunder sounded.

Madelyn laughed. "Is that so?"

"Oh aye, it 'tis." Hamish grinned. "I am sure you noticed the piles of rocks we passed along the way. Well, the story goes that the giants liked to live quietly. They raised cattle. Every night Wade had to bring in the cows for milking. He noticed they had a little trouble coming in across the bramble, so he decided to build a road for them. Bess helped, carrying the stones in her apron. But stones in these parts can get a little heavy and each time her apron strings broke, she dropped a pile of boulders. They are still visible today, as is the causeway old Wade built for his cows."

Madelyn laughed. "I have seen the piles of rocks, and the causeway, I think. But it sounds like a tall tale to me." She looked at Julian who gave her his crooked smile.

"All true," Julian said.

Hamish smiled, his eyes twinkling with mischief. "And finally, did you notice the gouged amphitheater of a valley a while back.

"I did." Madelyn answered, eager to hear his explanation.

"It seems the lovebirds did not always get along. Once, in the midst of a raging argument, Wade became so angry with Bess he gouged out a handful of land and hurled the mud at his wife. And that is how the valley came to be. It can be still seen today." Hamish grinned. "Of course, you are wondering if he hit her. Well fortune was on his side, and he missed, but the pile of dirt landed, creating Blakey Topping, still seen today."

Madelyn laughed, waiting to hear more tales. Hamish nodded and winked at Julian. "The land is rife with legends of every sort. It is the home of King Arthur and his worthy knights."

"I didn't know that. Here on the moors?"

"Oh yes. In fact, very near here is Richmond Castle, said to be the final resting place of King Arthur. There is a wild tale about that. But this one I will let Jules tell."

Julian leaned back in his seat, tipped his hat even further onto his face and chuckled. "Thank you for that Hamish." Julian began his legend in his soft melodic voice. "As Hamish said, Richmond castle is not far from here. It was built in the eleventh century by a Norman named Alan the Red. It is said to have been built over deep caverns. Well, one day, not long ago, a fellow by the name of Peter Thomas, a potter by trade, was wandering outside the castle walls. He chanced upon a cave; the entry only partially covered. Being a curious man, he pushed aside the stones and went inside."

Julian paused and grinned, shifting lower into his seat. He was relaxed, and amused. She smiled too. There was something wonderful in Julian when he let this side of his personality show.

"Well, when he entered the cave, the first thing he sees is a huge stone crypt; King Arthur's tomb. He knows this to be the case because lying on the lid of the stone coffin is Arthur's massive horn, and beside it, the mighty sword Excalibur.

The light is glittering off the sword, and he can't resist coming nearer and picking up the weapon. But the second he does, the room erupts in thundering racket. The scrape and screech of stone rubbing against stone is all around him as the tombs from every corner of the cave begin to open. It is deafening. Dust, long undisturbed, begins to swirl around the room. And then began the blood curdling clatter of armor, echoing through the cavern. He is terrified!

He quickly laid the sword back on the coffin.

As suddenly as it began, everything stopped. All is still but for settling dust, and there is an eerie silence. He turns to high tail it out of there.

As he fled, he heard, 'Potter Thompson, Potter Thompson, hadst thou blown the horn, thou had been the greatest man, that ever was born.' Well poor old Peter runs for his life, stopping only to cover the entry once more with stones, blocking the entrance so no one else would stumble upon the sleeping knights."

Madelyn looked at him appreciably, "That is a marvelous story. And is it all true as well?"

Julian chuckled. "It is." For a second they smiled at each other, the functioning side of his lips curling into a wide grin, before Julian turned to look out his window. "But now I see the rain has stopped, and Hamish and I will be needed to help with the wagons and horses. It will be a battle getting through this mire." Julian half rose and knocked on the coach ceiling. They came to a sliding halt.

"Oh aye," Hamish smiled. "But we're almost home missy. We might just make the rise before sundown."

When Julian and Hamish left the coach, it was as though the energy had been sucked out with them. The amber coach light no longer radiated the warmth it had. She pictured Julian, sprawled comfortably across from her, his hat pulled down low to cover his scarred cheek, and telling his story with relaxed ease. This was the husband she wanted to know.

The coach skidded sideways interrupting her thoughts. She wiped the mist from her window and peered into the darkening landscape. They were climbing a rise, on a narrow trail. The valley behind them was shrouded in fog, with gray clouds cloaking the heather and brambles below. The sun had set, and night was moving in quickly under the stormy skies. Low rumblings of distant thunder warned that another downpour may be eminent. She pulled her wool cloak around her, leaned back, and huddled against the chill.

A horse whinnying and shouting from outside had her back at her window, trying to look behind the coach to see what had caused the fray. The carriage stopped. She could make out distant shapes, struggling with one of the wagons. One of the baggage carts had slid from the trail and leaned precariously off the trail into a steep ditch.

Julian rode up to the coach, his black cloak swirled

around him, as he spun to a stop and spoke to the coachman. She slid open her window to hear.

"Carry on Briggs," he shouted up to the man, "take my Lady up to the Manor. We have lost a wheel and will be some time." Then he glanced at her from beneath his brimmed hat. "You are only a few miles from Montrose. Briggs will see you safely home." And he touched his hat before turning back to the chaos behind him. He looked for all the world like a highwayman, dark and mysterious against the night sky. Madelyn could not suppress a shiver.

The coach moved forward up the incline at a slow pace. The rain had started again. Heavy blotches could be heard intermittently hitting the coach roof. A flash of sheet lightning lit the sky. At the crest of the hill Madelyn slid back her window to look back once more at the wagons below. She could see several lanterns bobbing in the dark and hoped they would be able to right the wagons before the upcoming storm.

She peered forward as the carriage levelled out atop the rise. She could see a figure up ahead struggling in the mucky road. The heavy drops had begun to hit the roof with increased frequency. Another flash of sheet lightning illuminated the road.

A woman was hunched into the gusting winds just ahead, keeping to the edge of the road to avoid the worst of the mire. As they approached, she slid a little, almost losing her balance and falling into the path of the coach.

Without thinking, Madelyn rose and rapped firmly on the trapdoor of the carriage, then returned to her seat and pulled back her window to holler at the coachman. "Stop! Stop. She will need a ride."

The woman waited by the side of the road until the coach rolled to a halt, then walked the few paces to the door. Madelyn flung it open, and the woman wordlessly pulled herself up into the carriage. She plopped down on the seat, carefully opened her cloak, and pulled out a bundle, wrapped in a thin cloth and knotted to make a bag. She set it carefully on the seat beside her.

The coach jerked forward once more. Madelyn watched curiously as the woman pulled back her hood, revealing a wizened old face, tanned and wrinkled. Startling white-blue eyes gazed back at her. And then the old lady smiled. "Thank you for taking me out of the storm my dear." A crash of thunder interrupted her, and she waited for the echoes to fade away. "It was in the nick of time."

As if to validate her statement the rain began to drive against the coach with renewed vigor.

"My name is Elizabeth Heeds. But people call me Old Bess, and I like the title. I do a little midwifing and doctoring with herbs and such to cure whatever ailments my people have. And who might you be?"

"Madelyn Stallridge, Lady Montrose." It was her first time using the name, and Madelyn was pleased she had practiced it. "I am journeying to my new home."

"Ah." The woman leaned forward with interest, taking in her appearance. "We heard the Lord had gone to London to find a bride. And here I am the first to meet her." She chuckled, her eyes sparkling in the amber light of the carriage. "A pleasure to meet you, a pleasure indeed."

"Thank you."

"You have the look of a city girl about you. It will be a change for you to be out here in the wilds, I'm sure." The woman cackled, "Aye, quite the change. You won't find much city life out here."

"No. But it is a beautiful land. I look forward to becoming a part of it. It's to be my new home. I know I will love it."

"Oh, it is beautiful, that's true." Bess looked at her critically. She felt as though the woman was assessing her in some way. "But it can be mighty lonely. Especially for a young girl in your position."

Madelyn's stomach clenched with her words. "In my position?"

"There are few young women of your class in the area. Not a lot of neighbors. Of course, you'll have the Stallridge cousins across the way. There is Edwyn and Henry." The old lady suddenly smiled. "I had forgotten. There is Anne. She is widowed now and will come home to live with her brothers." She nodded. "She will be some company for you. She is a quiet lass from what I remember, but always had a good heart—an oddity in that family." The thunder rumbled and she paused once more. "But Anne would have at least a decade or two on you, still, she'll make a good friend to you."

Madelyn was pleased to hear there would be someone for her in this desolate place.

"Aye," the old lady continued, "And you may need a

good friend, given the curse that hangs over that Manor."

"The curse?" The coach lit up with eerie white light, followed by a loud clap of thunder.

The old woman again waited for the noise to dim, before saying, "Where's my head? It's not a time, nor a night to be sharing old wives' tales. And that's all it is. Old legends die hard in this country."

"A curse! But now you must tell me."

The old woman shook her head. "Nah, it's just an old tale."

"Oh please. You cannot just leave it at that. I must hear it."

Old Bess sighed. "I suppose someone will share it eventually. But mind, you are not to take it seriously."

Madelyn thought of the tale of King Arthur, and the giant Wade. She grinned. "I promise it will just be a story for me."

"All right. It began almost two hundred years ago. The Lord of Montrose had lost his first wife after many years. His children had grown; his daughters married, and his sons off to fight in the wars. He found himself to be lonely and decided to take a new bride. In the next county he met a young woman who struck his fancy. But she was too young for him, too young and too beautiful to be the wife of a lonely old man. Like all old men, he was too proud to admit his age, and took her to wife anyway."

The woman grinned at this. "It is the folly of many an old man. Anyway, the marriage began well. The Miss was a gentle soul, who nursed his ailments and graced his days with much joy. Katherine was the lass's name. It is said she was a healer, though some say she was a witch. Well, over time the young woman did indeed fall in love with her husband, despite his age, and cared for him as no other ever had."

Thunder rattled the carriage again, forcing the woman to pause. The rain was coming down harder now. Old Bess was forced to raise her voice to be heard. "There came a day when Katherine was called down to the village. A young man had been gouged by a boar and needed her ministrations. Katherine took her herbs, needles and threads, and tended to the man. It was a long healing, requiring Katherine to come again and again to drain and clean the wound.

Now it was around this time that Katherine had fallen with child. At first the Lord was happy. He invited everyone in the village to join him in a feast to celebrate his good fortune."

Bess stopped and looked at her. She seemed hesitant to continue. But Madelyn was engrossed in the story. "Go on," she said. She expected a tall tale like the two she had been told earlier tonight.

"Well, his joy didn't last long. Rumors began to circulate that the child was not the Lord's. It was said the Lord was too old to accomplish such a feat, therefore the baby must be the handsome young man's from the village. And sure, hadn't they spent hours alone together in his hut.

When the old man got word of the gossip, he was furious. He confronted his wife. And she, a proud woman too, began by first refusing to answer such slander. The old Lord took this as her admitting to the deed. Now, it so happened that there was a crew of bricklayers in the home, just finishing the repair of a crumbling fireplace, and maybe that is what put the worm into the Lord's head. In a fury he ordered that his wife be immured---bricked into an old priest's hole to suffer a long and painful death. Katherine began to deny the accusations, but it was too late. In his anger and damaged pride, the old lord would not rescind the order. He took the workmen to a hidden location in the dungeons, and they began the gruesome task."

Old Bess sighed. "It was said that as the last bricks were laid, the young wife uttered a curse. No Lord of Montrose would find love or happiness in a marriage until she was released from her tomb.

Well, the old man was sickened by shock and grief. He took to his bed that night and was dead by morning. The servants tried to find the hidey hole and release her, but the house has many secret passages and hidden rooms. All their efforts were in vain. The brick layers were itinerant laborers, and horrified by their part in the ghastly deed, had quickly moved on. She was never found."

There was a long silence. Madelyn sat wide-eyed in horror. This was not the tall tale she had expected. This was a curse which spoke directly to her. She had married a Lord of Montrose.

"I should not have told you this. Not on your first night. I must be getting old and foggy in the head. Forgive the ramblings of an old woman." Old Bess reached over and patted her clenched hands. “It is just an old wives' tale, not to be taken serious.”

Madelyn swallowed, suppressing a shudder. “And have the marriages been unhappy ones?” Her voice sounded strange to her, distant and high-pitched.

Old Bess refused to answer. She shook her head. “No more of that. It is sorry I am to have told you that old story. Every big house has one, and this is just yours.” She looked away for a moment, glancing out the coach window. “And see, the rain has stopped. In good time too, my lane is just ahead. Briggs will drop me here; he knows the place well enough.”

Madelyn shook off her lingering feelings of trepidation. Bess was right. It was just a story. It must have been the storm which chilled her so.

Bess reached over and patted her hand once more. “In time you will be happy here. I am a wise woman and I know these things.” She smiled, and Madelyn noticed again her startling blue eyes, now twinkling with a kind of mischief. “Some say I am a seer, and that is what I see.” She nodded, looking her over once more. “It's pleased I am to have been the first to meet you. You seem a fine young woman and good too, offering a ride to an old woman. My cottage is just across the lake. Come for a spot of tea once you're settled.”

“Oh, I will,” she answered. Despite the unsettling story, she liked the old woman. There was a kindness about her.

The coach slid to halt, and the old woman picked up her cloth bag. “My precious herbs,” she said, her clear blue eyes twinkling once more as she tucked them under her cloak, "always best picked before a storm." She opened the coach door, and slid down to the muddy earth, closing the door behind her.

The coach lurched forward once more. Madelyn slid back the window and raised a hand of farewell to old Bess. She turned to look forward, peering into the distance, hoping to see Montrose Manor. But night had swallowed the views, and she could see nothing but dark shadows ahead.

Her new home, and the life she would make there, were a mystery. She hoped old Bess was correct; that she would find happiness here. Her mind wandered to the curse of Montrose. She shivered, before quickly banishing the thought. Surely it was just as Bess said, an old wives' tale.

OTHER BOOKS BY CYNTHIA KEYES

The Smuggler

The Spy

The Meadows

Printed in Great Britain
by Amazon